Last Dance With Annie

Rochelle Wisoff-Fields

EBook ISBN: 978-1-958783-12-2
Paperback ISBN: 978-1-958783-13-9
Hardcover ISBN: 978-1-958783-14-6
Cover Art by Rochelle Wisoff-Fields
Cover Design by Maria Biondo (artbymb.co)
Published by Ozark Hollow Press
PO Box 4573
Joplin, Missouri 64803
Lia Wu, Publisher
Ozark Hollow Press Edition 2024
Printed in the USA

In memory of Wayne Clinton Witcher, my ever-patient therapist. I will always consider myself your success story.

To my husband, Jan Wayne Fields, who stood by me through the darkest times. You believed all things and hoped all things. Thank you for your stubborn loyalty, m'luv.

Contents

Chapter One	1
Chapter Two	6
Chapter Three	12
Chapter Four	14
Chapter Five	18
Chapter Six	22
Chapter Seven	25
Chapter Eight	31
Chapter Nine	35
Chapter Ten	42
Chapter Eleven	49
Chapter Twelve	56
Chapter Thirteen	61
Chapter Fourteen	64
Chapter Fifteen	70
Chapter Sixteen	73
Chapter Seventeen	77
Chapter Eighteen	80
Chapter Nineteen	83
Chapter Twenty	85
Chapter Twenty-One	88
Chapter Twenty-Two	90
Chapter Twenty-Three	96
Chapter Twenty-Four	102
Chapter Twenty-Five	109
Chapter Twenty-Six	114
Chapter Twenty-Seven	119
Chapter Twenty-Eight	128
Chapter Twenty-Nine	132
Chapter Thirty	138
Chapter Thirty-One	144
Chapter Thirty-Two	149
Chapter Thirty-Three	153
Chapter Thirty-Four	157
Chapter Thirty-Five	160
Chapter Thirty-Six	165

Chapter Thirty-Seven 169
Chapter Thirty-Eight 173
Chapter Thirty-Nine 177
Chapter Forty 182
Chapter Forty-One 187
Chapter Forty-Two 189
Chapter Forty-Three 191
Chapter Forty-Four 195
Chapter Forty-Five 199
Chapter Forty-Six 202
Chapter Forty-Seven 205
Chapter Forty-Eight 210
Chapter Forty-Nine 213
Chapter Fifty 217
Chapter Fifty-One 220
Chapter Fifty-Two 225
Chapter Fifty-Three 228
Chapter Fifty-Four 232
Chapter Fifty-Five 238
Chapter Fifty-Six 242
Chapter Fifty-Seven 247
Chapter Fifty-Eight 251
Chapter Fifty-Nine 255
Chapter Sixty 258
Chapter Sixty-One 261
Chapter Sixty-Two 265
Chapter Sixty-Three 268
Chapter Sixty-Four 271
Chapter Sixty-Five 273
Chapter Sixty-Six 275
Chapter Sixty-Seven 279

Acknowledgments 283
About the Author 285

The Dancer

The steps used to
   Be simple,
   Every leap and turn;
   Graceful, exultant dance.
   But now
   Annie leads me to murky depths
   Of despair
   And
   Threatens,
   In the most literal sense,
   To devour
   Soul, spirit and body.
   I'm tortured by
   Pain on the faces of those
   Who care.
   Helpless to halt this
   Insane choreography
   I seek resolution
   Via self-destruction.

Chapter One

"Who is she?"

"I was ringing her up and she keeled over."

"Bet she's a junkie. See how skinny she is?"

"Mommy, I smell stinky."

Elise's cheeks blazed against the cold tile. The last thing she remembered was writing a check at the register when a wave of nausea and lightheadedness swept over her. The helpless feeling of losing control as she lost consciousness rushed back. She squirmed, wishing she could dissolve between the cracks. How many of those "gentle action" pink pills had she taken in anticipation of dinner?

Heretofore she'd taken pride in having the cycle down to a science. Scarf a handful of laxatives at eleven. Eat at one. What she didn't chew up and spit into wadded napkins she'd squirt by two. Voila! Nothing sticks.

"You know you're too damn smart for your own good," her frustrated support group leader had snapped at her night before last. "Why do you even bother coming to meetings anyway?"

"To learn new tricks, of course," her demonic inner voice cackled.

Elise groaned. Her science had come back to bite her after dinner. House of Hunan had had something for everyone, including her husband, Tony. He'd filled his plate with egg rolls, crab Rangoon and bacon wrapped Rumaki. Plenty of fried food to keep him happy.

The voice had crooned, "Buffets are great places to hide."

She'd studied the mound of lettuce and sautéed green beans on her plate. How many calories? Two hundred? Maybe less. Iceberg only had fifty per head. Her empty stomach had roiled as the laxatives had kicked in. At the same time it had growled with hunger. She longed for beef with bok choy, her favorite dish.

"No! You can't. It's too much," the voice had sung. "It will make you fat. Porky as a pig. Enormous as an elephant. Huge as a hippo. Fat, fat, fat!"

Lying in her own filth, Elise now felt anything but smart. Someone touched her shoulder. "Ma'am?"

She turned her head, opened her eyes, and peered at the uniformed ambulance attendant who took her hand and pressed his fingers against her wrist. His dark eyes clouded with concern.

"Ma'am, do you know where you are? Do you know your name? The day? The year?"

She wanted to say, "My name is Stupid," but her aching lips and dehydrated tongue fought her. Rolling onto her back, she mumbled. "Elise—Elise Reeves. Salvation Army—Thrift Store. Kansas City, Missouri. February twenty-fifth, nineteen ninety-six. How—how am I doing?"

The paramedic wrote on his clipboard and read aloud, "Patient is awake and aware of surroundings." He turned back to her. "Pleased to meet you, Elise. Which hospital do you prefer?"

"No doctors, Elise," the unrelenting voice inside her head rasped. "They'll force you to eat. They'll turn you into a blimp."

"No—no hospital. I'm okay." Elise tried to sit up, but her heavy limbs refused to obey. Weak and dizzy, she fell back. "Or not."

The EMT's partner, a woman with intuitive eyes, arched an eyebrow. "Take her to Brookside Memorial."

"Brookside?" The EMT glanced at his wristwatch. "Any particular reason?"

"There's an eating disorder unit there."

Eyeballing Elise, he whispered, "I see what you mean. Isn't Belton Regional closer?"

The female paramedic lowered her voice a notch. "It doesn't have an eating disorder unit."

"Gotcha."

The two helped her onto a gurney. Elise squeezed her eyes shut to blot out inquisitive stares until they loaded her into the ambulance.

Once the doors shut and the vehicle began to move, the EMT picked up the ambulance phone and poised his fingers over the buttons. "Do you want me to call your husband?"

"Husband?"

The young man's cheeks flushed as he pointed at her wedding ring. "I assumed—"

Elise swiveled the gold band around her ring finger with her pinkie and thumb. They'd had a terrible fight at the restaurant about her dinner—or lack thereof—as always.

Tony had filled a plate with chicken and vegetables and plopped it front of her. "Dammit, Elise, eat something!"

When she'd shoved it away his icy gray eyes had flashed, and he'd clenched his jaw, his silence more terrifying than his yelling. A call from the ambulance would most certainly push him over the edge.

"Mrs. Reeves? Elise?" The paramedic's voice made her start. "The number?"

Rattling off the numbers, she found the edge of the sheet beneath her and twisted it between her fingers as he dialed the number.

"Mr. Reeves, I'm a paramedic with…"

Trying not to hear what he said, she focused on her surroundings. Neck braces, splints, oxygen masks, and various pieces of medical equipment-filled shelves. A fully-stocked emergency room on wheels.

The other attendant struggled to insert an IV needle into one of Elise's collapsed veins. After poking around, she found a spot and the needle slid into Elise's arm. How odd. It should've hurt but it didn't. She certainly deserved the pain.

The EMT handed her the phone. "He wants to talk to you."

"Hi, honey," she whispered.

"You've got no idea what you're doing to me." Tony's voice crackled through the receiver. "Elise, for God's sake, snap out of it. I don't know how much more of this I can take."

Elise let the receiver fall from her fingers.

Sirens squealed. Lights flashed. The ambulance doors swung open, and her stretcher slid from her safe cocoon. Florescent ceiling lights whizzed by until the gurney came to an abrupt halt.

The paramedics helped transfer her from the gurney to the ER bed and raised the bedrails. Elise lay back against the pillow, wincing at her own stench. At least Tony couldn't smell it over the phone. Shame flooded her. What about the children? What would they say when they found out?

The female paramedic, a full-figured blonde, squeezed Elise's hand, her blue eyes awash with compassion. "Don't let the beast win, Elise. It's not worth killing yourself."

Forcing a weak laugh, Elise squeezed the EMT's hand in return. "Don't be silly. I'm not going to die."

Beast? What a perfect name for it. It held her hostage.

"I'm not a beast, Elise. I'm your friend. Your ally." The voice escalated. *"Your protector and champion."*

The emergency room nurse, a chubby woman with a double chin, hovered over her. "Is this the forty-two-year-old anorexic?"

The words reverberated in Elise's head. Anorexic? A mixture of shame and pride welled up in her. Yet, she didn't feel worthy of the title. "I'm not—not anorexic."

"Right," said the pudgy nurse, "and I'm Miss America."

The male paramedic glared at her. "We all got our issues, don't we?"

"Hmm," she grunted in reply.

With frowns at the nurse and a wave to Elise, the paramedics turned to leave. Desolation wafted over Elise. Her swollen lips vibrated, and she ached from her fall. She couldn't remember ever feeling so abandoned and alone. The door closed behind the two. Elise shut her eyes and wished she could disappear.

The nurse's abrasive voice cut through her stupor. "Can you sit up?"

Propping herself up on her elbows, Elise forced a smile. "I... I think so."

"Good." She wrenched off Elise's soiled blue jeans and panties, stuffed them into a plastic bag, and tied it shut. "I don't get paid enough for this shit."

Elise bit her lip and laid back. Her cheeks blazed with shame. She trembled and fear gripped her. How could she ever face Ben and Gracie? What would they think of their mother?

"You're not done yet, honey." Scowling, the nurse tossed a warm washcloth across Elise's bare thighs. "Clean yourself."

Don't call me honey, you tub of lard. You heart attack waiting to happen. I'll bet you consume five-thousand calories a day. Ignorant cow! I hope you choke to death on a french fry.

Elise gritted her teeth and glared at the nurse's dark-rooted blonde hair. Her heart thrashed against her ribs. Grasping the bedrails, she managed to sit up. She gasped at the sight of the feces covering her lower extremities. Mortified, she shivered with embarrassment. It took three washcloths to clean it all. Still the stench remained.

Once finished, she fell back against the pillow, her strength sapped. The nurse's glare bore through her like laser beams. "Stand up and put this on."

The nurse helped her out of her blouse and bra and into a clean hospital gown and then wrapped a blood pressure cuff around Elise's upper arm. She wagged her head and clucked her tongue "Eighty-five over fifty-four."

Crunching her pincer-grip around Elise's elbow, she practically hoisted her onto the scales. "Eighty-seven pounds."

"Too heavy," the Beast murmured. "Too heavy."

The nurse shook her head, chins jiggling and tongue clucking. "If you want to die so badly, Mrs. Reeves, why don't you shoot yourself? It's faster." Then she mumbled to herself, "And wouldn't smell so damn bad."

Chapter Two

"Good morning, Mrs. Reeves. Rise and shine! Breakfast is served. Sunny-side up eggs, crispy bacon, toast and jelly, and piping hot, healthy oatmeal. Face this fine morning with bright eyes and bushy tail."

Elise rubbed her crusty eyelids and groaned, "Who called in the cliché brigade?"

Every inch of her body ached, especially her mouth, which had taken the brunt of her fall. Her empty stomach grumbled and begged for nourishment. Rolling onto her side, she shut her eyes and pulled the covers over her head. An IV needle poked her arm. She returned to her back.

Opening her eyes, she watched clear liquid drip from the bag into the tube traveling to the needle. She squinted at sunlight pouring through the venetian blinds and sat up.

Next to her bed, a heart monitor beeped to remind her she was still alive. Blood pressure: ninety over sixty. Heart rate forty. Elise beamed. A coach at the fitness center had told her that that was a very athletic heart rate. He'd quipped that it was something like one beat per day.

She glared at the breakfast tray. "I'm not hungry, Nurse Whatever-Your-Name-Is."

The nurse pointed to her nametag, which read, *Cassiopeia Chukwu, RN, MSN.*

"Cassiopeia? That's some handle."

"It's after the constellation. Nicer than 'Whatever-Your-Name-Is,' dontcha think? My daddy referred to me as his shining star. You may call me Cassie if you'd like."

Cassie's complexion shone like polished bronze. Willowy and tall with high cheekbones, her salt-and-pepper hair was buzzed like a man's. Not many women could pull off such a style, but it suited her oval face. Her eyes, dark crescents, twinkled. "Try to eat something, even if it's only a bite."

Resentment welled up like bile in Elise's chest. This woman probably never had to count a calorie in her life. She certainly didn't care what happened to Elise. It was just her job to act like it.

"Take the food. Leave the coffee," she hesitated, "Cassie."

The bacon's sweet, meaty aroma tantalized Elise. Fingering the fork, she imagined mopping mellow egg yolk with a piece of buttered toast and allowing it to melt in her mouth.

"Eighty-seven pounds," the beast purred. "You can eat when you get down to eighty."

Trembling with rage and panic, with the ball of her foot she shoved the tray table. It crashed into the dresser. Bowls, cups, and cutlery clattered to the floor. Juice made orange rivulets through the spurned oatmeal mound.

"Oops. My foot must've slipped." After a second, she added, "Don't bother yourself with bringing more. I'm not up to eating anything just yet."

Cassie bent, picked up a napkin, and dabbed at the coffee on her slacks. "You don't get rid of me that easy, girlfriend." She poured water from the pitcher on the nightstand into a glass, which she handed to Elise along with a paper cup full of pills. "Got meds for you."

Laying back against the pillow, exhausted by her outburst, Elise bit her lip. "Meds? What are the side effects? Do they cause weight gain?"

"Just your regular scripts. Weight gain? I could shine a light right through you. Why, I'd bet you haft-a run around in the shower to get wet. Get real, sugar. We gotta put some meat on dem bones, dem bones, dem *scrawny* bones."

Like a golden halo, sunshine crowned Cassie's head. Elise turned away from her effervescent smile. How could this woman be so freaking cheerful? Elise hated her with every fiber of her being.

"Alright, alright already." Elise swallowed a capsule and a pill. Chasing them with water, she crumpled the cup and flung it at her. "There. Satisfied? Now get lost."

Her smile undimmed, Cassie called for housekeeping, wrote something on Elise's chart, and headed for the door. Turning on her heel, she returned to the bed, sadness filling her eyes. "If you aren't willing to eat something, you'll force us to use a feeding tube to get some nutrition into you. You aren't dying on my watch."

The rest of the morning continued with a steady stream of technicians and hospital staff parading in and out. Some extracted vials of blood from Elise's arm after jabbing several times, while others came with clipboards and questions.

An attractive strawberry blonde, clad in a colorful, floral-print dress, appeared in the doorway. "Knock. Knock. You up for a visit from your favorite GP?"

Relief flooded Elise. Dr. Williams, Susan, had been her doctor for the past five years and had a knack for making her feel better about things. A recovering bulimic herself, Susan always understood and never judged. She would never threaten to turn her loose as some of Elise's support group companions' doctors had. For whatever good it did, Susan encouraged her to come in once a week to weigh in. She even phoned Elise a few times to check up on her.

Susan sank down on the bed, a wry smirk on her freckled face. "Congratulations."

As if she'd received a punch to her gut, Elise gasped, "Come again?"

"It's what you want, isn't it?" Susan's green eyes brimmed with tears. "I wish you could see how much you have going for you, Elise. I've never met anyone with so much talent. So much to live for. But you don't see it, do you?"

Elise focused on her folded hands to avoid Susan's searing gaze. A lengthy silence ensued, interrupted only by the heart monitor's rhythmic chirps. The smell of food wafted over her. Another meal to avoid. Her stomach growled.

Susan reached over. She squeezed Elise's knee and leaned into her face. "You're going to end up like Karen Carpenter—dead on the bathroom floor and there's nothing I can do about it."

"Don't be silly. I'm not going to die." Elise coaxed a smile. "Besides, eighty-seven pounds isn't underweight for five-foot nothing."

"Tell me that again when your organs start shutting down."

***

Elise nibbled a lettuce leaf and took a sip of tomato juice with a smug sense of victory. Not many calories in a dry salad and the juice would fill her belly. The aide took back the ham sandwich when Elise told her she was Jewish.

The hospital needn't know she didn't keep Kosher. If that didn't work, she'd claim to be a vegetarian. They'd bought it during her previous hospitalizations at Elmwood Psychiatric Center and Hilliard General. While those institutions were well-versed in treating depression, alcoholism, and psychosis, they were ill-equipped to address eating disorders. She'd manipulated the clueless techs with ease.

Picking up the remote control from the nightstand, she clicked on the television. A Prego spaghetti sauce commercial flashed across the screen. The sight of the tomato-drenched pasta activated her salivary glands. She wiped her mouth with a Kleenex.

"Mmm. Looks delicious," said a gentle male voice. "I'll bet a big plate would hit the spot right now."

Elise started and snapped her head around. A stocky, balding man with a friendly smile stood in the doorway. He wore a suit vest and lavender shirt with a deep purple bow tie under his white lab coat. She smiled at him until she eyed his clipboard.

"Gimme a break." Turning off the TV, she scowled. "More interrogation? Who might you be?"

"Dr. Wayne Picard. Not to be confused with Captain Jean-Luc of the

Enterprise." He patted his head as he took the seat beside her bed. "We do have the same charming hairline though."

"Somehow you don't strike me as a starship captain. But if you're a *Star Trek* fan, you can't be all bad. Let me make a wild guess. You're a shrink, right?"

"So they tell me. Let's engage. I'll be working with you once your cardiologists are sure your heart's out of danger and can get those electrolytes back in balance."

"Everything's hunky dory. Send me home."

"Not an option." He set his pen to his clipboard. "Birthdate?"

Elise nodded toward the end of the bed. "It's on my chart already."

"Humor me."

"September the fourth, nineteen fifty-three."

"Almost forty-three, eh?"

"So they tell me."

"Touché. Shall we proceed, milady?"

Although she tried hard not to, Elise had already taken a liking to the man. None of her smart aleck comments seemed to deter him. His calm, even voice and relaxed manner put her at ease. And those eyes. She'd never seen eyes that shade of blue. "Carry on, good sir."

"It says on your admittance form that you work at a grocery store. What's your position?"

"Sign maker slash cake decorator."

He raised an eyebrow. "Odd occupation for someone with an eating disorder."

She turned her head to avoid his inquisitive gaze. "It's an art form. Like painting. I love to make flowers like roses and daisies. I'd never eat my canvas, would I?"

"Good point, I suppose. If I worked in a bakery, I'd weigh three hundred pounds. Any family history of diabetes, heart disease, or cancer?"

"Dad was type 2 diabetic. Mom died of lung cancer. She smoked herself to death and he dug his grave with his teeth."

"You do have a way with words. Tell me. How many times a day do you purge?"

"Never. I've tried but I can't make myself barf."

He wrote something, then scratched it out. "What do you call what you do with those laxatives?"

"Saving my teeth." She hoped the subject of her two root canals within six months didn't come up. "Puking erodes them, right?"

"Frequent episodes of binging and purging... bulimic," he muttered as he wrote.

She bristled. "Cross that out. I *never* binge. I'm *not* bulimic."

A slight smile graced his lips. "What difference does it make? An eating disorder is an eating disorder is an eating disorder. I'd have to say—"

The pager on his belt mercifully interrupted.

He dialed the bedside phone. "Hello? Woah, Cassie! Slow down." His sunny smile dissolved, and he rolled his eyes. "She did what? Not again... be right there." He hung up the telephone. "Be back when I can, if not here, up there." He winked and pointed toward the ceiling.

"Up there? You think I'm at death's door?"

"Upstairs in the eating disorder unit. However, keep it up and you will be knock, knock, knocking on Heaven's door."

Chapter Three
Tony

Tony directed his flashlight beam in the direction of the voice. River water filled his boots. Mud rose to his ankles. He tried to move his feet but he sank deeper into the muck.

Another voice screamed. "Tony! My leg! I can't feel my damn leg!

"Hold on, Frankie." Tony choked. "I'm coming."

Try as he might, Tony couldn't budge his feet. Mud rose to his knees.

Short bursts illuminated the night sky. Frankie floated past him. Blood spurted from his hip socket, coloring the brown water. All at once Tony found himself surrounded by mangled corpses, American and Viet Cong, glazed eyes and severed limbs.

Mud rose to his waist. A woman's emaciated form drifted by him, face up. She turned to him and hollered, "Help me, Tony. I'm drowning."

He reached for her. "Elise, stay with me."

Mud rose to his neck. Viet Cong guerillas surrounded him.

Tony shivered and rubbed his wet palms together. "Frankie?" His comrade's screams faded and the water of the Mekong Delta receded. He turned his head to see an infomercial blaring on TV. His neck ached from sleeping in the recliner. "Holy shit. What a dream."

"Daddy?" Gracie's soft voice resonated in his ear. "Are you okay? It's six-thirty. Don't you have to be at work?"

He bolted upright. The taste of stale beer lingered in his mouth. Frankie's anguished cries reverberated in his head. "Damn. The whole fourth infantry division must'a marched their muddy boots over my tongue." He reached for the remote. Clicking off the television, he forced a smile. "I guess I conked out in middle of my movie. Last thing I remember, John Wayne rounded up all the wagons in a circle. It's okay, I've seen it a hundred times. The cowboys win."

Apparently, his attempt at humor fell flat, for Gracie didn't even crack a smile. "You've had a lot of nightmares lately, Poppo."

He shrugged. "Shouldn't you be getting ready for school?"

"It's Saturday." Gracie twisted a lock of her hair around her finger. "But I have a swim meet this afternoon. Will you be able to take me?"

He rubbed his neck. "Can't Ginger's folks take you?"

"Sure." She sucked in her lower lip and turned to leave. "I'll give her a call. I thought—"

As if seeing her for the first time, Tony stared at his daughter. Her russet curls skimmed her slender shoulders. When did a silky nightgown replace her Hello Kitty pajamas?

A lump formed in his throat. "I wouldn't miss your meet for the world."

"What's wrong, Poppo?"

"It don't seem like that long ago we brought you home from the hospital. Now you ain't hardly my little kitten anymore. Why, you're almost a—a woman."

Light glinted off the mouthful of the braces that was costing him a year's salary. Cheeks turning crimson, she pulled her terrycloth bathrobe around her. "Daddy? Can I ask you a question?"

"Sure."

"Am I getting fat?"

Chapter Four

FLIPPING through channels with the remote control, Elise settled back against her pillows. With supper behind her, she could relax and watch whatever she wanted. She was in control even if it was only of the television. She came across an old "I Love Lucy" episode and set the remote on the nightstand.

Five minutes later, Tony and Gracie burst through the door. Tony picked up the remote and changed the channel to the news. "I ain't watching that crap."

Elise clenched her teeth. Same old story, different day. She'd been here a week and he'd come to see her every evening after work. Even here, he controlled the remote.

"Look what I got, Mommy." Gracie skipped to the bed, flashing a shiny medallion on a ribbon.

"First place in Medley Relay. I wish I'd been there to see it." Elise cradled Gracie's medal in her palms. "I'm so proud of you, honey. Someday, you're going to take the Olympics by storm."

"You should'a seen her, Elise." Tony beamed. "Nobody but nobody could touch my little girl in the butterfly. She's half-fish."

"Like my mom," said Gracie.

"I never could do that stroke." Elise slipped the medal around

Gracie's neck. The scent of chlorine wafted from her hair. "Tony, will you be able to stop by Sally's for swimmer's shampoo? We don't want our daughter's beautiful red hair to turn green, do we?"

"Dammit!" Tony slapped his forehead with his palm. "Someone should'a reminded me before now. Things been pretty busy at work with Marco leaving and now with you pulling this crap again. I barely have time to catch any shut-eye."

Elise opened her mouth to point out that things had a way of slipping his mind but the look on Gracie's face begged her to avoid confrontation. "It's my fault. I didn't remind him, Mommy. Besides, sometimes it's hard to find in the winter."

Elise reached over to pat Gracie's hand. "You're right of course. Did you eat a good breakfast, Doodlebug? Something besides Pop-Tarts?"

"Maybe if you were home to cook breakfast, you'd know what I ate." Gracie frowned and stuffed both hands into her blue jeans' pockets. She plopped down in the chair beside the bed. "What did *you* eat for breakfast, Mom? A stalk of celery and black coffee?"

"Failure. You're a failure," the Beast intoned. "You can't even feed your family. They'd be better off without you."

Elise bowed her head and clapped her hands over her ears as if it would stop the beast's relentless accusations. For years she'd been a housewife and mommy, but with the added burden of Gracie's braces, a growing list of extracurricular activities, and Ben's college expenses, Tony insisted Elise find a job. When she did find a full-time position she enjoyed, Tony complained about her long hours.

"I wish I could be a stay-at-home mom, but with our finances, I need to work." Elise noted how her little girl had filled out over the past few months. "You're practically a woman. Healthy eating is important. I can start prepping your meals when I get out of here. All you'll have to do is pop them in the microwave in the morning."

"Yeah, right, Mom. Can we go home now, Poppo?" Gracie glared at her then turned to Tony. "I just remembered I have a paper to write for American history and I'm expecting a call."

He raised an eyebrow. "From who? That boy I caught you playing kissy face with yesterday?"

"That should be 'whom.'" She folded her arms across her chest. "His name is Doug and it was a peck on the cheek to congratulate me."

Elise forced a smile hoping to lighten the mood. "Doug Kaplan. He's the high-dive champ. You remember him, Tony. He took Gracie to Homecoming."

"Did I know about this? Isn't he a senior?" Tony's cheeks flushed. "He's too old for you."

"He's seventeen. What's wrong with a two-year difference? You're *seven* years older than Mom."

Color rose from Tony's neck to his forehead. "That's different. Different times. I'm still your father and I ain't letting you hang around with just anybody."

"I've had it!" Gracie jumped up from her chair and stomped to the window. "Why does everything have to be your way?" She turned her back to them.

Gracie's shoulders shook and she sniffled. Elise slunk down in the bed to shield herself against Tony's volcanic anger.

Instead of erupting, he wrapped his arms around Gracie and kissed the top of her head. "I'm just trying to protect my little girl. I'll kill anyone who lays a hand on you."

Melting into his arms, Gracie buried her head in his chest. Dejected and lonely, Elise fell back against her pillows. Might as well face it, Gracie was Daddy's little girl.

Gracie pulled back from him. "It's okay, Poppo, I can take care of myself. I'm a green belt, remember?"

"Yeah, yeah, and you'll kick any boy in the nads if he tries anything." Tony reached into his pocket and took out a handful of change. "Get yourself a Coke and wait for me in the lobby, kitten."

Gracie mopped her wet cheeks with her sweatshirt sleeve and leaned over to kiss Elise. Throwing her arms around her daughter's neck, Elise's eyes spilled over. "I'm sorry I'm not a better mother."

Wriggling out of her grasp, Gracie flashed her braces. "It's all good, Momette. Catch ya in a few, Poppo."

Tony's gaze followed their daughter as she flounced from the room. "What's with this 'Poppo' shit. What happened to plain old 'Daddy'?"

"Remember 'The Patty Duke Show'? One of the old black and whites." Elise shrugged. "Patty called her dad 'Poppo'. I guess Gracie thinks it's cool."

For a moment, Tony stared at the television, intent on a story about a murder in midtown. He groused under his breath about crime in Kansas City. Then he turned off the television. "She watches the same crap you do. You're rubbing off on her, y'know. She's afraid she's getting fat." The intensity in his expression paralyzed her. He reached under her nightgown and caressed her breast. "I miss you, baby."

She cringed at his touch. The handsome, devoted husband. Any woman would envy his loyalty. So why did she feel violated? She didn't have to dig too deep for the answer. It was always about *his* needs. The same way it had been through their entire relationship. What about her needs?

"How'd your session with Dr. Picard go?"

"Typical psycho-babble." He moved his hand down her torso. "He wanted to talk about me. But I told him I ain't going there, it's all about my *wife*."

"He means his property," said the Beast.

Elise pushed his hand away and rolled over on her side. "Is it?"

Chapter Five

"WHEN I WAS YOUR AGE, nurse's aides were called candy stripers. I loved their cute red and white striped pinafores and nurse's caps." Elise bit into a green bean. "But I couldn't do it after I heard they had to clean out bedpans."

"Ugh." The aide, who'd been assigned to Elise to watch her at mealtimes, wrinkled her upturned nose. "Mostly I deliver flowers and cards."

Elise set down her fork on the tray beside her untouched chicken. She took her sketchbook and Rapidograph pen from the table. "Mind if I draw you?"

The aide, with her flat stomach and blue eyes, smiled as she watched her likeness appear on the paper. "Wow, you're really good! I can't draw a stick figure."

Cassie entered the room. "Nice evasive maneuver, Elise." She turned to the aide. "Baby girl, go check on Mr. Grant in 406."

"He's so—" the aide made a face. "Okay. Good luck, Mrs. Reeves. You're a nice lady."

"You simply pecked at the dinner." Cassie pressed the fork into Elise's hand. "Take a bite of chicken for Cassiopeia and I'll stop hounding you—for now."

After dinner, Tony called to say he wouldn't be able to come to visit.

Thank heaven for small favors. A nurse came in to check her blood pressure and heart rate.

Finally, the day drew to a close. No more techs taking blood or nagging her to take one more bite. Elise curled up on her side, being careful of her IV and shut her eyes. She had almost drifted off when the phone on the bedside table rang. She fumbled for the receiver and, after dropping it twice, managed to bring it to her ear.

The tearful voice said, "Mom?"

Her heart leaped. "Ben!"

At twenty-one, his voice was deeper than Tony's and, unlike his father, his command of the English language was perfect. Majoring in journalism at Harvard, she had high hopes for his future in broadcasting. She could imagine his silky voice on national radio or his good looks on television. Perhaps he'd even have his own talk show.

The last time her eldest child—her best friend and confidante—had called from Boston was a week before Christmas to say he couldn't make it home. Tony had exploded and laid the proverbial guilt trip, demanding to know why. When Ben had refused to say, Tony had yelled louder. Gracie had rushed to the bathroom in tears and slammed the door.

Memories of the evening paralyzed Elise now as it had then. Her chest ached and her head spun. Beads of sweat broke out on her upper lip, and she fought to catch her breath.

Ben's voice broke through her musing. "Mom? *Mom!* Are you—okay? Gracie called me."

"Ben, it's so good to hear your voice." Her words tumbled over each other in desperate succession. "How's school? Do you have a girlfriend yet? Will you be home for spring break?"

"Mom. Stop it! Listen to me. I haven't said it lately, but—but I really love you and I…" He drew a raspy breath. "…don't want you to die." *Click.*

She set the receiver back in its cradle. Those words—death, die, cardiac arrest—had come out of several mouths over the past week, including the EMT, the horrid ER nurse, Elise's family doctor, and Nurse Chukwu.

Elise buried her face in her pillow, trying to laugh them off, but every time she closed her eyes, the memory of the thrift store swooshed about her in shades of blue and gray. Over and over, her bowels evacuated and the floor smacked her face.

Hot tears oozed from her eyes. What had she done? She didn't want to die. All she wanted was control over something.

More than anyone's, Ben's words haunted her. She couldn't bear his disappointment in her. Hearing him cry into the phone ripped her heart apart.

"Elise?"

She turned to see Cassie standing beside the bed with a cup of water in her right hand and a pill in her left. Snatching the pill, Elise gulped down the green and yellow capsule without water.

Cassie set the glass on Elise's tray table. Then she removed the IV needle from Elise's arm. Tossing Elise's laundered clothes on the bed, the nurse winked. "No more lounging around in your jammies."

Relief at not having the needle poking her at every turn flooded Elise. Then, sudden terror gripped her. Were they sending her home. Did she want to go home? Home to Tony's constant nagging? Home to a hormonal teenager? Home to be left to her own devices where she might, as Susan warned, end up dead on the bathroom floor?

As if reading her thoughts, Cassie said, "You're being transferred to EDU where the real work begins."

The Beast screamed. "They're going to force feed you until you weigh five hundred pounds!"

"Now? It's seven o'clock in the pee-em." Elise sat up to put on her bra. What was left of her breasts hung like empty tube socks. She bit back a satisfied smile. "At least I won't have you pestering me." The room spun around her as she stood to pull on her blue jeans.

"Steady, girlfriend." Cassie caught her and helped her sit in a chair. "Give yourself some time to get used to standing on those toothpicks. Didn't they tell you, sugar? You're my assignment."

Cassie picked up Elise's framed wallet-size photo of Ben and Gracie from the nightstand. She swiveled her head from side to side. "Mm hm. Seems to me you've got a lot to live for."

A lot to live for? Almost exactly what Susan had said. Elise took the picture of her children from the nurse. They'd inherited her deep brown eyes. Ben had her dark hair, while Gracie's was a riot of auburn curls. Ben's slender physique contrasted his sister's more rounded yet muscular shape. Both faces were so full of promise, reflecting their brilliant minds.

Tony's comment about Gracie's budding obsession with her weight set off alarm bells in Elise's head. *This is my fault. They would be better off without me.*

Cassie shook her head and muttered, "What happened to you to make you hate yourself so much?"

Chapter Six

OPENING the new drawing pad Daddy had given her for her seventh birthday, Elise imagined the masterpieces she would create on the twenty-five heavy pages. Before she had a chance to put pencil to paper, her cousin Nancy grabbed a crayon and slashed red streaks across it.

Elise wrenched the crayon from Nancy's chubby fingers and shoved her.

"Mommy!" the three-year-old squealed. "'Lise pushed me."

Aunt Vivian burst into the living room like a fire-breathing dragon in a floral muumuu. "Dammit!" she hollered. "I just got the baby to sleep."

Down the hall, two-month-old Danny began to wail. Aunt Vivian leaned into Elise. "See what you did? You're supposed to be watching Nancy, not picking on her."

Elise held her breath. Aunt Viv had a "distinct stink" as Daddy put it. She smelled of dirty diapers, B.O., and cigarette smoke. Mommy said it was because Aunt Viv was so fat, she couldn't properly clean herself. Daddy said it was because she was a slob, pure and simple.

It was hard to believe Aunt Vivian and Elise's tiny mother were sisters. Mom kept an immaculate house and worked in an office, while her younger sister lazed around most of the day watching soap operas.

"She didn't even know she was expecting until she went into labor," Elise had overheard Mom telling someone on the phone. "That pig must weigh every bit of three hundred pounds."

Elise blinked back tears. If Mommy and Daddy didn't like Aunt Viv, why did they always ask her to babysit?

"We can't afford to pay someone," Daddy would say. "Besides, she's your aunt and she loves you."

"If you lay a hand on Nancy again, I swear I'll tear off your arm and beat you over the head with it." Aunt Viv swept Nancy into her arms, all the while yelling naughty words and threats. "Do you hear me, Elise Jacobson?"

This is love? Only a deaf person couldn't hear her.

Engulfed in her mother's fleshy arms, Nancy peered down at Elise and stuck out her tongue.

Elise held up her sketchbook to show her aunt the page Nancy had scribbled on. "She ruined it."

Danny's shrill wails grew louder. Ignoring his cries, Aunt Viv plopped down on a pile of dirty clothes on the couch. She nudged Nancy off her lap and lit a cigarette. "Nancy wants to be an artist like her cousin. It won't hurt you to share. Turn on the TV for Mommy, Nancy."

Elise gathered up her art supplies and tucked them under her arm. She stared out the smudged picture window. Home was only two blocks away. She could walk the distance, but Mom said she was too young to stay by herself.

"They're not coming to get you until tomorrow morning." Aunt Viv shifted her girth and crammed some popcorn into her mouth. "You might as well settle in. Supper will be ready soon."

Nancy had gone to her room. Danny must've given up, for his cries had stopped. Heaving a sigh, Elise sat on the floor cross-legged and set her drawing pad, a pencil, and a kneaded eraser on her lap. Like a real artist. She tore out the page her cousin scribbled on and turned it over.

People were her favorite things to draw. Beginning with the eyes, she sketched a girl's face. Aunt Viv peeked over her shoulder. "Damn. You've got some kind of talent, kid. Your parents should send you to art school."

How quickly Aunt Viv's mood changed. She even offered Elise some of her popcorn. "Buttered. Put some meat on those skinny bones. Don't your parents feed you? Guess your fatso daddy eats it all." She roared with raucous laughter. "Don't know how he managed to *shtupe* my sister to conceive you and Eugene. Bet he has to dig deep to find Wee Willy Winkie now." She laughed louder, spewing bits of popcorn in all directions.

Uncle Leo, who'd been silently sipping his third beer, raised an eyebrow and chuckled. "You think it's so easy to climb the mountain with you, Viv?"

Chapter Seven

Elise buried her head in the pillow. Outside the room, carts rattled by and staff greeted each other with cheerful "good morning"s. She twisted the open end of the pillowcase around her pinkie finger. After Elise grew up, Mom had teased her about her childhood habit. Elise shrugged off the memories of Mom's ridicule. Why should she stop it if it wasn't hurting anyone, and it helped her relax?

The night before seemed like a dream. Once she had dressed in her street clothes, Cassie had taken her in a wheelchair to the ninth floor. There she'd steered her to a room with comfortable couches, a couple of overstuffed chairs, and a television. "Here you go, Elise. Your home away from home. I'll take your bags to your room."

A skinny teenager had handed her a bag of chips. "Here's your snack."

When Elise had protested, another patient had gone on to explain a bedtime snack was part of their nightly routine. It was munch or else. Or else what?

Obediently she'd opened the bag and removed a chip. She'd taken the teeniest tiniest bite possible. By nine, when attendants herded the patients to their respective room, Elise had triumphantly crushed and tossed the full bag of chips into the wastebasket.

Cassie had explained to Elise that her roommate had already gone to bed, so she needed to be as quiet as possible. The advice had proven unnecessary as the woman in the other bed snored like a jackhammer.

After a fitful night, Elise had drifted off at dawn, hoping for a few more moments of sleep.

Cassie's voice jolted her awake with, "Time for vitals, ladies. Dixie, you know the drill. I'm counting on you to show Elise the ropes."

Elise rubbed her eyes and moaned, "Go away. Lemme sleep."

"Better do as you're told, Suzie-Q," said an unfamiliar voice.

Opening her eyes, Elise looked up to see her roommate—a woman so emaciated she looked more like a Halloween skeleton than a living, breathing human being. Her thin blonde hair hung in her sunken eyes. The hospital gown swallowed her. Although she looked to be at least ninety years old her voice sounded much younger.

"Dr. Picard's Dixie?"

"That's my name, don't wear it out." Dixie's smile couldn't soften her skeletal face. "You tie the gown like this. In the front." She pulled one side over the other and tied the strings at the neck and waistline. "Then we follow Sassy Cassie to get folded, spindled, and mutilated."

Elise took her gown and followed Dixie's instructions. "What's that supposed to mean?"

"Y'know, the usual drill. Weight. Height. Blood pressure." Dixie smirked. "Every morning like clockwork. Then the staff stands over us while we gag down their sorry excuse for breakfast."

A week of languishing on the cardiac ward might not have prepared Elise for Brookside Memorial's eating disorder unit routine. During her former hospitalizations she'd been able to manipulate the techs and shrinks. She had an uneasy inkling it might not be such a snap here.

"Run!" the Beast hollered. "Hide!"

The Beast, her ally, her protector and her worst enemy. Elise's feet turned to stone.

"Take my hand," whispered the Beast. "Don't let them force you."

"Come along, ladies. Terry's waiting." Cassie held the door open. "Step lively." She slid her gaze to Dixie. "But not too lively."

Following them down the hall, Elise took in her new surroundings.

The walls were littered with framed motivational quotes and childish artwork, presumably done by patients. Besides Dixie and Elise, three young women, not quite as emaciated as Dixie, but thin enough, lined up by the nurses' station.

"Nice that you could join us, ladies." Terry, a stout lady with a mop of bottle-red hair and butterfly earrings, peered over her rhinestone half-track reading glasses. "Good morning, Elise. Step right up."

Heart thumping with anticipation, Elise raised her foot to step onto the beam scale. Terry held up her hand, palm flat against the air. "Turn around—everyone. Step onto it backward, Elise. We don't allow the number to control us, do we, girls?"

Elise backed onto the scale and strained her ears as Terry slid the weights across the scale's beam. Try as she might, she couldn't figure out where they balanced by the sound. The Beast roared in anger. Before she could sneak a peek, Terry slid the weights to the end. "Next."

After each patient had her weight and blood pressure recorded, Terry excused them to dress for breakfast. Dixie skipped a couple of steps and turned a perfect cartwheel, then a front flip. Landing on her feet, she puffed out her non-existent chest and raised her arms in a 'V'. She definitely wasn't anywhere near ninety.

Cassie grasped Dixie's rawboned wrist. "Don't make me put you in a wheelchair, Ms. Gymnast."

Back in their room Dixie and Elise dressed in silence. Staring at her roommate's protruding ribs, the lightbulb went on. Elise remembered reading an article a few months ago about an anorectic former gymnast in the *Kansas City Star*. It reported her weight to be around sixty-something pounds.

"They won't tell me what I weigh, of course," said Dixie. "I'm thirty-six in case you're wondering. You're no teenager either, are you? Forty-two I heard the nurses say."

Elise nodded and checked the size tag of her blue jeans. Still zero. The loose fit pleased her.

"That zero stands for your chances of getting out of here without swelling to the size of a house," whispered the Beast. *"Fritos are nothing but fat and oil that multiply and mutate into a thousand fat cells."*

Elise examined her reflection in the full-length mirror. The bruise on her upper lip had faded. She turned and peered over her shoulder. *My butt's too big. I'm developing a double chin like Aunt Vivian. It's only a matter of time before I look just like her.*

"Come on, Suzie-Q." Dixie poked Elise's shoulder. "You're a stick. Let's go make the Gestapo happy with our presence."

Elise surveyed the breakfast table in the cheerfully painted dining room. The same girls she'd met the night before gathered around the long table. They ranged in age from very young, possibly twelve, to one woman who looked like she could be Elise's mother or grandmother. Their stares made her squirm and the hard chair hurt her behind.

She poured her coffee. "Where's the sweetener?"

Cassie sat in the chair beside her. "You won't find that low-cal poison here. Honey, sugar, or maple syrup are your choices."

"Black then."

"At least put some honey in your oatmeal."

"I like it plain." Elise dipped her spoon in her oatmeal and licked a bit from the tip. She sneered at Cassie. "Yum."

With a nervous giggle, the perky blonde across the table said, "A little honey goes a long way. Hi Elise, I'm Marissa."

Dixie nibbled at her muffin. "This is Marissa's last week."

"Yup." Marissa shoveled scrambled eggs into her mouth. "Going back to school next week. I'm a senior at Center High."

"My alma mater." Elise stirred her cereal. "My daughter goes there, too. Maybe you know her."

"Marissa's a cheerleader." A tall young woman with jet-black hair, wire-rim glasses, and sallow cheeks rolled her eyes. "Cheerleaders are all airheads. Don't expect to hold an intellectual conversation with her." She gritted her gray teeth and offered her hand to Elise. "I'm Nyx."

Scars webbed down Nyx's dragon-tattooed arm. Elise noted her calloused fingers. "Unusual name."

"She named herself after the Greek goddess of death. She's a puker and a cutter," said Dixie. "But it doesn't take a rocket scientist to figure that out."

Nyx withdrew her hand and glared at Dixie. She opened her mouth then shut it and slugged back her orange juice. "To each her own toxicant."

A dark-haired girl with almond-shaped eyes sat at the end of the table—her expression stony and unchanging. She gripped her fork and jabbed her muffin until it was nothing but a heap of crumbs.

"Karlie? What did we talk about?" Cassie nodded at the nurses standing in the doorway. "It's time."

Karlie threw her plastic butter knife at Cassie. It smacked Cassie's forehead and fell in her lap. Without losing her composure, Cassie picked it up and placed it on the table.

With a loud shriek, Karlie leaped from her chair and lunged at Cassie, fingernails poised to claw her. Two nurses caught her from behind and dragged her, biting and kicking, from the room.

Cassie waited a few minutes before saying, "I'm sorry this happened on your first day, Elise. Karlie's being transferred today. I fear her problems are way out of our league."

Elise sat on her hands and searched the room for an escape. What kind of nuthouse had they put her in?

"Haldol time." Dixie circled her index finger next to her ear. "Loony toons."

Cassie shot a sidelong glance at Dixie and touched Elise's shoulder. "Your food's getting cold. One more bite—for me."

"You're one to talk about loonies, Dixie." A girl with taffy-colored curls and freckles, who reminded Elise of Gracie, stuck out her tongue. She cradled a teddy bear in the crook of one arm and grinned at Elise, revealing a mouthful of braces. "I'm Tina-Louise. Named for the actress who played Ginger on 'Gilligan's Island'."

Elise nodded at each of the girls, but didn't reply.

Under Cassie's watchful eye, she gagged on her cold oatmeal. *What the hell am I doing here? I'm old enough to be these girls' mother."*

"Too old and fat to be anorexic," the Beast hissed.

How could I be an anorexic? All I do is think about food.

"See? That wasn't so bad, was it?" Cassie's smile didn't reach her eyes. "Try the egg. You need the protein."

The wiry, gray-haired woman Elise had noticed earlier pointed a spindly finger at Dixie and snarled at Elise. "Or you could do what your buddy Dixie does and hide your half-chewed eggs under your plate."

Elise eyed the woman's bared teeth and puckered lips, then quickly shifted her gaze to Dixie.

The woman snarled at Elise. "What are you staring at?"

"You nosy old bat." Dixie stood, knocking over her orange juice. "Elise, meet Irma, the oldest patient on the unit—sixty-two going on eighty—and the biggest snitch. She tattles on the rest of us to take the attention off her own sneaky self. Half her food goes into her pockets or on the floor when no one's looking."

Elise smiled at the older woman. *At least I'm not the oldest patient in EDU.*

Elise's scrambled eggs swam in juice. The Beast cackled. Elise pushed her plate away and murmured a "Thank you" to Dixie.

"Breakfast is over. Nyx, Marissa, Irma, and Tina-Louise, good job this morning. You may be excused." Cassie turned to Elise and Dixie and narrowed her eyes. "Don't kid yourselves, ladies. You didn't get away with anything."

Chapter Eight

DR. PICARD SAT at his desk with his ubiquitous clipboard and notepad. "How are you settling in, Elise?"

Taking a sip of Ensure, she grimaced. It tasted like a thin, sweet chocolate milkshake. It tasted like too many calories. "Okay, I guess."

He nodded. "A little something extra? Trouble with breakfast?"

"Nah, cold oatmeal soaked in orange juice with a side of anxiety—over-not-so-easy. I'm sure you heard about Karlie."

Still shaken from Karlie's violent outburst in the dining room, Elise curled up in the wingback chair. What had happened to the child to cause such a melt-down? She couldn't be more than twelve or thirteen.

His cheerful smile faded. "I can't—"

"Patient confidentiality. I get it."

"When was the last time you ate three full meals in one day, Elise?"

"When was the last time you took a dump?"

He wrote in his notepad and said aloud, "Patient shows hostility... and rapier wit."

Elise's head throbbed. She resented him and this place. He probably went home to a perfect family and a beautiful wife. No cares or worries for him.

Searching for a place to stash her drink, she surveyed his office. It was on the east side of the hospital as evidenced by the morning sun streaming through the window. His desk appeared to be an antique; she guessed it to be carved oak.

On one pale blue wall hung a framed print of a ballerina. Elise recognized it as *The Star* by Edgar Degas. She had always admired that one and hoped to one day produce such a composition. Another wall boasted an ocean scene. She imagined herself beneath the waves. What bliss that would be.

The sun behind Dr. Picard put his face in shadow. Elise winced. "Do you suppose you could move? You look like a dark blob."

He rose and sank into a different chair. "That's a step in the right direction. Better?"

"Yes. What do you mean by that?"

"How often do you ask for what you need?"

"Often enough, I guess."

"How often do you ask Tony?"

Ask Tony? As if he'd ever have time to listen to me.

Acting as if she'd not heard Dr. Picard's question, Elise pointed to a framed medical certificate on the wall. "John Wayne Picard, MD, PhD," she read. Then she zeroed in on the doctor's silk bowtie. "Nice shade of cerulean. It brings out the blue in your eyes. Mind if I call you Wayne? Or do you prefer John?"

"Will it make you feel more comfortable?"

"Yes."

"Wayne it is, then."

He opened a folder in his lap and put on his reading glasses. "On that note, I've been meaning to go over the IQ tests you took at Elmwood. Remember those?"

"Vaguely. No one ever gave me the results, so I haven't really given them much thought."

"Would you like to know your scores?"

"Be gentle." Stiffening her shoulders, she braced herself. "I've two children between 125 to 129 IQs. Pretty sure mine will be in two digits."

"Room temperature, eh?" Shutting the folder, Wayne raised an eyebrow and shook his head. "Where do you think your kids get it?"

"My brother Eugene? He's the smart one."

Wayne took off his glasses and caught her in his gaze. "From *you*, my dear. They get it from *you*."

Fireworks went off in Elise's head. "I'm—I'm smart?"

"Elise, where did you get the idea you're not?"

She extended her legs in front of her and wriggled her feet. "The end of my junior year of high school, they sent us to our designated guidance counselors to discuss our post-graduation plans. It was the first time I ever talked to mine. He sat back in his chair. Hardly looked at me, but opened my file, citing my poor class performance and GPA as detriments to my future."

"What was your rank?"

"No clue. He didn't tell me, and I didn't ask. I wasn't a great student. Although I did get straight As in Spanish, art, and drama. I did well in German, too. My Language Arts teacher loved my poetry even though my grades in her class weren't the best. Math and science? Forget about it.

"Mr. Counselor, I don't even remember his name, suggested I either go to trade school or get married because I wasn't college material. I've always translated that to mean I'm stupid."

Wayne's focus on her intensified. "That lie stops here and now."

Elise's heart jumped, mulling over this new piece of information. Pride and anger warred inside her head. She smiled at the idea of being as smart as her genius brother who used to boast about his high IQ. At the same time, she blamed her nameless high school counselor for robbing her of her self-respect.

Wayne leaned back and crossed his legs. "What else do you want to talk about?"

"Nothing." She took a long sip of her drink, loathe to admit to herself it tasted good. "Nothing at all."

"While I'm thinking about it. In case no one's told you yet, you're not allowed visitors until the weekend."

An involuntary smile spread her lips and relief flooded her. She'd already refused three calls from Tony this morning. When she'd spoken to him the night before, he'd been hostile and demanded she stop this nonsense and come home.

Wayne checked his watch. "In the remaining time we have, why don't you tell me a little about you and Tony?"

Elise set her Ensure on an end table and drew her knees into her chest. "Well, we started going out when I was only sixteen. On more than one occasion he told me I was going to marry him."

"He told you?"

"That's his way." Elise shrugged and added, "We got engaged at my senior prom."

"How long after that did you tie the knot?"

"Six months. I was eighteen and thought I was so grown up." Elise bit her lip and sighed. "We moved the date up because we found out that our meager income as a married couple gave me a better chance at a hardship scholarship to the art institute—not because I was pregnant—which is what my mom's friends thought." Elise twisted a lock of hair around her finger as her memories of her wedding day filled her mind. "Do you believe in omens, Wayne?"

"My jury's still out. Go on."

"Well, everything was perfect the week before the wedding. The weather was unseasonably warm and sunny. Our wedding day? Cold, blustery, and drizzly. Mom complained the flowers and decorations weren't right. My pushy, orca-fat Aunt Viv griped about everything else."

The cuckoo clock on his wall sounded. Elise choked back giggles as the bird shot through the swinging doors ten times. "Seriously, Wayne?"

He shrugged and flashed a sheepish grin. "What else?"

Chapter Nine

After her session with Wayne and lunch, there had been a group session with Ronnie, the dietitian. She spent an hour going over things like necessary body fat, weight of head and bones, calories necessary to maintain a healthy weight. Elise yawned. There was nothing new under the sun. She'd read scads of books and magazines on diet. No doubt she could teach the class. There were good carbs and bad carbs. Good fats and bad fats.

Elise's heavy eyelids drooped, and the dietitian's voice droned into oblivion.

"Snap to, Suzie Q." Dixie's boney elbow poked her side.

Elise started, opened her eyes, and scanned the room. Tina-Louse curled up on her chair still clutching her Teddy bear. Nyx slinked down, her long legs stretched out in front of her. Marissa leaned forward, elbows on her knees and chin propped on her cupped hands, the picture of youthful enthusiasm. Irma, arms folded across her chest, pursed her lips as if to say, "Tell me something new."

Ronnie turned to Elise. "If we're not keeping you up, Mrs. Reeves, could you tell us how many calories a healthy, active woman should consume per day?"

"It depends on her age and height. In her twenties, at five-foot-five about 2,200 calories a day. Fewer if she's short like me." Elise yawned. "I'm sorry, I didn't sleep well last night."

The plump dietitian flashed a compassionate smile. "No doubt. Lack of nutrients can cause chronic insomnia. I'll bet you haven't gotten a full night's sleep in months."

And I'll bet you sleep like a baby, Ronnie.

Elise ground her teeth. "Why do you make us eat dessert?"

"Normal people eat dessert."

Normal fat people maybe.

Ronnie beckoned Marissa. "I've printed up some pages that will help answer your questions, Elise."

Now it's 'Elise'? Does this make us friends? Elise resented Ronnie's know-it-all attitude. The woman, at least twenty pounds overweight, didn't practice what she preached. Her body fat must be at least fifty percent. *Where does she get off telling me what and how much I should eat?*

Ronnie gave Marissa a stack of papers to distribute to the group. "These handouts list nutrients and vitamins necessary to maintain a healthy body. Without them, your hair will fall out, your brain won't function properly, and the rest of your organs could eventually shut down. We don't want that to happen, do we?"

Dixie tugged at a whisp of her thin hair and sneered at Marissa. She snatched the paper out of the girl's hand and crumpled it in her fist.

"Dixie, please." Ronnie shot her a disapproving frown. "Please take a moment to read these in your spare time. They could be enlightening."

Elise shrugged. "I already know this dreck."

Ronnie's gaze traveled from Elise's head to her feet. "Do you now?"

When the class ended, Elise received a message to meet Terry at the nurses' station. There, the gregarious nurse handed her a pad of water-color paper and a box of colored pencils. "Someone named Lynda who says she works with you thought you'd enjoy having these. Dr. Picard okayed it. He had her leave your airbrush and colors in the art room."

Elise hugged the paper and pencils to her chest like a long-lost friend. Her fingers itched. Drawing would keep her mind on other things besides her miserable situation. "Thank you, Terry," she whispered.

Elise lay on her bed, exhausted from her first twenty-four hours on EDU. Full day. Full stomach. She had eaten more at supper than she had actually swallowed in months. Three bites of fried chicken four hundred calories, green beans maybe a hundred, baked potato (not all that many unless one counted the butter she was forced to put on it), chocolate cake with fudge icing—she winced. Too many calories to accept.

A little disappointed the staff hadn't allowed her to see Lynda, she reminded herself that her friend probably would've delivered a tongue lashing. Over the past few months, she'd observed Elise with her granite-blue eyes and joked that she was saving the date for Elise's funeral.

Trying to shrug off the shame of letting down one of her closest friends, Elise propped the drawing pad on her knees and stared at the blank paper. "What should I draw?"

Dixie lay on her side doing leg lifts. "Forty-four... do a caricature of Terry... forty-five. That would be hilarious."

"I could do one of you. I'd only need half a sheet of paper."

"And you could use the other half for a self-portrait."

Elise drank in the delicious scent of the daffodils on the nightstand. It was sweet of her coworkers to send them up. She reread the card that said, "Fight the good fight. We love you."

"Nothing says spring like a daffodil." Elise sniffed.

"No, but make sure you never set them where Irma can see 'em. She goes bonkers around flowers."

"Why?"

"I'll let her tell it." Dixie flipped onto her back to do sit-ups. "We're supposed to concentrate on our own stories."

"Gotcha." The picture she wanted to draw popped into Elise's head. "And you're not one to break the rules, are you?"

Dixie fell back against her pillow. "Don't you dare rat on me."

"My lips are sealed." Elise sketched the outline of a child's profile, her own face. Thinking back on the article in the *Kansas City Star,* Elise asked, "What's your story, Dixie?"

Folding her arms behind her head, Dixie lay still. "I made it to the American Cup in Madison Square Garden in 1976. I was sixteen and destined for the Olympics. My forte was the balance beam. I was damned good, too. Four-foot-ten and one hundred pounds of solid muscle."

Elise drew daffodils around the child. "What happened?"

"Nadia Comaneci and Kathy Howard happened. I was competing with them instead of staying in my own head and kicking butt. I missed my mark and fell off the beam. Gave myself a concussion and broke my ankle."

Elise filled in the yellow flowers with colored pencil. "I'm so sorry."

"I was laid up for weeks, but still ate like an athlete. By the time I made it back to the gym, I'd gained ten pounds. My coach really got on my case about it. My boyfriend Jason, a football player, showed me how to barf after every meal so nothing stuck. He said it worked like a charm for him."

Elise stopped sketching and shuddered, her own gag reflexes threatening to kick in. "I can't make myself do that."

"It got so easy. After a while I didn't even have to stick my finger down my throat." Dixie heaved a deep sigh. "By the next competition, I'd lost twenty pounds. My coach was so complimentary, I dropped another twenty."

Resuming her sketch, Elise drew a bubble wand in the little girl's hand. "Did that make him happy?"

"Ha! I thought it would. Instead, he sidelined me. Would you believe he said I was too skinny to compete? That was the end of my gymnastic career."

"But why are you still starving yourself when you're—?"

"Too old to be a gymnast?"

"That's not what I was going to say."

"It's true. Whoever heard of a thirty-six-year-old gymnast? My shelf-life has expired."

"Couldn't you coach?"

"I did—for a while." Dixie twisted her lips to one side. "May I see your picture?"

Elise put the finishing touches on a bubble and held up the sketchpad. "What happened after you quit gymnastics?"

"Oh, I didn't quit, my folks put me in a psych ward where I put some of the weight back on... all the way up to ninety-five," she said as though it had been one of her greatest accomplishments. "I finished my senior year, went to college, and landed a job as a gymnastics instructor. Everything was perfect. Jason snagged a position at a college as a football coach. He proposed... got down on one knee, just like in the movies. Finally. Finally, little Dixie Granger was going to live happily ever after."

"What happened?"

"Jason dumped me for a voluptuous cheerleader." Dixie rolled over on her side and propped up on her elbow. Her dark eyes, recessed in their sockets, brimmed. "Guess you could say I lost my fiancé and my appetite. Enough of me, what about you, Suzie-Q? Did you always like to draw?"

Elise studied the little girl blowing bubbles in her sketch. The picture of carefree childhood. What was that like? Her mind traveled back to her tenth birthday. She remembered counting down the time on her new Cinderella watch with pride. It had been her favorite present. Mommy had promised she could have it when she could tell time. She had been sprawled out on the floor drawing pictures at Aunt Viv and Uncle Leo's house.

"Ten minutes after six o'clock."

Mommy and Daddy will come and get me soon.

Daddy owned a barbecue restaurant called JB's. Mommy worked there as well. Elise wished she was there, too, but Mommy insisted Elise stay at Aunt Viv and Uncle Leo's after school.

"How come Eugene gets to stay home by himself?" Elise pouted. "It's not fair."

"He's in junior high and has extracurricular activities. Besides, you said he's mean to you."

Mommy didn't lie. Eugene teased her and he was bossy, but Elise still preferred staying with him than at her smelly aunt's house.

Aunt Viv lay on the sofa and puffed away on her third cigarette in twenty minutes. *The news blared on the television. "Mr. Kennedy's one handsome man-full, isn't he, Elise? What I wouldn't give to bed down with him."*

Elise sprawled on the floor on her tummy beside Nancy. She concentrated on the coloring book, not sure of how to answer her aunt. "Here, Nanny, the grass should be green, not pink."

Nancy continued to color. "I like pink."

Elise shrugged. "Okay." She sat up and watched the black and white images on the screen. "I think Mrs. Kennedy is very pretty."

Uncle Leo took a swig of his beer. "She does sex me up."

The front door opened and Daddy stepped into the living room. Elise ran to him. He swept her up into his meaty arms. "Has my princess been a good girl?"

She wrapped her legs around the expanse of his stomach and buried her face in his chest, breathing in the aroma of barbecue.

"Elise is always a perfect angel. How's business?" Aunt Viv pointed to Daddy's grease-stained work clothes. "Looks like most of the profits ended up there. Have you gained weight, Bob?"

That night at supper Daddy bawled out Eugene for forgetting to take out the trash. Then he yelled at him about his poor grades. "What do you plan to do with your life? Be a bum?"

"Bob, please." Mommy pleaded in a hoarse whisper.

Eugene leaped off his chair, knocking it over. "I'm sure as hell not going to be a fat fry cook like you!" He stomped off to his room.

His face flushing to fiery red, Daddy raced after him. Mommy pushed her plate away and lit up a cigarette. Elise picked at her sandwich. Her brother's cries begging Daddy not to hit him ate at her.

When Daddy came back to the table, Eugene stayed in his room. Daddy crammed half a sandwich into his mouth. Barbecue sauce dribbled down his chin. "Elise, you haven't taken more than two bites."

"I'm not very hungry."

"You're too skinny, sweetheart." Daddy glared at Mommy. "Your son is sulking. As far as I'm concerned, he can starve. Why'd you have to have a boy anyway?"

Mommy stubbed out her cigarette and returned his glare. "It wasn't the immaculate conception, you know."

Elise pondered the words. "What does that mean, Mommy?"

"What it means is," Daddy finished his sandwich and took Elise's off her plate, "your mother thinks she's better than everyone else."

"You're meshuggeneh." Mommy muttered and took her dishes to the sink. "I should've listened to my dad."

"Your whole family looked down on me from day one." Daddy's voice grew louder. "Self-righteous, religious fanatics."

Mommy shook her head and turned to walk away. Daddy picked up a pop bottle and hurled it at her, missing her head by an inch. She whirled around and threw a napkin holder at him. Plates, cups, and utensils flew back and forth along with hollered words that made Elise's tummy hurt.

She managed to escape undetected to her room where she cowered under her bed, pressing her hands against her ears. Their hateful shouts faded as she imagined she was a gravely ill patient on "Dr. Kildare".

The handsome young doctor held her on his lap. "We'll take good care of you, Elise. I promise."

Chapter Ten
Tony

Tony paced the floor, checking his watch every few minutes. He moved the drapes aside and searched the empty street. *It's past eighteen hundred hours. Where is that girl? She should be home by now.*

He took his car keys off the hook by the door to go search for her, but then he remembered he had eggs boiling on the stove and a casserole in the oven. The aroma wafting over him told him it was almost done.

He heard a car and peered back out the window. The car sped past. He heaved an angry sigh and a growl. "Dammit."

A loud pop startled him. Two more bangs followed it. *Viet Cong! Hit the deck!* Tony dropped to his knees, covering his head with his hands. *A second explosion. Frankie, watch out!*

"Daddy? Are you okay?"

Tony raised his head and blinked. Gracie crouched beside him. He read her worried expression and counted her freckles. The echoes of bombings ceased, save the ones going off in his stomach. Forcing a smile, he whispered, "Hey, baby girl." Then he frowned. "Where've you been?"

"I told you this morning. Band practice 'til five—I mean, seventeen hundred hours. I waited for you. When you didn't come, Doug gave me a ride."

Wiping his damp palms on his blue jeans, Tony stood and looked at his watch. "It's eighteen forty-five hours. The high school ain't that far away."

Gracie rolled her eyes. "We stopped at McGrab and Gag for fries and a Coke."

"Just you and him?"

"Us and some of the kids from the team. Since none of us have a car, Doug's our chauffeur." Gracie jumped to her feet. "I'm sorry. I was going to call but the school office was locked and, by the time we got to McDonald's, I plum forgot."

"Next time you're gonna be late, you call. I'll come and pick you up. Get it?"

"Got it." She sniffed, nose in the air. "You still making your world-famous deviled eggs with macaroni and cheese for supper, Poppo?"

"Crap-a-doodle-doo!"

Gracie giggled at his expletive, which eased his tension to a small degree. He had picked up the habit when Ben was a toddler and Elise had begged him not to swear in front of the kids.

Tony hurried to the kitchen. "I forgot about the eggs."

He came to an abrupt halt. Switching off the gas burner, he moved the blackened saucepan. Scorched eggshells crunched under his feet. Pieces of yolk and white stuck to the stovetop and walls.

"Way to go, Poppo." Gracie pointed upward in awe. "There's even some on the ceiling."

Tony's heart thumped against his ribs. "It does look like a war zone, don't it?"

Grabbing a pair of hot pads, she took the casserole from the oven. The macaroni was blackened around the edges. She set it on a trivet on the table. "Dinner is served."

"Let's pray." Tony bowed his head and closed his eyes. "Lord, bless this food to our bodies..." It was the same prayer his father prayed over every meal. *What a hypocrite.*

After supper, Gracie went to her room to do her homework. More memories flooded Tony. He remembered how the winter wind buffeted the Reeves' tiny mobile home in Andover, Kansas the year he turned fourteen. He lounged on the Naugahyde sofa turned into a makeshift bed and watched the lights twinkle on the tiny Christmas tree. Some things never changed. He took a final drag from his cigarette and stubbed it out in the ashtray on the coffee table.

Aside from their tradition of putting up the tree, his birthday had come and gone without much fanfare. Dad promised he'd be home to celebrate. Tony snorted. It wasn't like his old man ever kept his promises. Of course, Dad chalked it up to his job as a crop duster which took him all over the country. He wasn't fooling anyone. Even Mom knew about his honey in California.

Tony lit another cigarette. His eight-year-old brother Woody snored away on his bed in the hallway. Jamie, who at twelve already turned male heads, shared Mom's bed in Dad's absence. In other words, almost always.

Drowsiness had washed over him. He put out the cigarette. It wouldn't do to set their miserable excuse for a house on fire. He remembered thinking that his poor mom had enough to deal with—four children, a full-time job, and a part-time husband.

He had fallen asleep until his father's voice woke him. "Son?"

"Dad?" Tony opened his eyes to see his father sit on the edge of the sofa. "I thought—"

Dad gently pressed his fingers against Tony's mouth and shook his head. "I wanted to wish you a happy birthday before I—. Tell your mom I'm sorry, okay?" Then he had vanished like smoke through a keyhole.

Unable to process what had just happened, Tony rubbed his eyes. "What a dream. It seemed so real." He shivered and pulled his blanket up to his neck, closing his eyes. "Or was it a dream?"

The next thing he knew, Mom shook him. "Tony, wake up. The police are here."

Even now, Tony's pulse thudded against his temples at the memory still sharp in his mind. His mind raced back to the six-pack he and his friend Alvin had lifted the night before. Surely Alvin wouldn't have ratted him out. Tony stretched out on the sofa. "Tell 'em they got the wrong guy. I didn't do it."

"Let me try, Mrs. Reeves," said a deep male voice. "Anthony, you're not in trouble."

Tony opened his eyes to see his mother sink into a chair and bury her face in her arms on the kitchen table. "Not my Billy… please, not my husband."

Tony gazed up at the uniformed officer. "What happened to my dad? Who finally took him out?"

"No one, son." Sitting beside him, the officer put his arm around Tony's shoulder. "His plane tangled in electrical wires, and he crashed into a pole. Death was instant. He felt no pain, I assure you."

"Too bad."

The next morning, after a fitful night of flashbacks and nightmares, Tony tried to check in on Elise. "I've had it!" He slammed down the receiver on his desk phone at the Military Entrance Processing Station, MEPS for short. "She's refusing to answer any of my calls."

Marco squeezed his shoulder. "Go easy on the equipment, Antonio. *¿Qué pasa?* She's going through her own battle. She'll take your calls when she's ready."

"Battle? Looks more like a vacation with nurses waiting on her hand and foot."

"Ya think? I've been in treatment myself. It wasn't such a cakewalk." Marco shuffled through a stack of papers. "Meanwhile, try and concentrate on the job."

"It ain't easy." Tony ran his hands through his hair. "I got a teenage daughter who's making me pull my hair out by the roots." He tweaked a lock of it and tugged. "She's out all hours and I'm afraid she's following in her mom's footsteps."

Desperation and fear seared his stomach. "Marco, she's trying to kill herself. What will I do if she actually succeeds this time?"

"Don't make funeral arrangements yet. Elise is a fighter. Look how long she's been married to you." Marco's smile under this thick black mustache faded. He paused and then lowered his voice. "You will do what you need to do for your daughter."

Tony looked into the eyes of his friend Chief Petty Officer Marco Sanchez. Marco's golden-haired fiancée sent him a 'Dear John' letter while he dodged VC sniper fire in Vietnam as a medical corpsman. When he came back to the states in 1970, he met and married Carla, only to have her succumb to ovarian cancer a few years later. Marco was left to raise their three sons. How Marco managed without losing his mind baffled Tony.

"Now pull yourself together, man." Marco handed Tony a folder. "Your first potential recruit of the day is here."

"How do you do it?"

"Sense of humor."

"There ain't a damn thing funny about cancer."

Marco shrugged. "Depends on how you look at it. Carla always told me if we divorced, she'd make sure I got custody of the kids. Said she'd hire 'lack-of-character' witnesses and prove she was an unfit mother." He turned his grin to the ceiling. "Guess you got the last laugh, Carlita." He turned to leave. "Lunch at Ruby's?"

Three hours later, Tony's stomach growled as he breathed in the aroma of fried chicken and greens. He never needed too much convincing to eat at Ruby's.

"You sailors sure do make my day." Ruby spooned a healthy dollop of chicken gravy over Tony's mashed potatoes. After drizzling more gravy over Marco's plate, she turned to talk to another patron. "You boys call if you need anything else."

"I'll need a crane." Tony bit into a chicken wing. "Just like Grandma made."

"Ruby's a Kansas City treasure. I wish I could take her with me." Marco's face turned crimson from the top of his bald head to his full cheeks. "Have some hot sauce, Antonio. It'll put hair on your chest."

"Apparently it doesn't do much for the hair on your head." Tony chewed and swallowed. "What d'ya mean take her with you. Going somewhere?"

"I've put in for an administrative position at the VA hospital in Palo Alto."

"Why?" Tony's stomach tightened. "I thought you liked it here."

"You know Jorge got that scholarship to Stanford, so I did a little digging," he took a deep breath and looked Tony in the eye, "Mijo, I got a transfer. Arturo and Rafael are all in. They're excited for the change." Marco's dark eyes glistened. *"Mi familia es mi mundo.* My family is my world."

Tony stopped shoveling the bacon-covered green beans into his mouth long enough to respond. "Yeah, I wish I could be with Ben. Hard to believe I grew up in an eight-by-forty-foot trailer in the sticks and now my boy is half a world away on a partial scholarship to Harvard. He'll be looking down his nose at his old man someday... if he don't already. That's the thanks I get."

"Ben's a smart young man. He knows how hard his father works."

"I wonder," Tony slathered one of Ruby's homemade biscuits with butter and bit into it, "if he gives his dear old dad a second thought."

He remembered Ben's last night at home over a year ago. Elise had only been home from Hilliard General a week. She had picked at her fried catfish fillet.

"Mom, you have to eat." Ben's brown eyes had filled. "Please. For me. For Gracie."

"And me." Tony took a swig of his beer and lifted the can with the sweeping gesture of a toast toward Elise. "Your loving husband."

Elise had taken a bite of her fish. "I'll try—for you, son."

Tony's gut had cramped as his children tried to coax their mother to eat as if she was the child. Her recent stay at Hilliard General hadn't seemed to have done a thing for her. Her thick, dark curls had obscured her narrow face. She'd never looked her age, but with all the weight loss she appeared even younger. It killed him that, try as he might, there wasn't a thing he could do about it. Anger had welled up in his chest and he had fought the urge to cram the whole fish down her throat.

"That's the thanks I get for going to the trouble of catching the damn fish. Not a damn word." Tony slammed his beer down on the table. "Ben's favorite for his farewell dinner and you won't even eat it! Does anyone give a rat's ass that I work fourteen-hour days to pay for all your crap?"

Gracie had burst into tears and run to her room. Elise had dropped her fork and covered her ears.

"Everything's about you, isn't it, Dad." Ben had jumped out of his chair. "You care more about your precious recruits than your own family."

"At least they respect me." Tony had pointed at Ben. "Y'know, the Navy ain't hurt us none. You'd do well to listen to me and enlist. They'd pay for *all* your school, not this half ride bullshit leaving your family in debt!"

The silence had crackled the next morning during the ride to the airport. Gracie and Elise's faces were blotched from tears. They each gave Ben lingering hugs before he boarded his flight. When they'd finished, Ben had given Tony a stiff handshake. "Take care of yourself, Dad."

Back in the present, Tony washed down peach cobbler with a long swallow of milk. "Marco, do you ever think about Nam?"

"Sure. Who doesn't?" Marco winced. "You haven't slept much lately, have you? Flashbacks?"

"Maybe."

"You know," Marco leaned forward and lowered his voice. "There's no shame in seeing someone."

"Hold on. Hold on. I ain't the crazy one here. It's bad enough I have to talk to Elise's shrink. The whole world don't need to know our business."

"I think you should take it into consideration, *mi amigo*. There are support groups at the VA specifically for Nam Vets. Couldn't hurt."

Chapter Eleven

EVERY TUESDAY AND THURSDAY, art therapy followed breakfast. Patients were encouraged to express themselves through the craft. Elise looked forward to these sessions.

The art room, set apart for the activity, bore no resemblance to the other rooms on the floor. It reminded her of what one would find in the pediatric ward. Each of the walls had been painted a different color—yellow, orange, bright green, and hot pink.

A large round table piled with tempera paint, crayons, and colored pencils sat in the middle of the room. A heavy sheet of paper had been provided for each patient. Elise guessed the paper to be one-hundred-forty pound. A good weight for tempera.

Breathing in the soothing aroma of Crayolas, she grinned inwardly. This was something she could sink her teeth into without having to imbibe calories.

Shifting her gaze from one patient to another, Elise sketched their portraits in her mind. Tina-Louise huddled in her chair, cuddling her teddy bear, her blue eyes red-rimmed and swollen from crying over a difficult breakfast. She stared at the page in front of her, making no move to participate.

Irma's iron-gray hair, pulled back into a severe bun made her appear more cross than ever as she hunched over her work in progress. She sucked in her thin lips until they seemed to disappear.

Elise couldn't help but notice emerging blonde roots in the part in Nyx's straight black hair. The girl seemed lost in her own world as she grasped her pencil in a white-knuckled fist. A tear trickled down her narrow cheek.

Irma scowled at her crayon drawing of a stick standing next to a big rectangle on two Xs. "It's not fair. Elise is a professional who draws for a living. She shouldn't be allowed in here with the rest of us."

"We all have different gifts." Elise's attempt at reassurance sounded feeble in her own ears. "I'm sure you're better at a lot of things than I am."

"*Like starving. Look how skinny she is,*" crooned the Beast.

Tuesday, they had painted ceramic coffee mugs. Today, Pam, the art therapist, prompted them to sketch something concerning their childhoods.

"I'm Jackson Pollock." Dixie splattered tempera paint on her paper. "Whaddya think, Suzie-Q?"

"Bright colors." Elise cocked her head one way and then the other. "What is it supposed to be?"

"A Rorschach inkblot. What else?"

"What does that have to do with your childhood?"

"I was a problem child even then."

"Pam?" Elise opened her sketchpad to the picture of the child blowing bubbles. "Would it be okay if I keep working on the one I already started?"

"Why, this is delightful, Elise." Pam took the pad from her and looked it over. "Tell me about it."

Avoiding eye contact with Irma's glare, Elise sharpened her colored pencils. "It's going to be mixed media with some airbrush and pen and ink."

"Why the bubbles?"

"It was one of my favorite things to do when I was a little girl."

"Good." Pam returned the pad. "This is exactly what I'm talking about. You're getting in touch with your inner child. Something we all need to do. We'll chat more about this when we have our one-on-one this evening."

She bent over Irma's shoulder, concern replacing her good-natured smile. "What's in the box?"

Irma rolled her eyes and flipped her paper over. "What do you expect to find in a coffin?"

"Why a coffin?"

"You'd have to ask my inner child and her lips are sealed."

Nyx held up a rather decent likeness of herself in yellow pigtails with ribbons. "How'd I do, teacher?"

With a sidelong glance at Irma, Pam turned to Nyx's picture. "Elise isn't the only talented one here. Very nice, Nanette."

"Don't you ever call me that!" Nyx bared her pitted teeth. She grasped a black marker in her fist and scribbled across her self-portrait. "Nanette is dead!"

"I'm sorry—Nyx. I didn't mean to upset you."

Careful to avoid Nyx's menacing scowl, Elise turned her attention to Marissa, who had been unusually sullen. She showed promise with a sketch of two little girls dressed alike in front of a yellow two-story. One girl was holding a puppy.

The mother in Elise wanted to give her a hug and tell her everything would be okay. Instead, she said, "Very nice. Is this your home?"

"Yes." Marissa put her head down on the table. "I'm afraid to go back."

Pam glanced at her watch and sank down beside Marissa. "The rest of you may go to your rooms and get ready for supper."

Elise set her new sketchbook on her dresser. She left it open to her latest picture, in which an airbrushed rainbow splayed forth from a daffodil. Magic Daffodils, the perfect title for the story budding in her mind.

During lunch, so pleased with her art, she had even enjoyed a few morsels of pizza and a lettuce salad with a smattering of dressing. No taunting voice bothered her, which frightened her a bit.

In anticipation of supper, she gave her reflection a quick glance, expecting puffy cheeks and broadened thighs. To her relief, her blue jeans still wrinkled in the right places and her cheeks boasted pale hollows. She turned from the mirror, stepped out into the hallway, and headed for the dining room.

Sitting down to the table, she looked around for Dixie. Her roommate had been called from art therapy halfway through the session. She hadn't returned from lunch. From the looks of it, she wouldn't be making an appearance for dinner, either.

Elise flagged down Cassie. "Where's Dixie?"

"She'll be back by bedtime."

"Is she okay?"

"It's nice that you care so much, sugar, but why don't we concentrate on you for now? Mm-mmm, that cheeseburger looks good. Try a bite."

Elise scrutinized the cheese melting on the succulent burger. It didn't resemble the cardboard hospital food she remembered when she had had her babies. The aroma tantalized her. Perhaps one bite wouldn't hurt.

With her mouth watering, she lifted it to her lips. She flinched when the Beast cried in a voice so loud, she was almost sure everyone else heard, *"Too many carbs. Once on the lip, forever on the hip."*

Setting the burger back on the plate, Elise slipped the meat from the bun and nibbled at a pickle.

Questions regarding her missing friend's whereabouts nagged at her. When Dixie had stepped on the scale this morning, Terry and Cassie had exchanged frowns.

Elise picked at a tomato slice. She scowled at the plateful of pink-iced cupcakes placed in the middle of the table because "normal people eat dessert."

They put her in mind of one of her many therapists telling her she didn't have an eating disorder because she ate cake. The therapist, who herself looked like a poster child for anorexia, had told Elise no anorexic she had treated would eat cake. It didn't make any difference to her that Elise worked in a bakery and a few crumbs might be all she ate in a day's time.

A sense of accomplishment coupled with a tinge of remorse welled in Elise's chest, thinking back to a mandatory occupational therapy session three years ago at Hilliard General. It was a group activity, and one Elise didn't have the option of skipping.

A perky blonde, yet totally clueless OT, had adorned a table with the usual equipment—bags, tips, colored icing. "We're going to decorate cupcakes. Won't that be fun?"

Fun? As a fulltime designer, Elise had lost any sense of fun. It had become a miserable job that smacked of crabby customers and demanding managers. Obediently, she did what came naturally. In no time, she frosted her cupcake and topped it with a pink icing rose.

In a syrupy, patronizing voice, the OT had ooh-ed and ah-ed over Elise's talent. "That's lovely, Mrs. Reeves. Such pretty roses, Mrs. Reeves. So much detail, Mrs. Reeves. Let's eat it now, shall we, Mrs. Reeves?"

That did it. Elise smashed the cupcake with the palm of her hand and hissed, "I'm a professional cake decorator."

Stomping back to her room, she had expected the techs to come running. No one did.

In one of the other mandatory groups the following day, the group leader had instructed patients to share the reason for their hospitalization. When it came to Elise, she'd decided to be honest and had blurted out, "I feel like I'm a piece of shit and I'm killing myself through starvation."

The facilitator had said something to the effect of, "Interesting. Next."

Back in the present, Elise glared at the cupcakes, tempted to repeat her Hilliard performance.

"Sugar and fat, sugar and fat," sang the Beast. "No, no we will not eat that."

"Care for some herbal tea?" Pam offered as Elise took a seat in the wingback chair she'd been led to.

The aroma of chamomile permeated the air. Zero calories. "That would be nice. Thank you."

Elise had looked forward to the evening meeting with Pam since showing her the sketch of her inner child with bubbles earlier in the day.

Pam returned the teapot to the hotplate on her desk before setting their cups on an end table next to a lamp that cast a soft glow on the pale blue walls.

"I hate the harshness of fluorescent lights." Pam sank down in the chair across from Elise. "I think they should be outlawed."

"So do I." Elise tucked her feet underneath her. "I work under them all day, every day."

"Oh, that's right! You're a 'cake decorator slash sign maker' at a supermarket. Can you tell me what that's like?"

"As long as you're not going to make me decorate cupcakes."

"Why on earth would I do that?"

"I'd rather not talk about it."

"As you wish. Let's forget about your job and concentrate on your artwork." Pam reached over to take the sketchbook. "May I?"

Elise nodded. "I started another one."

Pam opened it to the third page, which showed a picture of a little girl sitting in the grass. With her hand extended to catch a bubble, the child pouted.

Tilting her head, Pam asked, "Why is little Elise so sad?"

"She's kind of a lonely kid. And a daydreamer."

"Was she now?" Pam pointed to Elise's notebook. "Is that your journal?"

"Actually," Elise passed it to her, "this might sound silly. I have this idea to write a story about little Elise. Kind of a children's book for adults doing inner child work."

"What a stellar idea. I wish I'd thought of that."

Pam's validating comments encouraged Elise. She envisioned more illustrations for her story. Perhaps her younger self would meet a fairy or an angel. Her head filled with ideas as she opened her bedroom door.

Dixie greeted her with, "I thought you ran away from home."

Dropping her sketchbook, suddenly guilt-ridden at her own happiness, Elise gasped at the sight of a wheelchair by the end of Dixie's bed. An IV stand beside the head of the bed held a bag of pale brown substance attached to a tube that went into Dixie's nose.

Shockwaves with a touch of envy swept over Elise. She silently reprimanded herself at her jealousy. What kind of sicko would envy a living cadaver?

"She does anorexia better than you, Elise. Can't you do anything right?"

"What on earth happened?"

"Like my new wheels? That jerk Dr. P put me in the chair so I won't burn any calories." Dixie's lips quivered. "He's threatening total bedrest if I lose any more weight." She darted her hollow eyes to the IV. "I really messed up this time, Suzie-Q."

Chapter Twelve

Elise braided and unbraided her long hair. As she applied her makeup, she sucked in her lower lip. No amount of concealer hid the dark circles under her eyes. *At least the bruise on my lip is gone.* She tried to stop her hands from shaking. One week on EDU down, three to go. If CHAMPUS approved. Damn insurance companies. Red tape and bureaucracy. They didn't care a fig about people. She brushed away a tear.

Last night was the first time since leaving the cardiac floor on Sunday that she had accepted one of Tony's calls. Since he and Gracie planned to be at the family sessions this morning, Elise figured she'd better speak to him—at least once.

"How are you and Gracie getting along?" she had asked, trying to keep her trembling to a minimum.

"Fine. Fine." His voice had grown louder. "I'd be finer if you'd do what I tell you and stop this nonsense. You need to think about what this is costing."

"Are—are you and Gracie coming tomorrow?"

"Do I have a choice?"

Elise had held her breath and counted to ten, then exhaled. "I'm so glad. I can't wait to... to see you, Tony. Could you bring my ink cartridges for my Rapidograph pen? Gracie knows where I keep them." Tony had grunted an affirmative and then the conversation petered into silence.

Dixie's voice brought her back to the present. "You're gorgeous, Suzie-Q. I wish I had your hair." She ran her skeletal fingers through her thin hair. A clump fell out in her hand. "Oh, joy… not."

"Dixie, why do you call me Suzie-Q?"

"It's from a 1930s song I found in a box of my mom's old records. It was love at first listen. So much energy and spunk. I worked up a floor routine to it. Scored high marks with it, too. I asked my mom to bring the video for you to see."

"Will the staff allow it?"

"Cassie says it shows progress and that maybe it'll motivate me to get better. Up until now, I haven't been able to watch it, much less let anyone else see it."

"But what does that have to do with your nickname for me?"

"You have the same energy as the singer and the song. Oh, you don't think so now, but look at the talent God's given you. He wants you to live and share it."

"Stop talking like your life is over. You're still young."

"Think so?" Dixie rolled her chair to the door. She smirked. "Your husband and kids are the reason you haven't offed yourself. I'll never—"

Before Dixie could finish, Cassie stepped inside the doorway and behind the wheelchair. "Uh-uh, girlfriend. I'm in the driver's seat today. Breakfast and, after that, visitors."

The unit's community room teemed with patients and family. Elise searched for Tony among them. She checked the wall clock. 9:55. He still had five minutes and it wasn't like him to be late. If anything, he would show up before anyone else to any function. He often chided her for her procrastinating ways. Maybe he'd do her a favor and not show up at all.

Chairs had been lined up in rows for what Elise hoped wouldn't be a boring lecture. She set her pillow on a chair in the front row. The hard seats hurt her backside when she sat for long periods.

"See?" crooned the Beast. "You're still skinny. But you won't be for long."

Marissa, who would be going home tomorrow, chattered away with her identical twin sister, Meredith. Elise marveled at how much they looked alike. They both had blonde curls pulled into ponytails, turned up noses, and the exact same blue eyes. However, it was easy to tell them apart since Meredith was heavier than Marissa.

Nyx's family surprised Elise. For all her goth tattoos and piercings, her mother could've walked out of an issue of *Good Housekeeping*. She stood a head shorter than Nyx and was a little on the chunky side. Nyx favored her dad, a slight man with thinning hair and horn-rimmed glasses. He wore a silver ankh around his neck. She'd shared at one of the sessions that he taught myth and ritual at UMKC, the local university.

Dixie's parents had arrived shortly after breakfast with a box of VHS tapes and miscellaneous items. Her silver-haired father looked every inch the athlete Dixie told her about. He'd gone to college on a basketball scholarship and now coached Southwest High School's team. Dixie's mother, a slender woman, probably in her late 50s, moved with balletic grace. She had danced the lead in *Swan Lake* during her Conservatory days. Her dark, silver-streaked hair, pulled back in a tight chignon, reflected her past.

Mr. Granger frowned and knelt beside his daughter's chair. "What's this about you losing more weight, Trouble?"

Mrs. Granger squeezed his shoulder with one manicured hand and cupped Dixie's sallow cheek with the other. "You can't possibly think you're fat now. You're barely fifty pounds, for crying out loud."

A hush fell over the hall. Elise's heart plummeted to her stomach. Mrs. Granger had broken the cardinal rule of the unit. Never discuss numbers, weight, or calories with anyone but your therapists. Dixie slunk down in her wheelchair.

Cassie dropped open her mouth. "Mrs. Granger!" She lowered her voice to a stage whisper. "One more outburst and I'll have to ask you to leave."

Elise pressed her palm against her stomach. Poor Dixie. Surely her parents meant well. Their concern and the tears in Mr. Granger's eyes made Elise's heart ache. She could only imagine how Tony would react if it were their daughter.

"You're nearly forty pounds heavier than Dixie," screamed the Beast. *"You're no anorexic. You're a pathetic failure."*

"Hey, good looking. May I have this dance?"

Elise lifted her head to see Tony with a bouquet of daffodils in a purple vase. His gray eyes twinkled. The eyes she'd fallen in love with. Her pulse raced. His muscular physique and thick brown waves with a few grays at the temples gave him a distinguished look.

A few female heads turned. Elise couldn't help but notice their admiring glances.

I should consider myself lucky to be married to such a hunk. He would be better off without me. I should—

What was it Dr. Picard said? "You've got to stop 'should-ing' all over yourself, Elise."

"Mommy!" Gracie nearly squeezed the wind out of her with her embrace. "I miss you."

Elise returned the hug and gave Gracie a slight shove. "Let me look at you. How are you doing in school? Did you swim this morning? Is that why you're late?"

"Nah, Poppo had a meeting or something downtown. I'm quitting the swim team."

Duty always came first, didn't it? She glanced over at Tony and then turned back to her daughter. "But you love to swim. What did Dad say?"

"He's not very happy about it." Gracie tugged at her oversized sweatshirt. "Can we not talk about it right now?" She took the vase from Tony and set it on a table.

Sitting near it, Irma narrowed her eyes at Gracie. "Get those smelly things away from me."

Tony cocked his head and cast a sidelong glance at Irma. "What's her problem?"

Elise grabbed his forearm. "Shh. Not so loud. She doesn't like flowers." She smiled an apologetic smile at her fellow patient. "Sorry, Irma."

"So now I can't bring flowers to my wife because of some loony, old broad? That's B.S. She needs to get a grip."

"It's okay, Poppo." Gracie whisked the vase from the table. "The nurse says I can take them to Mom's room. B.R.B."

"My baby's growing up, ain't she?" Tony followed her down the hallway with his eyes. "B.R.B?"

"Computer chatroom lingo," said Elise. "'Be right back'."

Chapter Thirteen
Tony

Gripping the armrest of his chair in Dr. Picard's office, Tony eyed Elise, who seemed less than happy to see him. She sat cross-legged in her chair, her eyes downcast. What had he done to make her reject him like this? He'd always been loyal, never had honeys on the side like his old man. He kept a roof over her head and put food on the table. Didn't that count for something? No way was he going anywhere. She belonged to him. Until death do us part.

His stomach twisted into a knot. "Elise, please," he whispered, "you need to think about what this is doing to our finances."

She refused to look at him. He heaved a sigh. At least she had a little more color in her cheeks than a week ago.

"So, this is where Marissa's been. Her sister's been real tightlipped." Gracie drew her legs up on her chair. "I don't get why she's here, though. She's not all that skinny."

Setting his clipboard on his lap, Dr. Picard frowned. "We're not here to discuss Marissa."

Gracie formed her lips into an 'o' and nodded. "Bet she's a barfer."

"Bulimia can be worse than anorexia and not as easy to spot since the sufferer might not be unusually thin." He pointed to an orange pottery bowl on his desk. "Care for a Tootsie Roll?"

"They stick to my braces." Gracie made a face. "I get it. I thought Mom was skinny, but that lady in the wheelchair... she's spooky skinny. Is she going to croak?"

Tony glanced at Elise. She looked plenty skinny to him. Had she lost some weight since her admittance? He couldn't tell from her baggy sweatshirt, but her legs looked like twigs in her black leggings. A lump caught in his throat.

Dr. Picard linked his fingers behind his neck, a tangible sadness in his blue eyes. "Let's hope not."

"What about Mom?" Gracie wrapped her arms around her legs. "Is she going to die?"

Elise reached over and squeezed her daughter's hand. "Of course, I'm not going to die."

Gracie pulled back her hand. "Dr. Picard?"

Tony analyzed the doctor's body language. As a Navy recruiter he could spot little things that indicated someone not telling the truth to someone outright lying. Would this so-called professional be honest with the girl?

"That's up to her." Dr. Picard's half-smile vanished. "What did you glean from this morning's session, Gracie?"

Gracie pursed her lips and looked up at the ceiling. "Our society has a screwed-up sense of what's pretty and what isn't. Thanks to the fashion industry. Poppo, did you know that Marilyn Monroe wore a size twelve, maybe even a fourteen?"

"Yeah, I heard." Tony gritted his teeth and glared at his wife. "And if Barbie was alive, with her proportions she'd have to be a French Poodle."

Dr. Picard leaned forward. "Do you think Miss Monroe was fat, Gracie?"

Gracie squirmed in her chair and tugged at her sweatshirt for the fourth time since they'd arrived at the hospital. She twisted her mouth to one side and cast her eyes downward. "Um... no?" Her stomach rumbled.

Panic thudded Tony's forehead. Had he been too busy to pay attention to the signs? She had lost a few pounds. He'd noticed her exercising more but he had chalked it up to training for swim meets.

First his wife, now his baby girl? He scrutinized Gracie's pale cheeks and peered into her brown eyes. Rubbing his sweaty palms together, he managed to croak, "Did you eat breakfast?"

"Yes, Poppo." Gracie fumed. "I ate breakfast."

"What did you have, Gracie?" asked Dr. Picard.

"What's it to ya?" She scowled at him and folded her arms across her chest. "What did you have for breakfast, Doc?"

"An omelet with cheddar cheese and green onions, a slice of buttered pumpernickel toast, and black coffee. Your turn."

"Half a granola bar."

"Only half?"

"I wasn't hungry."

Chapter Fourteen

Sundays were laid-back times on the unit. After breakfast, the staff allowed Elise full reign over the art room. She took the opportunity to finish the illustration she had discussed with Pam at her last session. The child in her story, "Little Elise", sat beside a stream. She held up her hand to catch bubbles floating in the air, a pout on her face.

"Why so sad?" Pam had asked.

Why wouldn't she be? A forgotten night from her own childhood flashed through Elise's mind—one of the nights when she babysat her cousins. She trembled at uninvited images.

She remembered how Aunt Viv said she'd had enough of depressing news so Uncle Leo suggested they go to the Strand Art Theater. Back then, Elise had known nothing of the place other than what Daddy had said. According to him, there was no 'art' about it. He'd referred to it as "unadulterated pornography. Pure filth".

Elise bristled at the pictures in her head. Who would leave a ten-year-old with small children? Certainly no one in this present day and age. Although Elise never liked spending the night in her aunt and uncle's dirty house, they would pay her a whole dollar for babysitting. While she'd never cared much for Nancy, she did love her youngest cousin with his golden curls and huge hazel eyes.

Reading to him was fun. "Someone's been sleeping in my bed and there she is!" Elise had read in her most dramatic Baby Bear voice.

Danny had squealed and clapped his hands. "An' Goldilocks runned all the way home! The end. Read it again, 'Lise. Peeeze."

Elise remembered the way six-year-old Nancy folded her arms and sniffed. "Time for night-night. Elise and me gots to go to school tomorrow. You're just a baby."

"Am not!" Danny had puckered his lips into a tight knot. Then he'd waved three fingers. "I'm this many."

Nancy wagged her finger in Danny's face and said in a singsong voice. "Mommy will get real mad if we're awake when she comes home."

Danny had huddled in his bed, clinging to his threadbare monkey. "Will you sleep in my bed, 'Lise?"

"Okay."

Nancy had stuck out her tongue as she crawled into her bed across the room, clutching her Chatty Cathy doll. "Danny is a baby. Danny is a baby."

"And you're a fat brat." Elise made a face. "So there!"

"Umm, I'm gonna tell Mommy you called me fat."

A hollow chill swept through Elise. She had to think fast. Few things frightened her more than her aunt's explosive temper. "Better not or I'll tell her you ate one of her Milky Way bars."

Nancy scowled. "You're not the boss of me."

"I am until your parents get back."

Danny had snuggled close to Elise and popped his thumb in his mouth. Turning her back on Nancy's blubbering, Elise curled her arm around him. Soon, she drifted off.

The next thing she remembered was waking up to Uncle Leo's alcohol-laden breath and tongue hot in her ear. Even now she stiffened. Not again. She would never forget how she'd squinched her eyes tight and hoped he would think she was asleep. However, her involuntary sob had given her away.

With his arm wrapped around her, he'd pressed his body against hers. "Shh, don't cry. Uncle Leo's here." Then he pinched her nipple. "Someone's getting boobies."

Even in the present, all these years later, she wanted to throw up. This was wrong. Daddy would never touch her like this. Desperate to escape, then and now, she imagined herself in a happy place filled with fairies and rainbows.

The group gathered in the chapel. Afternoon sun poured through a stained-glass window, making colorful patterns on the wall. Everyone sat on the front two pews watching Cassie and a stout, white-collared man beside her in front of the pulpit.

"What a grand afternoon for a coining out ceremony," said Cassie. "For you newbies, this gentleman is our own dear Chaplain Charlie."

She took a bronze coin from her pocket, held it up between her thumb and index finger. Next, she beckoned Marissa. "Please come up front, sugar. This is your golden moment."

Blushing, Marissa stood before the pulpit, between Cassie and the chaplain.

Then Cassie handed the coin to the chaplain. "Chaplain Charlie, will you open our festivities with the prayer on the coin?"

"With pleasure, ma'am." He winked and read aloud, "'God grant me the serenity to accept the things I cannot change. Courage to change the things I can, and the wisdom to know the difference.' Amen and amen."

Cassie took back the coin and grinned. "For those of you who've never been to a coining out, the rules are simple. We pass this little gem around, beginning on this side of the room." She gave it to Tina-Louise. "Each person holds it and says something positive to Marissa, then passes it to the next person until it reaches the honoree."

"Marissa, you're a good friend." Tina-Louise clutched the coin and held it to her chest. "I hope you stay healthy."

She passed it to Nyx who rolled her eyes. "Happy rah-rah on the outside, M. Don't barf on your pom-poms."

Next came Irma. Licking her withered lips, she heaved a deep sigh. "You've got your whole life ahead of you, sweetheart. Be well."

"Surprise." Dixie leaned into Elise. "The old bat actually said something nice."

Cassie's pointed glare said she'd heard Dixie's whisper. "You're next, Dixie. See if you can be as nice."

Dixie took the coin and flipped it. "Call it, Marissa."

"Tails," said Marissa.

"Wrong. It's heads. Okay, Marissa, here goes nothing. Jump off the beam, flip off the bars, follow your dreams, and reach for the stars." She pointed to her chair's wheels. "Don't let this happen to you."

Elise wrapped her hand around Dixie's and pried the coin from it. "My turn." She inspected the coin on her palm. Meant to be a symbol of victory, it only reminded her of how many coins she had from her previous hospitalizations. Coining was supposed to be the gateway to the road to recovery. It was a road full of potholes and pebbles. Elise's pulse thudded in her ears. Who was she kidding? She'd never had any intention of recovering. She had only coined out at the end of her previous hospitalizations because the insurance ran out.

She scrutinized the girl who would be leaving with her parents and twin sister in less than an hour. Only a year ahead of Gracie. Marissa folded her hands in her lap, her expectant baby blues fixed on Elise.

"Marissa—" Elise swallowed, "... you're beautiful the way you are. Believe it, because it's true. You don't have to be a fashion model to be acceptable."

"Hmf!"

Elise turned to see a young woman on the end of one of the pew. Her gray-green eyes, framed by perfectly arched eyebrows, flashed. She puckered her full lips, which accentuated her high cheekbones and caramel complexion.

Cassie lifted the coin from Elise's hand. "Everyone, this is Felicia, the new kid on the block."

"Lemme guess," said Nyx. "You're a fashion model."

"She is indeed." Handing the coin to Felicia, Cassie nodded. "You're up, Miss Thang."

"I'm—at a loss, since I don't know you, Marissa." Felicia wrapped her manicured fingers around the coin. "I wish you well. That's it."

"And that's enough." Cassie took the coin, handed it to Marissa, and embraced her. "Don't let me see you back here unless it's just for a visit, Missy."

Marissa bid a tearful goodbye to Elise with a hug. "Don't worry about Gracie. I'll watch out for her."

Cassie picked up Marissa's suitcase. "We've kept your momma and daddy waiting long enough. Thank you, Chaplain. I'll leave the rest to you."

Chaplain Charlie held up a plate. "Those who would like to take communion are welcome to stay. The rest are excused to your free time."

Nyx, Tina-Louise, and Felicia went their separate ways, leaving Elise with Irma and the chaplain.

His white collar accentuated his ruddy complexion. Tight rust-colored curls framed his round face. His gray-blue eyes twinkled as he gave Irma a sip of wine. Then he passed the cup to Elise. She took a small sip of the sweet grape juice as he said, "The blood of Christ shed for you."

After setting the cup aside, he took a round wafer, broke it, and laid it in Irma and Elise's open palms. "The body of Christ broken for you."

After munching the cracker, Irma crossed herself. She rose and shook his hand. "Thank you, Father."

"You're quite welcome, ma'am, but I'm merely a deacon, authorized by the Church to administer the sacraments to shut-ins."

"That would be us." Irma twittered. "See you at… ugh… lunch, Elise."

Elise swallowed the remains of her wafer, contemplating the calorie count.

At least sixty between the grape juice and the cracker, the beast whispered.

"Are you Jewish?" The chaplain angled his head toward Elise's Star of David necklace. "May I sit with you?" When she nodded he asked, "Why did you stay and take communion?"

Elise drew her legs up on the padded pew, unsure of what to say. Would this very Christian man think she'd lost her marbles? She took a deep breath. What did she have to lose? "Yes. Messianic actually, which means I accepted Yeshua, Jesus, as Messiah. However, these days I'm not sure what I believe."

"You know our Lord was a Jew." He grinned, revealing a slight gap between his two front teeth. "So, you're Jewish *and* Christian?"

"Something like that. My dad called me his Yiddisheh shiksa when I came to faith. My mother called me meshuggeneh."

"Yiddisheh shiksa?" Chaplain Charlie furrowed his bushy brows. "What is that?"

"Yiddisheh meaning Jewish. Shiksa is a derogatory term for a gentile woman. Meshuggeneh means crazy. In other words, they weren't pleased. Although, my mom came to believe before she died."

"I'd love to hear more about this when we have more time. Is there anything you'd like me to pray with you about?"

Elise lowered her eyes. Did God care about her after she had let him down so many times? "Nah, He and I haven't exactly been on speaking terms lately."

"May I see?" He pointed to the sketchpad on Elise's lap. "Cassie tells me you're something of an artist."

"I like to scribble."

Taking it from her, he flipped through the pages, his eyes widening. "These are more than scribbles." He chuckled. "You've certainly captured Nurse Terry's likeness. Our Lord has bestowed a magnificent gift on you."

Elise's face heated. "It's nothing."

"Oh, my dear, it most certainly is something. I can't draw a straight line with a ruler." With an attitude of reverence, he closed the book and handed it back to her. "Thank you for sharing this with me."

"Chaplain Charlie? Quite the handle. I'll bet you get teased a lot."

"I get more about this nose and red mop on my head." Taking Elise's hands in his, he bowed his head. "Dear Lord, bless this Thy child with peace and a will to live. In the name of the Father, the Son, and the Holy Ghost. Amen."

Chapter Fifteen

Monday afternoon marked Elise's first full week on EDU. Terry and Cassie gathered the residents in the patient lounge for what Elise had come to know as a weekly tradition. According to Dixie they did a different activity each week. Sometimes they would share concerns or frustrations. Other times it would be a time to get acquainted.

Last Monday, Elise hadn't paid much attention to her surroundings. The walls were painted powder blue—a comforting color. At least that's what she had read. A sofa, two upholstered chairs and a few colorful bean-bag chairs had been arranged in a semi-circle around a table and four folding chairs.

Tina-Louise curled up in a red bean-bag chair. Nyx, Elise, and Irma sat on the sofa. Cassie wheeled Dixie's chair next the sofa.

Terry pointed out a variety of objects, such as a coffee pot, plates, and silverware on the table. Curiosity piquing, Elise scrutinized the table setting. It appeared to be set for a meal. But the plates were empty and there was no food in sight.

Nyx elbowed Elise and pointed. The room seemed to come to attention and all heads turned to see a slender boy sitting on one of the upholstered chairs. He stared back at them, his mouth lengthened into a taut line. He reminded Elise a little of her naturally skinny Ben.

This boy, on the other hand, weighed a good ten pounds less than Ben.

"Why is a boy up here?" Tina-Louise puckered her brow. "Boys don't get eating disorders."

"Ladies, meet Lucas." Cassie placed her hand on his shoulder and addressed the patients. "It's a gross misconception that only women struggle with body image. Sadly, that is why men with eating disorders go unnoticed and undiagnosed all too often."

"Are you an athlete like a basketball player?" asked Dixie, pointing out his lean frame.

"Dancer. I dance seven hours a day." He raised his voice and became more animated with each statement. "People like my mom and Dr. Picard don't understand what it takes to be the best."

"I get it. It takes hours upon hours of training and discipline to be a successful gymnast."

"Dixie," Cassie pressed her index finger against her lip. "Enough."

Lucas dropped open his mouth. "You're Dixie Granger. I saw you on *The Susan Powter Show*. The gymnastics champion. You're a celebrity."

Terry moved to the center of the room.

She stood beside the table. "Let's get back to the matters at hand, shall we?"

"How many of you are familiar with role play?" asked Cassie.

Nyx groaned. "The game where we act out and spill our guts."

Terry nodded, setting her butterfly earrings to flight. "That's one way of putting it. In essence, the idea is to travel back to a time in your life that might've caused pain for you. The subject will play herself. Today, Irma will be our star. Elise and Nyx, her costars. Nyx will portray Irma's mother. In this scene Irma is eight and Elise is Irma's six-year-old sister." Terry instructed them to sit around the table. The girls would be served breakfast by their mother.

Nyx dragged her feet as she walked slowly and deliberately to the table. Elise's heart thumped with relief at not having to be the lead. She joined Nyx and Irma at the table.

Irma leveled her gaze at Nyx. "I'm not hungry, Momma. Alma can have my egg."

"Nonsense," said Nyx. "You haven't had anything to eat today."

Irma sat with a distant look in her pale gray eyes. Attempting to prompt conversation, Elise spoke in her best little girl voice. "Did Daddy go to work already?"

Folding her arms across her chest, Irma hissed, "I hope he never comes home. He can stay at the funeral parlor forever."

"Is that where Daddy works?" Elise whispered.

A tear trickled down Irma's cheek. "He's a funeral director—an undertaker."

"Is he a bad dad?"

"How can you ask such a question?" Irma curved a trembling hand around Elise's wrist. "Don't you remember, Alma? He used to dress us in frilly dresses and lay us out in caskets with flowers all around. Then he'd take pictures of his 'pretty cadavers'. One night, you cried and told him you didn't want to play the game anymore. 'Shut up, you little demon,' he hollered and pressed a pillow over your face."

Nyx gasped and stopped pretending to cook.

Irma's grip tightened. "You fought so hard. Oh, Alma. My poor baby sister. He buried you in that same dress and coffin." Throwing back her head, Irma wailed. "Daddy, Daddy, please, kill me, too!"

Terry gently pried Irma's fingers from Elise's throbbing wrist. Curving her arm around Irma's stooped shoulders, Terry escorted her from the room. Irma's cries and epithets could be heard all the way down the hall.

In the ensuing stunned silence, Cassie sank onto the sofa, tears glistening on her bronze cheek. Nyx eased into one of the bean-bag chairs and dropped her head into her hands.

"Wow, I didn't see that coming." Elise wound her shirt hem between her fingers. "I thought my uncle was bad."

"I hope the bastard paid for his crime." Dixie picked at the tape holding the feeding tube to her cheek. "Hanging would be too good for him."

Tina-Louise hugged her teddy bear. "Do you know if he went to jail, Cassie?"

"Sorry sugar. That's Irma's story to tell, not mine."

Chapter Sixteen

After the usual song and dance of their sessions with Wayne asking questions and Elise evading them, he peered over his reading glasses. "Let's shift our focus for a moment. I'd like to discuss your daughter."

"Gracie? What about her?"

"Do you know why she dropped off the swim team?"

"She told me she'd rather devote her time to Taekwondo and painting. She's very talented."

"I'd say she comes by it honestly. I'm concerned that she feels uncomfortable in her swimsuit. 'Beached whale' is the term she used."

"That's preposterous! She has an adorable figure. I should be so lucky. When I was her age, I was already into a thirty-four double D."

Wayne's eyes widened. "I'm no expert on the subject but for a woman of your height and build, it seems it would be hard on the shoulders."

"Hard on the shoulders?" Elise set down her drink and drew her legs up to her chest.

Images flashed through her mind. The Sno-Ball dance when Michael Gordon, one of the most popular boys, had asked her to be his date. Her joy at being asked had quickly turned to humiliation when he'd cupped his hand around her breast.

Heat rose to Elise's face and tears oozed out the corners of her eyes. She hugged her legs in tighter. "You have no idea."

Wayne wrote something on his notepad. "In our last session you told me you love to swim and went every morning before work until you landed here. I find it odd that someone with your skewed body image should enjoy a sport involving skimpy attire."

Elise contemplated his observation. How could she explain it? Her mind traveled back to the summer she turned seven. Elise's family had joined the Jewish Community Center, which boasted two Olympic size pools, one outside and one inside. Mom enrolled her in swimming lessons. From the beginning, Elise took to the water like a fish.

Mom had used the pool as a babysitter during summer vacation. She'd drop Elise and Eugene off on her way to work and pick them up on her way home. Rain or shine. She charged Eugene with the care of his little sister.

Eugene would congregate with his friends and stayed as far from Elise as he could. Occasionally, she had someone to play with. More often than not, she swam alone and entertained herself. She enjoyed the cooler, cloudy days because she would virtually have the pool to herself.

Diving under the water, she would imagine herself to be a mermaid with iridescent fins. The rhythm of lap swimming relaxed her. Immersed in her watery world, she didn't need playmates.

By the time Elise turned fourteen, bikinis were all the rage. She envied her classmates whose non-existent chests allowed them to wear the skimpiest suits. If a suit bottom fit Elise, the top most certainly would not.

Elise went swimming less often as her developing body embarrassed her. Eugene had joined the Air Force. Mom decided she could no longer justify the expense and let their JCC membership lapse.

As the years passed, she had had all but forgotten about swimming. Marriage and children demanded her full attention. During the summer, the closest she came to a pool were kiddie pools.

When Tony started his new job as a Navy recruiter, he decided they should join a fitness center. The facility had provided a nursery so Elise would be able to work out. He had insisted they go every night after he came home from work. Any plans she had would be cancelled.

Elise never complained. She had discovered aerobics, weight machines, and strict dieting helped her drop weight. In fact, she often went during the day to get in twice the workouts. She did enjoy a swim to cool down after a strenuous workout.

Then her parents died within three years of each other, victims of their own bad habits—smoking and overeating. Elise ramped up her exercise routines. If she could control nothing else in her life, she could control her fitness and what went into her mouth. She took pride in achieving sixteen percent body fat.

As far as she could tell, Tony had become so obsessed with his personal workout program he never seemed to notice she had a problem. In fact, he often praised her new slender form and stamina.

When the fitness center closed a couple of years later Tony turned to running with his Navy buddies on his lunch hour. Elise worked out at home as best she could and jogged in the early morning hours with her neighbor.

Elise's flashbacks of childhood abuse had surfaced in her mid-thirties. Each memory suppressed her appetite—exacerbating her hatred for her body. When she had sought help from a professional, Tony fumed and said their problems were nobody else's business.

In the midst of it all, Tony had been deployed to the Persian Gulf for two years. Abandoned, saddled with a teenager and preteen, Elise plummeted into a deep depression. Elise's therapist admitted her to Elmwood Psychiatric Center. There Elise rediscovered solace in the pool.

After her release, she had joined the nearby YMCA. When Tony returned from the Gulf and she found a job, she committed to swimming every morning before work. Heretofore, she hadn't equated body image with swimming. She chose modest suits that covered her ample breasts. At the Y, she would go straight from the locker room to the pool.

Elise finally replied to Wayne, "The water's my safe place. Like a cocoon."

"I see." He rested his note pad on his knees. "Let's get back to Gracie. Do you ever criticize her appearance?"

Heat flooded Elise's cheeks as she remembered a shopping trip with her daughter to find a dress for Homecoming. Gracie had claimed she could die of happiness then and there when Doug asked her to be his date. Guilt riddled Elise as she remembered what a buzzkill she'd been.

"Whaddya say, Momette?" Gracie had twirled out of the dressing room in an outfit with a burgundy midi top and matching short skirt. "Is this the cutest or what?"

Elise had pinched Gracie's bare midriff. "I'd say easy on the onion rings."

Her eyes brimming, Gracie had put the outfit back on the rack, opting for a pink dress with a Peter Pan collar and a looser fit. "This one works. Doug likes pink."

Back in the present, Elise wound and unwound a lock of her hair around her index finger. "I might have suggested she should be more careful about her diet once or twice."

Chapter Seventeen
Tony

"Is your homework done, kitten?" Tony set a bowl of popcorn on the coffee table in front of Gracie, who was curled up on one side of the sofa, intent on the television. In her fuzzy robe and bunny slippers, she still looked like his little girl. "Cheese, our favorite. You didn't eat much at supper. I thought you might need something more."

Heaving a melodramatic sigh, she glared at him. "Da-ad! Can't you wait until the commercial?"

"What's the show?" He plopped down beside her and reached for the remote. "Looks like one of those stupid sitcoms."

"There's only a few minutes left." She frowned. "It's *Wings.* You might like it. It's about pilots and airplanes." She giggled at something said on the show and reached her hand into the bowl. "Antonio cracks me up." Shoveling some popcorn into her mouth, she munched and then grimaced. "This crap gets stuck in my braces." Her cheeks turned red. "Sorry, Poppo, I didn't mean to swear." The show ended and she handed him the remote. "Yes, my homework's done. Signed, sealed, and delivered. The TV's all yours."

Tony set the remote on the coffee table. "Your granddaddy was a pilot."

"Yeah, you told me. A crop duster. Died on the job when you were fourteen. You had to raise your sister and brothers while Grandma worked."

"He was a daredevil." Tony downed the remainder of his beer and belched. "I'll never forget the time your granddaddy took me and your Aunt Jamie up in an old biplane. I was ten and she was nine. Dad says, 'Make sure them seatbelts is fastened real tight'." Tony remembered his father's ornery grin. "Well, the next thing I know, we was flipped upside down. I'm here to tell you your Aunt Jamie had a powerful set'a lungs on her."

"What about you, Poppo? Weren't you scared?"

"Not a bit. Daddy did loop-de-loops and pretended we was about to crash." Tony flattened his hand and swooped it up in the air like a plane. "Then *woosh!* Back up in the air we went. He took me up a few more times, but Aunt Jamie wouldn't have no part of it again. I'd almost qualified for my pilot's license when he got killed. Your grandma surrendered her own license and begged me not to get mine."

Gracie kissed his cheek. "Maybe you should do it now."

"Nah. I'm afraid that plane's left the hangar. You best get to bed, kitten."

She slipped off the sofa and straightened. Carrying her pillow under one arm, she padded down the hallway to her room. The door shut behind her.

Tony picked up the brown paper sack he'd set on the floor when he came home from work. It contained a few things Marco had given him as he cleaned his desk. Tony hated to see his good friend transfer, but the man had to do what he had to do.

He reached into the sack and found the eight ball Marco had insisted he take. Rolling it around his hand, he remembered Marco's comment. "This is a reminder that no one came back from Nam unscathed."

Finishing the last swig of beer, he set the ball on the coffee table. He reached into the bag and took out a navy-blue coffee mug with gold letters that said, "Brothers in Arms". How many times had he seen Marco drink out of it? Five, maybe six cups a day.

Thinking he should go to bed himself, he fished the last gift from the sack—a VHS Dire Straits video. After removing the outer wrap, he popped it into the VCR and picked up the remote. He told himself he'd catch a music video or two to relax.

Pencil-drawn images on the cover reminding him of some of Elise's work flashed across the screen to the song "Brothers in Arms". Soldiers battling in wind and rain. Billowing waves. The ethereal music and softly sung words lulled him.

"Tony, I'm hit!" Frankie's panicked face flashed before him, barely visible above the muddy water. He clung to the side of the boat by his fingertips. Sniper fire came from everywhere.

As Tony reached for him, Frankie's hands slid off and his head disappeared beneath the stagnant water.

Tony's own anguished outcry startled him back to the living room. Early morning light poured through the living room window. Static and snow filled the television screen. Sweat sluiced between his shoulder blades. He fished his wallet from his trouser pocket and flipped through a clump of business cards until he found the one Marco had given to him. "Henry W.L. Rodgers, PhD, LCP." He reached for the phone on the end table.

Chapter Eighteen

The group gathered in the lounge to view a video recording of Dixie's glory days.

Marissa, who now attended as an outpatient, had come to watch. At Dr. Picard's invitation, Gracie had also come. She and Marissa exchanged pleasantries and appeared to be on the road to friendship.

Lucas sat apart from everyone else. He was still technically part of the group, but riding the outskirts. At breakfast he had announced that he would be turning eighteen and, as an adult, he would no longer be under his parents' jurisdiction. He clasped the seat cushion beneath him, twirling his slipper clad feet in front of him. He had a tragic elegance about him. His melancholy brown eyes reminded Elise of her Ben, who would never walk in his father's military footsteps.

Time seemed to be passing Elise by. She asked herself if she'd made any progress. On the other hand, did she really want to?

She surveyed her fellow patients, who had become a sort of family in a mere week and a half. Tina-Louise's face had filled out nicely. A good sign, said her motherly instincts. She hoped some of Tina-Louise and Marissa's positive attitudes might rub off on Gracie, overriding Elise's less-than-maternal influence.

Irma sat on the couch, her lips pulled into a taut line and an unopened bag of potato chips on her lap. Sitting beside her, Nyx leaned over and whispered something. Irma raised an eyebrow but said nothing.

Interrupting Elise's musing, the night nurse, Bruno, a sturdy woman sporting a frosted updo, entered the room. She refused to divulge her first name. When asked, she shook her head and claimed she'd be laughed out of the town if anyone knew it. At any rate, Bruno fit her forthright personality. Elise liked her. She always had time to talk in the wee hours of the night when Elise couldn't sleep, offering chamomile tea and graham crackers.

Bruno slid a tape into the VCR. "We have a treat tonight."

"Can't wait!" Elise reached for Dixie's hand. "You sure about this, roomie?"

Dixie pinched Elise's cheek. "No worries, Suzie-Q." She sat cross-legged in the wheelchair. "Prepare to be entertained."

Before she started the recording, Bruno glanced at Dixie. "You're sure about this? It's okay to call it off."

Squeezing Elise's hand, Dixie shook her head. "Nah, I'm good with it."

"Now we go into the floor exercises." A male announcer's voice filled the room. "From the USA's team, sixteen-year-old Dixie Granger. At present she's holding in third place behind Kathy Howard on the parallel bars."

On the screen, young, athletic Dixie, her thick hair styled in a pixie cut, stood poised on the mat. Her form-fitting, red sequined leotard accentuated her toned stomach and flat chest. Elise envied her trim, muscular physique.

"Dixie's solid," said the female commentator, former gymnast Cathy Rigby. "A firm contender."

As the lively trumpet music started, Dixie did a few jaunty steps before turning two cartwheels, a back flip spiraling into a front flip. The crowd cheered.

The singer on the scratchy recording sang, *"Now you swing over here, now you swing over there."*

Dixie hopped and did a series of high kicks before going into her second series of tumbles. Her thigh muscles rippled. Elise felt dowdy and clumsy by comparison.

"Great form and control," cried the male announcer.

"Yes," said Cathy Rigby. "She manages to go high on those flips. Great balance with her own unique style."

Elise bit her lip as onscreen Dixie performed an aerial cartwheel and tripped upon landing. The crowd let out a collective gasp and hushed. Dixie blinked several times, but maintained her smile as she finished her routine. Elise groaned when Dixie ended with a final stumble.

"That's going to cost her," said Rigby.

"Dixie Granger," said the other announcer. "Four feet, ten inches. One hundred pounds. Next up, Romania's Nadia Comaneci."

"I didn't stand a chance. Nadia was four eleven and weighed eighty-six pounds. She scored a perfect ten," said Dixie with a sob in her voice. "Not like little ol' Thunder Thighs here. Please turn it off, Bruno."

After shutting off the television, Bruno knelt before Dixie's chair. "Would it be okay if we all discuss this?" Dixie gave a slight nod. Bruno patted Dixie's knee and asked the group, "Who would like to comment?"

Lucas's Adam's apple bobbed. "You were magnifico, Dixie. You could've been a prima ballerina."

Dixie cast her eyes downward and shrugged her knobby shoulders. "Thanks. But I was probably too fat for that, too."

Bruno stood and leveled her probing gaze at each one of her charges. "Who thinks Dixie looked fat in the video?"

No one spoke at first. Irma drew a deep breath and exhaled so everyone could hear. "Not an ounce of flab. That was pure athleticism. Whoever said you were fat should've been drawn and quartered and fed to sharks."

"Only my coach," Dixie murmured. "He told me I lost my balance because I was carrying too much weight on my thighs."

"I hope he's dead."

"Nope, he's still coaching."

Chapter Nineteen
Wayne

WAYNE READ LUCAS'S CHART. "Unless I have a court order, I can't keep you from checking yourself out Saturday." Wayne couldn't help but feel irresponsible for releasing Lucas, but had no jurisdiction in the matter. The boy was severely underweight when he was admitted and had dropped more weight since then. Not only had he lost weight, but he had become more withdrawn than ever.

"Candy?" Wayne held out his bowl of Tootsie Rolls. Lucas recoiled.

"Suit yourself." Wayne took a piece of candy for himself. What more could he say? "What are your plans?"

Lucas crammed his hands in his pockets and paced like a lion in a cage. "I'm renting an apartment with my friend Yaakov, a dancer from Tel Aviv. We go into rehearsals for *The Nutcracker* in two weeks."

Wayne forced a smile. Lucas hadn't offered this much information in the short week he'd been at Brookside. "That's terrific."

"It's a small role, but I'm pretty pumped about it."

"How are your folks handling your moving out?"

"Mom cries a lot and Dad says I should give up the 'fairy stuff' and join the Army. Says it will make a man out of me."

Taking a deep breath, unsure of how far he could take the conversation, Wayne asked, "May I ask a personal question?"

"Shoot."

"Are you and Yaakov in a—relationship?"

Stopping mid-pace, Lucas frowned. "Not all dancers are gay. I have a girlfriend and Yaakov is, as he puts it, a rooster on the prowl in the henhouse."

Wayne glanced at a picture of a dancer he kept on his desk and swallowed an expanding lump. Poised in tulle dress and toe shoes, her rail-thin arms arched in position, her golden hair pulled back in a tight chignon. She had danced with the likes of Dame Margot Fontayne under the direction of George Balanchine. What a shame she never realized her dream of partnering with Nureyev.

"Who's that?" Lucas pointed to the photo.

"My sister, Elizabeth Picard."

"She's exquisite. Perfect form. She must be a marvelous dancer."

"She was."

Wayne remembered her infrequent visits home when he was a boy. Even at eleven he had noticed how she seemed thinner each time. When Mom put supper on the table Elizabeth would find reasons to skip out. Rehearsal. Going to a movie. Or the biggest lie—meeting friends for dinner. One day she collapsed in a rehearsal and was rushed to the hospital. One by one her organs had shut down.

Wiping a tear from his cheek, Wayne asked, "Is your girlfriend a dancer, also?"

Lucas' pasty cheeks colored. "Prima ballerina."

"If you don't mind my asking, when you go on dates, do you take her out to eat?"

Chapter Twenty

ELISE EXAMINED her reflection in the bathroom mirror. Was her face rounder than when she had been admitted? How much weight had she gained over the past almost two weeks? Ten pounds? Twenty? She lifted her nightgown and poked at her bare chest. With a satisfied smile she noted she could still see her ribs. She curled her thumb and index finger around her wrist.

The staff had ordered in pizza for supper. Cassie had kept her under scrutiny, making it impossible for her to spit chewed bits into her napkin. Resenting the feeling of being full, she pressed her hand against her stomach. She wished she had hidden some laxative pills in her cosmetic case. If only she could throw up, but that was something she never could make herself do.

"You swallowed a thousand calories tonight. All that cheese and grease. Yuck!" the Beast screamed. *"Fat. Orca fat."*

"Trust me, Suzie-Q, you're plenty thin."

Elise startled to see Dixie standing in the bathroom doorway. "So says the skeleton from her closet." Elise repositioned her gown. "Where do you get off sneaking up on me?"

"I wasn't sneaking. I need to use the facility. I see you're doing the bone check." Dixie grasped Elise's shoulders. "Don't listen to her, Suzie-Q." With that she gave Elise a gentle shove and shut the bathroom door.

Elise padded to bed and picked up her sketchbook. Leaning back against her pillows, she propped it on her knees. She decided she wasn't in the mood to draw tonight and put it back on the nightstand next to her untouched glass of *Ensure*.

"More calories," whispered the Beast.

Dixie plopped down on her bed and picked up her *Ensure*. "Mm. Chocolate."

Lying down, Elise turned on her side and watched her roommate. While Dixie was still wretchedly skinny, she did look better than she had a week before. Elise rose on one elbow, resting her head on her hand.

"Dixie, what did you mean 'don't listen to her'? Who is 'she'?"

"You know her voice. We all do. Annie-Wrecks-Ya. Annie for short."

Elise recalled what the paramedic said the night she was admitted. "Don't let the Beast win."

"I call her the Beast."

"She's a B word all right. A lying one at that."

"Don't listen to her, Elise," whispered the Beast. "I'm your guardian. Annie. Your best friend."

"Annie-Wrecks-Ya." Elise repeated. "That's cute. Hello, Annie."

"Are you listening? There's nothing cute about her. She makes us think we're in control. Until we find out who's controlling whom." She sucked the remains of the drink through her straw, making loud slurping noises. "It's so good to have that nasty feeding tube out."

Biting her lip, Elise stopped herself from saying anything about her roommate's weight gain. "That has to be uncomfortable."

"Keep doing what you're doing, and you'll find out."

"What's that supposed to mean?"

"I've seen you spit food into napkins when you thought no one was looking. And when you do swallow, it's one, maybe three bites. I'll bet you've lost five pounds since you've been up here."

"You really think so?" Elise couldn't keep from smiling.

"I didn't mean it as a compliment." Dixie dabbed her lips with a tissue. "But I get it. As for your nasty habits, I'm not the only one watching. Your pretty daughter studies your every move. Is this what you want her to inherit from you?"

Elise laid on her back. Hugging her pillow, she twisted the open end of the pillowcase around her pinkie. Even in the dim lamplight, Dixie's eyes seemed brighter.

Her determined gaze shot through Elise. "I'm not dancing with her anymore."

"Who? Annie?"

"Yeah. Annie. When I watched myself tonight on the video—it was like a light went on. Just because my half-baked coach called me 'Thunder Thighs' didn't make it so. I let the lying butthead rob me of twenty years I'll never get back." Dixie's bony jaw set and her eyes in their hollows flashed. "I'm going to get well, Suzie-Q. From this day forward, no more two-steps with Annie!"

Chapter Twenty-One
Tony

"Salúd!" John Ponak set a pitcher on the long table. "Enjoy some liquid attitude." He slapped Marco's back. "For you, the first pitcher is on the house. *Mi casa es su casa.*"

"Ponak's Mexican Kitchen serves the best Margaritas this side of Southwest Boulevard." Marco embraced him. *"Gracias, mi amigo."*

"Anything for a fellow vet."

Sitting in his wheelchair beside Tony, Hank Rogers raised a glass of seltzer. "A toast to the US Marine Corps and John Ponak, the greatest Marine to come back from Viet Nam. Semper Fi!"

"Oorah!" John grinned. "Back to the kitchen for me."

Tony licked salt from the rim of his glass with the tip of his tongue and sipped his drink. He savored the sweet and tart flavors while Dr. Picard's words reverberated in his mind. *"If Elise doesn't stop what she's doing, she'll be dead in a year."*

One by one, the guys toasted Marco with bad jokes and good wishes. Raucous laughter echoed off the walls. Tony finished his first Margarita. He poured a second and tossed it back. Tears stung his eyes.

"Stop that crying, boy," said Dad, unbuckling his belt, *"or I'll give you something to cry about."*

The waitress brought out a second pitcher. Tony filled his glass and gulped it down. *"I'm glad you're dead, Dad. You bastard, I hope you're rotting in hell."*

"Hey, Tony, why so glum, chum?" Master Chief Matthews' crimson nose and cheeks reflected his love for the drink. "You're empty. That won't do." He refilled Tony's glass. "Time to celebrate your latest gold wreath. How many does that make? Six?"

Clenching his tongue between his teeth, Tony held up eight fingers.

"To Chief Reeves, the best damned recruiter in the district. You make me look good."

"I tell them kids the truth." Tony forced a smile and finished his Margarita. As he poured another, Frankie's face popped into his head, uninvited. "Join the Navy. See the world."

He hadn't thought about Frankie in years. Why now did that kid turn up in every nightmare? Tony took a long drink from his glass. Hundreds of sailors perished in the jungle, serving on patrol boats. He had gone over knowing it was virtually a suicide mission.

Seaman Recruit Franklin Murphy. Typical boy next door. No one ever called him anything but Frankie. Frank just didn't fit. Freckles, blond hair, and big brown eyes like a calf. He was barely eighteen, looked thirteen and would never see nineteen.

Hank nudged Tony back to the present. "How 'bout I give you a ride home, Chief?"

"I'm not even feeling a buzz." Raising his glass, Tony turned toward Marco. "To the best friend a man can ask for. Fair winds and following seas." The room spun. "On second thought..." Tony handed his car keys to Hank. "9912 Campbell. Thanks."

Chapter Twenty-Two

UNABLE TO SLEEP, Elise turned on the lamp over her bed. She glanced at Dixie to see if the light bothered her. With her covers pulled over her head, Dixie didn't budge. If it weren't for her snoring, Elise would have checked her to make sure she was breathing.

Picking up her sketchbook, Elise turned to a blank page. Pam had suggested she draw herself as a teenager to get in touch with her feelings. Elise put pen to paper and began with her face and her long frizzy hair that no amount of ironing or rolling on soup cans could tame. After she finished her face, she continued with her body, drawing herself in her Dairy Queen uniform. It was white and accentuated her breasts that, between her thirteenth and fourteenth birthdays, had gone from a 32C to a 34DD.

Not many kids were hired for regular jobs at fourteen, but the owners of the Dairy Queen had made an exception because they liked Dad. Elise hoped she wouldn't let him down. At any rate, she'd be earning a whopping dollar an hour. Twice what she had made babysitting her cousins. The less she saw of her aunt and uncle the better.

She had enjoyed her job and had taken great pride in her ability to make the sundaes and cones look like the pictures on the signs. Her enjoyment had turned to embarrassment the day she heard a boy at the counter say, "Check out the short chick with the humongous knockers."

Her thirteen-year-old self, arms covering her breasts in her sketch, looked as miserable as Elise remembered being. She closed the sketchbook and turned off the light. Burrowing her head in the soft pillow, she drifted off to sleep.

Thanksgiving dinner. Dad had spent the day preparing the cornbread dressing, turkey, and sweet potato pie with real whipped cream. Elise enjoyed the mingling aromas. No one could cook like her father.

Even though Dad couldn't stand Mom's sister, he relented and agreed to invite them. Elise's heart cratered to her stomach. She wasn't too fond of Aunt Viv and Uncle Leo. Eugene refused to come home for the holiday, saying he would rather eat in the chow hall where it was peaceful.

As Dad carved the turkey, Elise set the table and Mom put out serving dishes piled with mashed potatoes and green beans. Elise's mouth watered in anticipation of the meal.

When company arrived, Elise modeled her new tent dress she had bought with her earnings. The crepe fabric flowed and made her feel quite feminine.

Aunt Viv laughed and said it looked like a maternity dress. Dad pointed out her girth and told her she was one to talk since she had all of her clothes made by Omar the Tentmaker. Things only worsened from there. All the while Elise tried not to make eye contact with Uncle Leo who leered at her like a ravenous wolf. She wished she was old enough to join the military like Eugene.

The bickering continued through dinner, making everything taste like cardboard. Elise asked to be excused. Not waiting for an answer, she retreated to her room. There she tore off the dress and flung it to the floor. After changing into a pair of jeans and a sweatshirt, she scowled at her reflection in her dresser mirror. Her curly hair defied relaxers and her breasts had grown larger than those of most girls her age. She switched on the radio to drown out the voices coming from the dining room. Plopping down on her bed, Elise opened her sketchbook to a portrait of Paul McCartney she'd been working on.

Mom came in to check on her. Looking over Elise's sketch she pointed out that one of the eyes was off. Elise turned the sketch over. Couldn't Mom ever say anything good about her drawing?

After an exchange of angry words, Mom insisted Elise come out to say goodbye to their guests. Dragging her feet, Elise followed Mom to the front door where Uncle Leo embraced her. When she needed them most, her parents were oblivious.

"Suzie-Q. Wake up!"

Drenched in sweat, Elise opened her eyes to see Dixie's concerned face hovering over her. She licked her chapped lips with her parched tongue. "I woke you. I'm sorry. What time is it?"

"Two-thirty in the aye and em." Dixie poured a glass of water from the pitcher on the night stand. "Here's something to wash away your nightmare. That must've been some dream."

Sitting up, Elise gulped the water to swallow the bile rising in her throat. "More of a flashback than a dream. It was so vivid."

Setting the water cup on the nightstand, Elise shuddered. She could still smell his alcohol-soddened breath and cringed at his tongue slipping between her lips.

"I'm okay now, thanks." She lay back and folded her arms behind her head. "Sorry I woke you."

"No problem, Suzie-Q. If you need me again, just holler." Dixie crawled back into bed. "But not too loud."

Closing her eyes, Elise remembered her bat mitzvah. Her crowning moment. Mom and Dad had beamed with pride and even Grandpa— Smiling Sam, which Daddy called him because he hardly ever did— flashed an ear-to-ear grin. In his thick accent, he praised Elise. "A gut girl. You vas alvays a gut girl." He handed her a check for eighteen dollars. A dollar for each line of the *Sh'monah Esrey*, the eighteen bless-ings she had recited as part of her bat mitzvah ceremony.

Elise couldn't believe the day she'd planned and worked for since she was six had come and was almost gone. The synagogue hall had glowed with candlelight. Her Hebrew school classmates cheered for her. The rabbi sang her praises. "Such wonderful diction and pronunciation. Elisheva, you're a natural!"

Elise always loved it when he'd called her by her Hebrew name. "*Todah Rabbah.* Thank you."

Uncle Leo had raised a crystal cup. "To my beautiful niece on her triumph over the Torah. *L'chaim.*" He gulped it back. "Delicious punch."

Of course, it was. He'd added his own "flavoring" from his personal flask.

Oblivious to her husband, Aunt Viv had helped herself to the sweet table, heaping her plate with petit fours and fruit. "Nothing like sitting through a dull service to whet one's appetite. Yvonne and I never had a bat mitzvah." She crammed a cookie into her mouth. "Girls didn't do the Bat Mitzvah thing back then. Can't say I feel deprived."

"That pig is anything but deprived." Dad had stage-whispered in Elise's ear.

"Bob." Mom hissed. "Not here. Not now."

"Why we have to invite the fat slob to every family affair is beyond me."

"She's my sister."

"She isn't mine." Dad had growled. "I'd do a jig if she dropped dead here and now."

Hands over her ears, Elise had walked down the darkened hallway to escape their bickering. Hearing heavy footsteps behind her, she stepped up her pace. The footsteps also sped up.

"Not so fast, bat mitzvah girl." Uncle Leo's speech slurred. "Wait for me."

She had ducked into one of the empty classrooms. Before she could reach the light, Uncle Leo circled one arm around her waist and shut the door with his other hand.

Wrenching out of his grasp, she backed away from him. He lunged forward and pinned her against the wall. She opened her mouth to scream. He clapped his hand over it. She kicked his shin. Instead of letting go, he unzipped his fly with his free hand and pressed himself against her. She would never forget how the light streaming through the window from the parking lot illuminated his leering smile. "You little tease. You know you want it."

Her heart had thrashed. "No! No! No!"

Danny banged on the door and yelled. "Daddy? Are you in there?"

"Go away! Daddy's busy."

Danny burst into the room. "Daddy, Mommy said to ask you—" Elise remembered his bewildered expression mixed with fear.

"Dammit!" Uncle Leo stepped back and tugged at his zipper. He gave Elise's breast one last painful squeeze. "You tell anyone what happened in here, you'll be in trouble, big trouble." He backhanded Danny's cheek with a loud slap. "That goes for you too, ya little momzer."

Dixie's voice snapped her back to the present. "Who's Uncle Leo?"

Elise flinched. "How do you know about him?"

"You've mumbled his name in your sleep quite a few times this past week. Each time you were crying."

"Doesn't matter, he's dead to me. Haven't seen him since Aunt Viv's funeral."

"Would you cry if it didn't matter? You know, no man's worth starving yourself to death over." Dixie grinned at her own revelation. "No one is. Not even an idiot gymnastics coach."

"At least your coach didn't… touch you." Elise snapped.

Dixie scowled. "So, your pain is worse than my pain? Is that it?"

"I'm sorry, I didn't mean to minimize you. It's just that I didn't even remember being molested until four years ago. Once the flashbacks started, they kept coming and coming. They're relentless. How on earth did I block those things out? Maybe it's all my imagination and those things never happened."

"You *want* to be making them up." Bruno entered the room carrying a tray with steaming tea in Styrofoam cups and cellophane-wrapped graham crackers. She set them on the nightstand. "I'm sorry to eavesdrop, but I heard Elise crying. It's amazing what a child's mind can block out."

"But I remember my childhood in great detail—things like reading right through a morning spelling lesson in the fourth grade. My desk was right next to my teacher's. The book was *On the Banks of Plum Creek*. I mean, I remember minute details from when I was three. How could I block out such horrid things?"

Elise trembled. She blinked back hot tears. The shame seared her as if she were twelve years old once more.

"Here, drink it while it's hot." Bruno handed Elise a cup. "Mind you, I'm only a psych tech so I don't have the creds to back my theory, but I'd guess you're creative enough to reinvent your childhood. Much like selecting the colors and details you want to include in your paintings."

Dixie tore open a pack of graham crackers and popped a whole one into her mouth. "Mm. I'd almost forgotten how good food tastes. I think Bruno's onto something, Suzie-Q."

"Seems to be a pattern, flashbacks in your late thirties or early forties." Bruno slipped a notebook and pencil from her scrubs pocket. "Here I go practicing back-alley psychiatry. Did something happen over the past few years to trigger buried memories, Elise?"

"My flashbacks… they started…," Elise fought to still her chattering teeth, "…while Tony was overseas."

"Ah. It was safe with him out of the way. Was he your perp?"

Elise curled up on her side and hugged her pillow. "No. Uncle Leo was."

"Isn't that the way? A brother. An uncle. A father." Raising an eyebrow, Bruno wrote in her notebook and stuffed it back into her pocket. "Does Tony know?"

A wave of exhaustion swept over Elise. She wound the edge of the pillowcase around her index finger and shut her eyes. "Can we please talk about it later?"

Chapter Twenty-Three

With her head resting on her left hand, Elise poked fork-prints in her pancake with her right. Thunder rumbled and rain pelted the windows. The perfect morning to sleep in. She'd had precious few hours of sleep the night before.

Dixie had kept her up until midnight expounding on the joys of recovery. Elise's emotions defied logic. While she rejoiced in her roommate's newfound hope, it challenged her. Panic seized her stomach. Did this mean she had to gain weight, too?

At the same time, she worried Dixie might not gain enough. How could someone be so thin and live?

Elise envied the attention the world seemingly gave Dixie, the Olympic-class gymnast who'd been featured on talk shows and in magazines.

Why should she be jealous of Dixie? Wasn't she trying to disappear? Nothing made sense.

A clap of thunder startled Elise. Beside her Dixie groaned and covered her mouth. "Can I go back to bed?"

"That's what you get for talking the night away." Elise stabbed her egg and watched the yolk seep into her pancakes. "You can't go back to bed unless I can, too."

Dixie shook her head and moaned. "I'm not kidding. I'm really sick."

Irma sneered and dabbed her lips with her napkin. "That's your best performance yet, Dix. What do you do for an encore?"

"Irma!" Elise scowled. "How can you be so mean?"

"And how can you not see what a drama queen she is? Anything to stay in the spotlight."

Dixie lurched forward and threw up all over her eggs. Nyx screamed what sounded like might be a spell of some sort. Tina-Louise jumped up from her chair and ran out of the dining room with Nurse Terry close behind her.

Cassie placed her palms on Dixie's cheeks. "Lord in Heaven, you're burning up."

It was all Elise could do to keep her own stomach from emptying. She glanced at Dixie, who had gone from chalk-white to pale green. Her grip tightened on Elise's wrist. "I'm so sorry, Suzie—" She turned her head and vomited on Elise's sleeve. Her eyes rolled back. Going limp, she fell to the floor.

Another wave of nausea coupled with shock swept over Elise. The possibility of her friend dropping dead at her feet terrified her.

"Code blue on EDU in the dining room!" blared over the loud-speaker.

Nurses and an intern rushed into the room. They lifted Dixie's life-less form onto a gurney and hooked her up to a heart monitor. Elise breathed a sigh of relief to see the line peak and hear the machine beep at intervals. She swallowed hard as they wheeled her roommate out the door.

After breakfast, Elise had trouble keeping her mind on her sketch in art therapy. Nyx and Irma refrained from their usual bickering. Tina-Louise squished a lump of Play-Doh while cradling her Teddy Bear.

Lunch tasted like cardboard. Elise traded her sandwich for *Ensure*. No one on the staff offered any information about Dixie. Elise couldn't help but fear the worst.

After lunch, Elise roamed the hallway, not wanting to go back to her empty room.

Supper came without news. No amount of coaxing from Cassie could make Elise eat. She gagged down another serving of *Ensure.*

After supper, Elise joined the others for TV time. Clutching an opened bag of Fritos, she tucked her feet underneath her on the sofa beside Lucas and Tina-Louise until their choice of programs, "Friends" mercifully came to an end.

Cassie shut off the television. "Okay, ladies and gentleman, it's bed time. Toss your snack bags in the trash can and head for your rooms. We'll be around with meds shortly."

Once in her room, Elise changed into her favorite flannel nightgown —the purple one Tony said made her look like his grandma. He didn't like it and nagged her about wearing something sexy to bed.

She turned on the lamp beside the bed and propped her sketchbook on her knees. With her Rapidograph she drew little Elise skipping. A tiny, winged pixie flitted overhead. *Oh, to be so free.*

"Knock, knock. May I come in?"

Elise looked up to see Cassie standing in the doorway with a pill cup in one hand. "Don't you ever go home?"

"This is my home away from home." She flashed Elise a wide smile as she set the pills on the tray table and poured a cup of water. "Here's your nightcap, sugar."

Swallowing her meds, Elise watched Cassie, but couldn't bring herself to ask the questions plaguing her. "Thank you."

Cassie clucked her tongue. "There's a reason the Lord gave you such a gift. If I were you, I'd—"

"You'd what?" Elise braced herself for a sermon. "You aren't me, are you?"

"No." Taking the drawing pad from Elise with an expression of awe, Cassie shook her head. "No. I most certainly am not you."

Elise bit her lip, afraid to ask. "Is Dixie, is she—?"

Handing the sketchbook back to Elise, Cassie's smile didn't hide her concern. "No. She's not dead. But she's a sick little girl. Bad case of the flu."

"But she was fine yesterday. In fact, she bent my ear for half the night."

"That's how influenza works. One minute you're fine and then…" Cassie snapped her fingers. "Next thing you know you're sick as a dog." She fluffed Elise's pillows and pulled the covers up around her shoulders. "You'll be alone for a few days, unless you want a new roommate."

"No!" Elise closed her eyes. "I'm a military wife. I'm used to being alone."

"Tell me about it. Takes one to know one."

Elise opened her eyes. "Oh? Does your husband bark orders at you like you're one of his subordinates?"

"He tries. But I'm a retired Army captain, so two can play that military game." Cassie chuckled. "Kind of tough being the wife left behind, isn't it? How was it when he came back from Vietnam?"

Elise wiped her eyes with the back of her hand. "Oh, I was still in high school when he was in Vietnam. I didn't meet him until after he was discharged."

"I'm confused. I thought I saw him in uniform when he came to visit."

"You did. He joined the Reserves right before Ben was born. He went full-time in '82 and became a recruiter. In '89 he got deployed to the Persian Gulf for two years. Went back to recruiting when he returned."

"That must've been hard with two youngsters."

"It was, but honestly," Elise tightened her arm around her pillow, "I never missed him."

Elise waited for an "Oh, you don't mean that."

Instead, Cassie sat on the chair beside the bed. Leaning against the back of it, she linked her fingers behind her head. "I get it. My husband served in the Marine Corps in Nam. When I got pregnant with twins and was sent stateside, I resented him. Tell me more about you and Tony. How did the two of you meet?"

"I'm keeping you from your job."

"You're last on my list."

"My dad managed a restaurant called Sirloin Stockade. I went to work for him after some of the kids who worked for him were killed in a car accident. It really shook my dad. He adored his kids.

"One of those kids, Jamie, was a single mom who married her son's daddy when she was sixteen. When they divorced, her son's paternal grandparents gained custody of him. She was devastated. Dad took her under his wing. She looked up to him like the father she never had, and I saw her as the sister I never had.

"Anyway, Tony was her brother. We met through her and he would come into the restaurant just to get a coke, although Jamie swore it was because he had a crush on me. I thought she was crazy because he was twenty-two and I was only fifteen." Elise yawned.

"A real Methuselah." Cassie yawned, too.

Elise giggled. "I suppose he wasn't old enough to be compared to the oldest man in the Bible, but seven years was a lot back then."

Cassie glanced at her watch. "I best be going so we can both get some shut-eye."

As the door closed behind Cassie, Elise shut her eyes, allowing the sleeping pill to take effect.

Drifting off to sleep, Elise dreamt of the first time she met Tony.

Elise and Jamie were hiding out in the car so Jamie's mom wouldn't catch her smoking when the front door of the house burst open. Little Brian ran to the car brandishing a toy pistol. "Bang! Bang!"

Jamie threw open the car door and collapsed on the ground, clutching her chest. "Ya got me."

Brian dropped to his knees beside her and pointed to the gold star pinned to his plaid shirt. "You're under arrest for robbing the bank."

Gathering him into a gentle headlock, she kissed his nose and tickled his sides. "You'll never take me alive, Sheriff!"

The boy giggled and squirmed out of her arms. A tall, handsome man with wavy, brown hair swept him up onto his broad shoulders. "Time for tacos, Marshal Dillon." He opened Elise's door. "And who's this pretty little girl?"

Brian's grin vanished and his huge brown eyes focused on her. "I 'on't know."

Standing and brushing grass out of her hair, Jamie pointed to Elise. "This is Mommy's friend from work. Can you say 'hi' to Elise?"

"Huh-uh." He hid his face in Tony's shoulder.

Meanwhile, Tony hadn't shifted his gaze from Elise. The same shade as the sky on a cloudy day, his eyes held her captive. His slow smile revealed straight teeth and deep dimples. He held up his left hand in a two-fingered peace sign and offered her his right. "Hello, Gorgeous."

Chapter Twenty-Four

A SPECIAL BREAKFAST of Belgian waffles with real maple syrup, fresh fruit, and butter had been served for patients and their families this Saturday morning. Elise noted how little Gracie ate. Tony and Dixie's observations of her daughter following in her footsteps haunted Elise. As for herself, she ate half a waffle with strawberries.

After breakfast, the patients dispersed for some free time to visit with their families. Elise walked down the hall to Wayne's office with Gracie at her side. Tony had called earlier to beg off breakfast, but promised to be there for their session. It didn't surprise her that he claimed he had an important matter to attend to. Everything was more important than she was.

Wayne's door swung open and Lucas leaped into the hallway. Then he did a pirouette and, with balletic grace, bowed. "*Bonjour*, Madame Elise. Mademoiselle Grace. I'd like to say I will miss you, but I'd be lying."

Elise stepped backward. "You're leaving?"

"Correctamundo! It's Saturday, March sixteenth—my eighteenth. As of today, I'm free as a bird. After my coining out, I shall waltz, piqué, and leap right through those revolving doors in the lobby." All color drained his hollow cheeks, and he clutched his chest.

Acting on maternal instinct, Elise reached out and grasped his arm. "Lucas, you're ill. Gracie, go get a nurse."

Lucas heaved a deep sigh and yanked back his arm. "I'm fine." His sallow face turned crimson. "Nothing's wrong and you're not my mother." He pivoted and headed toward his room.

Elise's feet turned to stone as she watched Lucas disappear. She'd never heard him talk like that. "I wonder what's really bothering him."

Gracie curved her arm around Elise's shoulder and whispered, "We're going to be late."

As they entered Wayne's office, his clock cuckooed eleven times. Slouched behind his desk, Wayne sat gazing at a photograph of a ballerina, his expression one of abject despair. Elise suspected it had much to do with Lucas.

She approached him with caution. "Wayne? Should we come back later?"

Setting the photo face down on his desk, he smiled a forced smile. "No! I mean, of course not. It's your appointment." He stretched his arms over his head, then rubbed the back of his neck. "Isn't Tony coming?"

"He's going to be a few minutes late."

Gracie flashed a broad smile. "Buenos morning, Captain Picard."

"Ah, a fellow *Star Trek* fan. Welcome, Number One," he said in a phony British accent. Standing, he held out his bowl of Tootsie Rolls. "Someone's had her braces removed. Enjoy."

She took one of the candies and unwrapped it. "Thanks." She popped it into her mouth and chewed. "It feels weird."

"You look positively lovely." He turned to Elise. "Tootsie Roll?"

Elise reached for one. She loved the chewy chocolate candies. They had been among her favorites for as long as she could remember.

"You've eaten way too much this morning," cooed the Beast that Elise had dubbed Annie.

Elise jerked back her hand. "No, thanks."

Setting the bowl down, he sat on the desk beside it. "Of course not. Must watch our girlish figure."

"Doctor Picard, don't you know that patronizing comments like that can diminish my ability to think clearly or make sound judgements?" Elise sank down in a chair. She pulled her feet up and hugged her knees. "In other words—do you really want to get on my bad side?"

Wayne tilted his head and raised an eyebrow. He held her in his gaze for a moment before applauding. "Brava, Elise! I apologize." He turned his attention to Gracie. "I'll start with you, my dear. You came to the meeting Wednesday night. Any thoughts? Feelings?"

Plopping into a wingback chair, Gracie picked at a loose thread on Tony's Navy sweatshirt sleeve. "I don't know why I should go to it. I don't have an eating disorder." She tapped her toes on the floor.

He pointed. "What are you hiding under those baggy clothes? Are you cold?"

"No."

"Then you won't mind taking off the sweatshirt—provided you have another shirt under it—for a moment. Could you stand?"

Rolling her eyes, she huffed and stood. She slipped off the sweatshirt and flung it in Elise's lap. Underneath it she wore a tank top, showing off her flat abs and well-muscled arms.

With a combination of pride and envy, Elise hugged the sweatshirt and breathed in her daughter's scent.

Wayne sat on the edge of his desk, his blue eyes brimming with concern. He motioned for Gracie to sit. "Are you dieting?"

Gracie flopped back down. "I need to lose a few pounds to look good at swim meets."

"I thought you quit the swim team."

"My coach talked me into sticking with it. He says I have Olympic potential."

Leaning forward, Wayne frowned. "Did he indicate that he thought you needed to lose weight?"

"Well," Gracie wagged her head from side to side, "no. But, the other girls on the team are so thin."

Elise's pulse thudded against her temples. A slender, toned young woman had replaced her chubby little girl. Diet? Why did Gracie feel the need to diet? Did Elise need to ask? Guilt-ridden, she bowed her head and leaned her forehead against her knees. Maybe she should pull

Gracie out of sports. Elise couldn't bear the thought of her baby girl following Dixie's path—starving herself for an Olympic medal.

Elise ground her teeth. "Did your coach compare you to them?"

"No!"

"How tall are you, Gracie?" asked Wayne.

"Five feet and four inches." She gave Elise's ponytail a slight yank. "Four inches taller than my five-foot-nothing mommy."

Elise raised her head, shifting her gaze from Gracie back to Wayne, who trained his focus on Gracie. "No need to toss out numbers, but I'd say you're right in the weight ballpark for your age and height. Tell me. What did you have for breakfast this morning?"

"Why are you interrogating me?" Gracie folded her arms across her chest. "I'm not the patient. Besides you asked me the same stupid questions last week."

"And I believe your answer was half a granola bar."

Elise interjected her observation. "She might have eaten a strawberry and a bite of her waffle. Not much more than that."

He tossed Gracie another piece of candy. "You're too young to remember Karen Carpenter, aren't you?"

"We have lots of her records." Gracie caught the candy in one hand. "Pity she's gone to the Great Beyond. She had such a badical voice."

"Do you know anorexia is what killed her?"

Gracie unwrapped her candy and sucked it into her mouth. Her dark eyes widened. "No. Mom? Did you know that?"

Elise nodded.

The words her doctor, Susan Williams, had said haunted Elise. *"You're going to end up dead on the bathroom floor like Karen Carpenter."*

Wayne slid off his desk onto his feet. He went to the door and opened it. "Okay, Gracie, I'll let you off the hook for now. See if your dad is out there."

Gracie seemed relieved to be off the hot seat. "Good luck, Mommy." She stood and walked to the door. Elise stood and followed her. Gracie winked and inclined her head toward Wayne. "He's in a mood today, isn't he?"

Opening the door, Gracie stopped and turned. "Oh, I forgot to tell you. Ben called this morning and wanted me to tell you at breakfast, 'Eat, dammit!'" She stepped out into the hallway.

Elise's heart leaped at the mention of her son. The apple hadn't fallen far from the maternal tree. Like his mother and his Uncle Gene, Ben used humor as a defense mechanism.

Long before Gracie was born, she made Ben her companion. Her confidante. Too much responsibility to put on a child. Nonetheless, he seemed to understand her better than Tony ever had.

Wayne sank down into Gracie's vacated chair. Leaning back, he folded his arms. "Here's a riddle for you, Mrs. Reeves. How many therapists does it take to change a lightbulb?"

"I don't know. Tell me, oh bright one."

"Just one. But only if the lightbulb is willing to change."

Tony entered the room. Elise met him with an obligatory hug. "Where have you been?"

He shrugged and planted a gentle kiss on her lips. "I had an important meeting with friends."

"What friends?"

"When I'm ready, I'll tell you." Putting his hands on her shoulders, he held her at arm's length, his gaze traveling from her feet to her head. "You ain't gained an ounce. Ya gotta get a handle on this, girl."

"I'm—trying." Elise sank back down in her chair, bracing herself for a lecture about medical bills and his stress.

Instead, he wrapped his arms around her and whispered, "Me, too."

"Won't you have a seat, Chief." Wayne held out the orange bowl. "Tootsie Roll."

Tony scooped up a handful and eased into a chair. "Thanks. Been a couple hours since breakfast."

Elise couldn't put her finger on it, but he seemed different. Calmer. Less defensive.

"Anything in particular you want to talk about, Chief Reeves?"

"Just one thing." Tony unwrapped a second piece of candy and popped it into his mouth. "How do you think my wife is doing?"

Wayne wrote something on his notepad. "She's made some progress, although not as much as I'd like to see."

Tony reached for Elise's hand. She braced herself for a tirade.

His eyes brimming, he squeezed her hand until it throbbed. "Elise, you've got to get well. Can't you do something, Dr. Picard?"

"I can't make her do anything. It's up to her." Wayne steepled his fingers and focused on her. "Healing is a process. Not an event. And the truth is, if Elise wants to die, I can't stop her."

Wayne's words hit like a hail of bullets. Tony's tears unnerved her. She searched his face for anger and found none. "What do you need from me?" he asked.

* * *

"We're gathered here for a coining out." Cassie's eyes didn't share her mouth's smile. She put a chair in the middle of the room. "Lucas, you are the man of the hour. Come ascend your throne."

It didn't take a genius to figure out why. Lucas was eighteen and the hospital had no legal right to hold him.

He sat on the chair and flourished a lithe hand. "Genuflect at will, my loyal subjects."

Cassie gave the coin to Nyx who closed her fingers around it and raised her fist. "All hail to the king who's dancing his way to Hell. I'd say I'll miss you, but I'd be lying." She passed the coin to Irma.

Irma eyed the boy and twisted her wrinkled lips to one side, shaking her head. Then she took a deep breath. "I realize I don't have a lot of room to preach to you. But you've got a lot going for you, young man. Apply yourself and you could be the next Baryshnikov."

At the mention of one of the most renown male ballet dancers, Mikhail Baryshnikov, Lucas puffed out his chest. His pasty cheeks flushed. "Thank you, madam."

"Don't thank me, kid. I'm not finished. I said, 'could be.' The fact is you won't, and you know why." A tear trickled down her weathered cheek as she passed the coin to Tina-Louis. "I've had my say. I hope I'm wrong, Lucas."

"I hope you get better, Lucas." Tina-Louise handed the coin to Elise.

Turning the brass disk in her hand, Elise skimmed the serenity prayer with her thumb and puzzled over what to say. What advice could she give? A few hours ago he'd seethed and told her in so many words where she could stick her advice. Elise's emotions warred between dislike and motherly concern for a gravely ill boy. Raising her head, Elise forced herself to smile at Lucas, wishing she could backhand some sense into him instead. "You've been given a great gift, son. Don't waste it."

As she passed the coin to Tina-Louise, Cassie's intense gaze seared through her. She could almost hear her say, "What about you, Elise? Aren't you wasting yours?"

Cassie handed the coin to Chaplain Charlie who said a prayer for Lucas to end the ceremony. Not waiting for any final farewells, Lucas made a hasty exit, slamming the door behind him.

"May God have mercy on that child," whispered the chaplain.

Irma stood and stretched her arms over her head. "That boy's got one foot in the grave and the other on a banana peel. I've seen cadavers in my Daddy's funeral home who looked more alive."

Elise's heart thumped against her ribs.

"Lucas is almost there," whispered Annie. "The ultimate success. What about you, Elise? Isn't this what you want for yourself?"

Tina-Louise drew her knees into her chest. "I don't want to die. I want to get well."

Cassie knelt beside the girl's chair and curved her arm around her shoulders. "That's the first step to recovery, sugar." Cassie glanced at Elise. "The decision."

Supper had no taste that evening as Elise thought back over the past few hours. Not even the good news of Dixie's soon return to the unit could wash away the sour taste of Lucas's departure. For the first time in years, she longed for Tony.

Chapter Twenty-Five

"Tʜᴀᴛ's ᴀᴍᴀᴢɪɴɢ, Nʏx."

Elise pointed to the clay dragon the girl had been working on for two days with bright-eyed enthusiasm. This morning, she'd been adding the finishing touches, detailing each scale with diligence. She had even chosen the colors for it.

Nyx flashed a rare smile. "Thanks."

"High praise from the maven. Too bad we can't all be artists like Her Highness Elise," Irma snarled.

Heat rose to Elise's cheeks. She had almost come to dread art therapy, at least when Irma showed up. The old biddy had a knack for sucking the joy out of it. Was it simple jealousy or had she done something else to make Irma dislike her so? As always, Elise avoided eye contact and tried her best to ignore her.

Nonetheless, Irma singled her out. Peering over Elise's shoulder, she sniffed. "Wake up and smell the coffee, honey. There's no such thing as pixies or angels."

Pam tried to intervene. "Elise is getting in touch with her inner child. Her drawings are to help with her healing."

Irma glared at the art therapist. "Pfft. Inner child, my eye."

Nyx bared her teeth. "Lay off her, ya old bat."

Taking Irma's arm, Pam tried to lead her back to her own art piece. Irma wrenched out of her grasp and pushed Nyx's sculpture off the table. It shattered. The girl shrieked, then jumped up from her chair and, before Pam could stop her, raked her fingernails across Irma's cheek.

"You black-lipped daughter of Satan!" Irma shrieked. A thin stream of blood trickled down her face. "I'm gonna sue your butt off. You *and* this quack-filled hospital."

Elise admired Pam's self-control. Although her cheeks blanched to chalk-white, she never raised her voice. She picked up the phone. "Terry, Irma needs medical attention for a scratch." Hanging up the phone she nodded at the tech who appeared in the doorway. "Take her to the nurse's station."

Irma seethed. "Scratch? Ha! I'll probably die of rabies."

The room took on an eerie silence in the wake of Irma's departure. Elise feigned concentration on her sketch to allow Nyx time to gather herself. Unable to resist the motherly instinct, Elise finally spoke softly. "I'm sorry about your statue, Nyx."

"No biggie." Nyx bit her lower lip and formed the moist clay into a ball. "I didn't like it anyway."

***

"These illustrations are coming along nicely, Elise." Pam thumbed through the small stack on her lap. "I could see these winning a Caldecott Award."

The thought of ever being awarded the coveted medal for her art pleased Elise. Heat rose from her neck to her face. "Oh, I don't think so."

"That isn't false modesty, is it?" Pam's Payne's gray eyes twinkled. "Tell me about this one." She held up the painting Elise had finished earlier in the day. In the foreground a pair of hands tossed a huge bubble in the air. Visible behind it was a mime face in the grass. A pixie sat on the edge of one of the eyeholes. "Why a mask?"

"Hope, the pixie, is showing little Elise what she found. The mask symbolizes the way we hide our true feelings."

"Brilliant. And how does grown-up Elise feel about this?"

Tucking her feet underneath her, Elise focused on the octagon-shaped aquarium in Pam's office. A school of six neon tetra swam toward the top of the tank. Four black mollies swam in the opposite direction. A catfish busily pecked at the colored gravel at the bottom. Two angel fish gleamed under the tank's light.

"Elise?"

She eyeballed the therapist's high cheekbones and square jaw. Her chin-length, blonde pageboy gleamed in the lamplight. What shade would she use to paint Pam's lips?

"Earth to Elise."

"I—that is—I'm sorry, what was the question?"

"How's your recovery coming?"

Elise fingered a lower button on her blouse. "Um. Food still scares me."

"I'd say I understand." Pam pinched her thigh through her slacks. "But obviously, I don't. I could stand to shed a few pounds. Can you share your diet secrets with me?"

"You're teasing, aren't you? You're not fat at all."

"Sounds silly when I say it, doesn't it?" Pam winked and set Elise's picture on an end table. She positioned herself in front of the full-length mirror on the back of her door and beckoned Elise to join her. "Tell me what you see."

Tilting her head, Elise scrutinized their reflections. Pam wasn't much taller than Elise. Pam's fitted, navy-blue pantsuit complemented her slender figure. "I see that we're almost the same height. What are you? Five-two? My brother's only five-two and he hates it. I guess it's different for a man."

"Elise." Pam arched an eyebrow. "When you look at yourself, what do you see? What do you *really* see? Not your skewed perception."

"I thought this was art therapy."

"Isn't an artist supposed to pay attention to detail?"

"You're shrewd."

"It's why they pay me the big bucks." Pam nodded at the mirror. "Go on."

Elise shifted her gaze to her own reflection. Her brown curls obscured a good part of her colorless complexion. Dark circles ringed her eyes. Her long-sleeved, plaid shirt hung to her knees. "You can't see my breasts at all. I'm down to almost an A-cup." Her tights made her legs look like black dowel rods in high-top, purple Converse sneakers. She repressed the urge to smile. "I'm too thin. I don't look healthy, do I?"

"Perfect timing, Momette. I just got home." Gracie's excited voice blared in Elise's ear. "We practically drowned the other teams. And I took first in the 100-meter breaststroke. Coach says I'm poetry in motion in the water."

"That's awesome! I'm glad you decided not to quit the swim team." Looking up and down the deserted hallway, Elise determined no one was listening to her phone call. "What did Dad say?"

"He's not home yet. Said he's meeting a friend for dinner. Hank Something-or-Other."

"Dinner, huh?" Elise clenched her teeth and glanced at her watch. "Coupled with a few beers, no doubt." Tony could never stop at one or two.

Realizing it was past nine o'clock, Elise asked, "Did the meet go late? Why are you just getting home?"

"Oh!" Gracie's voice raised an octave in her excitement. "Doug took me to dinner at Bo Ling's. You know how much I love their egg rolls!"

"You shouldn't be out so late on a school night, Gracie."

"You're not entirely wrong, Momette. Except it's spring break."

"Oh—right." Elise felt shame for being so out of touch with home and family. "He's never—tried anything—has he?"

"Mo-om. I wish you'd stop saying things like that. We doubled with Marissa and Kent. Speaking of... Marissa's going to call me at nine-thirty. Bye."

"Tell her—" *Click.*

Elise hung the receiver on the hallway wall phone. Where was Tony? Not that it wasn't like him to go out on a work night. However, as a rule, when Gracie had a date, Tony would plant himself on the sofa until she came home.

Different scenarios of where Tony could be whirled through Elise's mind as she padded to her room. She sank down on her bed and stared at Dixie's empty one. Her twenty-four-hour bug had spread out over four days and four lonely nights. Had she lost weight from her illness?

"You'll never be as good at it as Dixie." Annie laughed. "You saw yourself in the mirror and told Pam what she wanted to hear. Good girl. But, you're still too fat! Wouldn't it be nice if you could get sick with the flu and be unable to hold down all the crap they keep forcing on you?"

Elise turned on the light and opened her notebook. On the front page she had written in scrolling calligraphy, "The Magic Daffodils by Rosemary E. Jacobson-Reeves."

She turned the page to pick up where she had left off that morning. It was time to write the story to go with her illustrations. Putting pencil to paper, she wrote, "Elise drank in the aroma of fragrant daffodils. She lay down in the cool grass and watched the fluffy clouds overhead. They took on all kinds of delightful shapes. Some looked like furry puppies or angels with wings. Soon she fell sound asleep, dreaming of cream-puff clouds that sailed far away."

Chapter Twenty-Six
Tony

TONY HAD NEVER CONSIDERED himself a candidate for therapy. He'd always believed all that psychobabble was hogwash and hooey. However, in the last couple of weeks, since he'd met Dr. Hank Rogers at the veterans' support group meetings, his opinions had begun to change. He'd even agreed to private sessions with the psychologist.

It came as a surprise when Hank had called him at work and invited him out for a burger at Winstead's. "Just us brothers in arms," he'd said.

Tony breathed in the greasy aromas of tater tots and onion rings. Perfume to his nostrils.

Hank sucked the dregs of his chocolate soda through his straw. He wiped his mouth with his napkin. "Winstead's still has the best steakburgers and tots in KC."

"No argument here." Tony slid his last tot through a mound of ketchup and popped it in his mouth. "The atmosphere hasn't changed since I was a kid and my dad brought me here. A special trip in his plane —just him and me—to Kansas City."

The waitress brought the ticket and laid it on the table. He reached for it, but Hank beat him to it. "My treat, Chief. Please add two coffees to that, Ma'am."

She shook her head and winked at Tony. "Two coffees on the house. I never could resist a man in uniform." Patting Hank's shoulder, she added, "Always a pleasure to see you, Gunny."

Leaning back in his wheelchair, Hank rubbed his rounded belly. "Guess I eat here a little too often."

Tony had great respect for Hank, a Vietnam veteran who'd lost both legs in battle. He was the recipient of two Purple Hearts, a Bronze Star, and a Distinguished Service Cross.

At their first meeting, trying not to stare at the therapist's stumps, Tony had focused on the medals in their shadow box. "You must have some stories to tell."

"You bet, but we're not here to discuss my service history, Chief." Hank had shrugged. "Surely you have a few medals of your own. Nightmares?"

"Some of both."

"Tell me about them."

"I see how it is." Tony had bristled. "What's this gonna cost me, Doc?"

"Nothing, save some emotional baggage."

True to his word, Hank had probed Tony's dark places and challenged him to face his demons. Had never let him off the hook.

Back in the present, Hank fixed his gaze on Tony. "Enough chitchat. Tell me what's going on with you, Chief."

"Hey now. You said we was meeting for a casual evening and a couple of burgers. If I'd known this was going to be a session, I'd'a never agreed to it." Tony checked his watch. "It's twenty-one hundred. Gracie should be home by now."

Settling back in his wheelchair, Hank motioned for Tony to calm down. "She's sixteen, right? She'll be fine. If she's anything like my daughter, she's happy to have the house all to herself."

"Yeah, that's what worries me."

The waitress came and set two steaming cups of coffee on the table. "Anything else, gentlemen?"

Handing her the ticket and a wad of bills, Hank shook his head. "That'll do us for the evening. Great service as always, m'dear."

"Thanks, Gunny." She turned and headed for the cash register. "I'll bring back your change."

"Nope. It's all yours."

Tony stirred creamer into his coffee. Events of yesterday's session with Elise came flooding back. After two weeks in the hospital, Elise hadn't gained an ounce. When he'd pointed it out, she'd hung her head and sobbed. Guilt at making her cry ate at him.

"I wish Elise would snap out of it."

Hank leaned forward, elbows on the table. His gaze shot lightning bolts through Tony. "Think you can fix her?"

"Wish I could. She changed while I was over in the Gulf." Tony chewed a toothpick. "She don't listen to reason no more."

"*Your* brand of reason." Hank leaned back and took a sip of his coffee. "You resent her not falling in line and seeing things your way."

Anger welled up in Tony's chest and buzzed like a swarm of hornets. "Hey! Are you insinuating that her problems are my fault?"

"Do you think they are?"

"Cagey, Hank."

"How did you and Elise meet?"

Tony's tight jaw relaxed at the memory of the first time he had seen her. She wore long dark pigtails, looking even younger than her sixteen years. "My sister Jamie worked for Elise's dad at the old Sirloin Stockade."

"Sounds familiar." Hank took a small notepad from his shirt pocket. "The one in Grandview?"

Tony craned his neck to see what Hank wrote. "What's that you're writing?" He caught a couple a table away staring at him. Lowering his voice, he said, "Not a session, huh?"

Hank shrugged and winked. "Can't help myself when we're making progress."

"Keep writing, then." Picturing young Elise in his mind, Tony felt a hint of giddiness. He couldn't keep from smiling. "This is good stuff."

Hank grinned. "Sounds like I might need a bigger notepad. Carry on, Chief."

"Yeah, Sirloin Stockade in Grandview, right off 71 Highway. 1969, I'd just gotten out'a the Navy. Sis and Elise hung out a lot and, once in a while, Jamie'd bring her home for supper. Elise was something. Pretty. Smart. Funny." Tony traced an hourglass shape in the air. "Mind you, I wasn't in the market for a little girl, although she was fun to flirt with. I guess you could say I was hooked the minute I saw her, but it didn't occur to me to date her. She was just a kid. A sophomore in high school. It's all my sister's fault we went out in the first place."

"How so?"

"One night I lean over the counter and say, 'Hey, good lookin', when you going out with me?' Elise turns all rosy. God, I loved that about her. Then, Jamie starts going on about this great movie called *Easy Rider* playing at the Plaza. 'You should take her, Tony.' Next thing I know I'm sitting in the theater with her."

"So, she was only sixteen. Her parents let her go?"

"I don't think they were all that thrilled but Bob, Elise's dad, trusted Jamie. He always treated her like a daughter."

"Interesting." Hank turned the page of his notepad and continued to write. "I take it one date led to another."

"Yeah. Everything about her impressed me, not just her looks. You wouldn't think we'd have much in common. Her being a sheltered little Jewish girl from the suburbs and me being a wild man from the trailer park. But we liked the same books and art. I liked to draw, but not like her. Once, she drew my portrait. Looked just like me."

Hank set his pen down for a moment and took a sip of his coffee. "How did her parents take it when you proposed?"

"Not very good." Tony took a final swallow from his cup. He'd never forget the disdain in his future mother-in-law's eyes. It still made him shudder. "Not good at all."

"But they gave their consent to your marriage?"

"I wouldn't say that exactly. We waited until Elise turned eighteen and didn't need their permission."

"You're not Jewish, are you?"

"Not even close. But I agreed to get married at the New Reform

Synagogue to keep the peace. It was a circus. Rabbi Davis was the only one in town who'd marry a mixed couple and Elise's grandpa wouldn't come unless we were married in a synagogue. My family on one side. Hers on the other. My mom crying. Her mom glaring at me like I'm Jack the Ripper."

Chapter Twenty-Seven

Lying still, Elise watched the flashlight beam traverse the room. She waited for the nurse to finish her nightly search. Rolling over onto her back, Elise stared at the ceiling and heaved a frustrated sigh. While her body craved sleep, her mind wouldn't shut off.

A sharp pain surged through her stomach. She bolted upright and rushed to the bathroom, relieved to find the door unlocked. Sinking onto the seat, she doubled over and let nature take its course. No need for laxatives.

With a sense of relief, she padded back to her bed. She slipped under the covers. Shivering, she pulled them up around her neck and rolled onto her side.

A light shone across the bed, and she looked up to see Cassie. "Elise, what's the matter?"

"It's nothing. I had a bad dream and a little Montezuma's revenge, that's all."

Shutting off her flashlight, Cassie laid it on the nightstand. She pressed a warm palm against Elise's forehead. "No fever. I suppose it could be stress related. But I'm gonna keep my eye on you. You might be coming down with that nasty flu. All we need on this floor is an epidemic." She picked up her flashlight and turned to leave. "If you get sick again, you call us, y'hear?"

Elise reached out and grabbed the nurse's wrist. "Could you stay with me for a while?"

"I suppose I could. Bruno's got the desk and everyone else is off in Dreamland." She sank into the chair beside the bed. "I'm all yours, girlfriend."

In a low voice, Cassie sang, "Wade in the water, wade in the water, children, wade in the water, God's a'gonna trouble the water."

Hugging her pillow, Elise wove the edge of the case between her fingers. A delicious fatigue flooded her as Cassie's lilting voice eased her anxiety. Her eyelids grew heavy.

"If you get there before I do, God's gonna trouble the water," Cassie continued. "Tell all my friends that I'm a-coming, too. God's gonna trouble the water."

Elise yawned. She loved the image of wading in the water. Where would God take her on her journey. Would he trouble the water for her? Would she and Dixie reach that magical place together?

"You should've been a singer." Without opening her eyes, Elise smiled. "That's a Negro spiritual, isn't it?"

"I suppose I'm stereotyping myself, but my momma used to sing it to me when I was a child. And I sang it to my babies. Sang it to my man when he came back from Nam. It helped chase away the night terrors."

"Does your husband talk about the war? Tony won't. He claims he's put it all behind him." Elise opened her eyes and raised up on one elbow. "He says I need to do the same thing with stuff that happened to me. 'Don't dwell on it,' he says."

Cassie arched an eyebrow. "Can you tell me what has you so upset tonight? Flashback?"

"Yeah. When I was a teenager, I drove my mom crazy trying to straighten my long hair. This particular night I remember kneeling beside the ironing board so she could iron it. I was going to the Sno-Ball dance with Michael Gordon. He was one of the most popular boys in school, so everything had to be perfect. And—drumroll—he was Jewish, which made my mother happy.

"My brother Eugene had recently been discharged from the Air Force. I still remember how it hurt when he said, 'Maybe you should try that to flatten your chest, Dee-Dee.'"

"Dee-Dee?"

"For my bra size. I stuck out my tongue and told him to DD—drop dead."

Lying on her back, Elise stared at the ceiling. Her mind traveled to the winter of 1970. Every detail came back with vivid clarity as she recounted them to Cassie.

"Rosemary Elise Jacobson." Mom had tutted. "That's no way to talk to your brother."

Nevertheless, Eugene's words pierced Elise. Shopping for a new bra that afternoon had been difficult. And why did her brother have to go with them anyway? Oh yeah, he had said he needed to buy socks and Macy's carried his favorites.

He had found his socks and returned to the lingerie department in time to catch the conversation between Mom and the clerk.

"A double-D is a lot for such a tiny girl." The flat-chested saleslady had folded two brassieres, one white and one black, to go under Elise's black semi-formal and wrapped them in tissue paper. "I wish I had half of that. I'm jealous."

Mom had nodded in agreement. "It's difficult to find bras to fit her."

"I understand. Most of us aren't lucky enough to be so well-endowed by our Creator, are we?"

Doubling her fists at her side, Elise had wished she could send them crashing into the clerk's ingratiating smile. Behind her, Eugene had snorted. "I didn't know they made parachutes in black."

"There." Mom finished ironing Elise's hair. She handed Elise a hairbrush. "See what you think."

Elise went to the full-length mirror on the bathroom door. Brushing her hair that hung to her waist, she growled at the kinks along her hairline that refused to be ironed out. She admired her new dress with its black V-neck top, flowered waistband, and colorfully striped skirt two inches above her knees. She tugged at the neckline trying to cover the unavoidable cleavage.

"Call Hefner." Eugene's gaze traveled from her toes to her head. "Dee-Dee, maybe you'll be the world's first Jewish centerfold."

Elise's face blazed. "Quit calling me that, Jerk-Wad."

Mom turned off the iron. "Gene, dear, don't you have something else to do besides torture your sister?"

Dad, who had been watching television in the bedroom, burst into the living room. He glowered at Eugene. "Dammit, I can't hear a thing over all this racket." His expression softened as he shifted his gaze to Elise. "My little girl is growing up."

"And out," Eugene mumbled as he sauntered down the hall to his room. He stopped at his door and made a vulgar gesture toward Dad's back. "Have fun at the dance—Dee-Dee."

Eugene's door slammed. Dad kissed Elise's cheek. "Back to the news. Have a good time, Doll Face."

Mom followed him down the hall with her eyes. Then she smiled at Elise. "I'm glad you've come to your senses and broken up with that Tony. He's too old for you."

Elise's stomach jumped at the mention of Tony's name. How she wished he was her date to the Sno-Ball. It hadn't been a matter of her "coming to her senses" as Mom wanted to believe. Tony had broken it off, saying Elise was still a child and he wanted a woman. What he really meant was he wanted to have sex and she refused.

Last she'd heard from Jamie, Tony was dating a classmate at Wichita State. He'd brought her home for Christmas. Jamie said she looked like a slut and their mother didn't like her at all.

Elise smoothed her skirt and turned, peering over her shoulder at her back. "My tush is too big."

Mom slipped her arm around Elise's waist. "You're fine the way you are. A little top-heavy perhaps. You get that from Grandma Jacobson." A shadow of disgust darkened Mom's face. She gave Elise a squeeze. "I'm glad you're going out with a nice Jewish boy for a change. The Gordons are big makhers at the Jewish Community Center, you know."

Admittedly, Elise had been surprised when Michael Gordon had asked her to the dance. He'd never given her a second look until they were both cast in the drama department's production of Rip Van Winkle *the year before. She had appreciated the way he refused to join his buddies in taunting her when her breasts had to be "diapered" to portray one of the children.*

This year, he chose art as an elective. Her turf. He often asked her for her opinion of his work and laughed when she winced as she searched for something encouraging to say. "I'll never be the artist you are, Elise. You're my hero."

She enjoyed their comfortable friendship. He considered her one of the guys. They shared silly jokes and commiserated about their unrequited loves.

Winding a lock of hair around her finger, Elise turned from her reflection. "Don't get too excited, Mom. Michael only asked me to the dance because his cheerleader girlfriend dumped him."

Mom sat by the end table and lit a cigarette. "You never know. What's he need with a shiksa cheerleader anyway?"

Elise rolled her eyes. "She's blonde, blue-eyed, and skinny. Not a zaftig wallflower like me."

"Stop it. My daughter has inner beauty. He asked you to the dance, didn't he?"

"Humph. Inner beauty. Thanks, Mommy."

"What'd I say?"

Elise rolled her eyes again just as the doorbell rang. "Nothing"

Mom stubbed out her cigarette and went to open the front door. Elise ran to the kitchen to take Michael's boutonniere out of the refrigerator.

"Michael. Don't you look handsome." Mom's enthusiasm grated Elise's ears. "Please come in and make yourself comfortable."

Elise entered the living room to see him holding a corsage with sweetheart roses and a large carnation. Her breath caught in her throat. His suit accentuated his broad shoulders and narrow waist. Long lashes fringed his deep brown eyes under dark brows. His olive complexion and thick black hair boasted his Mediterranean background.

"Wow, you clean up nicely, Michael." Oh man, what a dorky thing to say.

He stared at her chest. "So do you."

Her cheeks warmed as he pinned the corsage to her dress.

Did he just cop a feel? Must be my imagination. Do I smell alcohol on his breath? Surely not. He's only seventeen and good Jewish boys don't drink. And pigs have wings.

Michael hadn't driven a block when he took a bottle swaddled in a brown paper bag from the glove compartment. He took a swig and offered it to her. "This will help us both survive the evening."

"No thanks. I don't drink."

"Of course not. Only cool kids partake." He rolled his eyes. "Bet you're a virgin, too."

"Gimme that." Crossing her legs, she took the bottle and drank. The booze burned her throat. She coughed. "Ugh. Tastes terrible. Guess I'll have to settle for being uncool."

After they arrived at the school, Elise marveled at the decorations that transformed the cafeteria into a winter wonderland. She tried to put the drive out of her mind. Michael sauntered over to the punch bowl to greet one of his football teammates who poured from his own brown-bagged bottle and stirred the dipper. Michael ladled spiked punch into two cups and handed one to Elise. He led her to a table. "Hold my place for a minute."

Heart sinking to her stomach, she watched him approach his former girlfriend, who had been crowned Sno-Ball queen. Leslie Gore's "It's my Party" played in Elise's mind.

"May I have this dance, Your Highness?" Michael bowed and kissed Kerry's hand. "That is, if I'm not too Jewish for you."

She cast a sidelong scowl at Elise and wreathed her arms around his neck. "One dance won't hurt anything, will it?"

He grinned at Elise over Kerry's shoulder. Elise's heart pounded. This wasn't the Michael she joked with in art class. Dr. Jekyll and Mr. Hyde.

Maybe I should call Dad to come and get me. *She sipped her punch. Cherry 7Up and sherbet overpowered the alcohol taste. An unfamiliar, yet pleasant buzz filled her head.*

Michael returned to the table and picked up her empty cup. He winked. "Looks like someone could use a refill."

Before she had a chance to say she'd had enough, he was back with a full cup. Setting it in front of her, he sat beside her and took a sip of his own. "Could use more vodka."

Elise couldn't stop a giggle from erupting. "I like it the way it is."

"My Girl" played over the PA. Michael squeezed her knee. Glancing over

his shoulder at Kerry in the arms of her Sno-Ball King, he heaved a resigned sigh. "Might as well make the best of it. Shall we dance?"

Elise stood and the room spun around her. "How can a girl resist such a charming invitation?"

Steadying her, Michael pulled her into his arms and led her onto the dance floor. "I'm sorry, Elise. I shouldn't lead you on. My mom made me break up with Kerry."

"Because she isn't Jewish. I know the drill." Elise leaned her head on his shoulder, breathing in the scent of English Leather. "Mom's delighted Tony dumped me."

Michael tightened his embrace. His hot breath made her shiver. "What a fool."

"He went back to Wichita to go to school. Good riddance." Peering around Michael's shoulder, she saw his teammate wink and give him a thumbs up. "What does that mean?"

"What? Oh, Bobby's congratulating me on being here with the prettiest girl in the whole school."

"Oh? But you're not here with Kerry."

Michael kissed her forehead, then slid his lips to brush over hers. "You have no idea how beautiful you are, do you?"

The song ended. Michael pulled back and grabbed her hand. "One more glass of punch and then what say we go somewhere to talk."

"Where? All the classrooms are locked."

"My brother has a pad on Troost, a couple of blocks from here. He lets me hang out there when our parents get to be too much. Besides, he's in Mexico right now, so we'll have the place all to ourselves."

"I don't know if that's such a good idea." She downed her punch and stood. Losing her balance, she plopped down on his lap. "Whoa! What a rush!"

Ten minutes later, Michael hefted her over the threshold of his brother's empty apartment. Black light paintings hung on the walls. The aroma of patchouli incense engulfed her. Michael slid his tongue into her ear as he carried her to the bedroom.

She squirmed and tried to break free. "Please... Michael—take me home."

"You tease, you." He dropped her onto the bed. "What do you expect after you've flaunted those sensational tits all night?" He stripped off his trousers.

"Do you think you can seduce me and not put out?" He fell on top of her, tearing at her bodice. "Time for this boychik to cash in."

Once home, she threw her blood-soaked panties in the outside trash can, burying them under yard waste. She changed into her pajamas and slunk under the covers, too stunned to cry. How could she face her friends? Her family? Or Michael?

The next morning, Mom's anguished cries woke her.

"Elise! Something terrible's happened."

Digging grit from the corners of her eyes, Elise opened them to see Mom hovering over the bed, tears streaming down her cheeks. Elise winced at the cigarette odor on her mother's breath. She buried her face in her pillow and groaned. "What did Dad do now?"

Mom grasped Elise's shoulders. Her words came in sputtering puffs. "It's Michael. Car accident. He's—he's dead."

Waves of nausea swept over Elise. Pushing her mother aside, she rushed to the toilet and dropped to her knees. She retched until there was nothing left. Leaning her forehead on the cool porcelain edge, events of the night before flashed through her mind in lightning-bolt fashion.

"Elise, are you hungover?" Mom pulled Elise's hair away from her face.

"Why would you ask me such a thing?"

"The police said Michael had been drinking. Since you might be the last person to see him alive, they want you to go down to the station to answer a few questions."

Cassie shook her head. "Either way, that boy would have been dead cause my daddy would have killed him. Did you ever tell your momma or daddy?"

"I—I couldn't." Elise's jaw tightened. "After all, he was the 'nice Jewish boy' my mom wanted me to date. Up until my flashbacks started, I really believed I was a willing party."

"And that's just what Michael wanted you to believe. He certainly got his reward."

"Funny, the biggest fights Tony and I had when we were dating were over sex. I was a virgin and wanted to keep it that way. He loved to hold that 'girl in every port' thing over my head. Those women knew how to please a man. Not me. I was a child." Hot tears stung Elise's eyes. "When

Tony and I got back together, the first thing we did was go to bed. After losing my virginity to Michael, saving myself for marriage didn't matter anymore."

A heavy silence filled the room. Elise rolled over on her side. Cassie stroked Elise's hair and whispered, "For all he's said and done, that man's stuck by you for twenty-five years. He loves you and I believe you love him."

Cassie resumed singing and Elise drifted off to the lyrics of "Wade in the Water."

"See those people dressed in black, they come a long way and they ain't turning back."

Chapter Twenty-Eight
Wayne

WAYNE'S HEAD throbbed after a long night in the ER. His heart ached even more. "I should never have discharged him."

Cassie squeezed his arm. "He was eighteen. You had no legal grounds to detain him, Dr. Picard. Are you sure you're up to this?"

"I have to." He pushed open the door to Dixie's room and forced a smile as he entered. "How's my favorite patient?"

"Hey, strangers!" Dixie turned off the television with the remote and raised the head of her bed. "I could get used to this. Really comfy. You just missed the dinner hour. Chicken, mashed potatoes, and, everyone's favorite, green beans. Oh, and a side salad with French dressing. I'm stuffed."

"You actually ate it?"

Dixie tucked her chin and raised her eyes. "Well, maybe not all of it."

Although still skeletal in appearance, the few pounds she had put on made her look radiant. This gave him a sliver of hope as he reached into his pocket to retrieve a Tootsie Roll.

"How about some dessert then." He tossed it and Dixie caught it.

She unwrapped the candy and popped it into her mouth. "Mmm. They took the IV out a bit ago. So, I'm sufficiently hydrated and ready to head back to EDU. What brings you two here on your time off?"

Cassie took a card from her purse. "For one, I came to bring you this."

Wayne peered over her shoulder at a sketch of a little girl floating in the sky, clinging to a bunch of colorful balloons. Across the top it read, "Get Well, Dixie!"

"Mrs. Reeves did a nice job," he said.

"That's my Suzie-Q." Dixie's cheeks flushed. "I'll bet the card was her idea."

"You know it was." Cassie handed it to her. "She's missing you something awful."

"Thanks, Cassie." Dixie gazed at the card. "Looks like everyone signed it, including the nurses." She squinted and moved the card closer. "Did you get some visitors to sign as well? I don't who these two are."

"Let's just say business is booming," Wayne rubbed his throbbing cheek and moved to take a seat in a nearby chair.

Cassie turned to him. "We should go back down to ER. You might have a concussion."

Dixie set the card on her bed table, her eyes widening. "Hey, Doc, how'd you get that shiner?"

"Guess you could call it a delivery from a dissatisfied customer." He sucked in a deep breath and exhaled. "You'll find out sooner or later. Lucas—"

"He kicked the bucket, didn't he? That's why you're here on your time off." Dixie lowered her eyes and scooted her index finger along her blanket. "There was a story on the news about an eighteen-year-old male ballet dancer who collapsed during a rehearsal. They said they were withholding his name until the family could be notified, but it didn't take a rocket scientist to put two and two together." She winced. "That poor mixed-up kid."

"Oh, his family's been notified all right." Wayne's vision blurred. He rubbed his eyes with the heels of his hands. "Sometimes I hate this job."

Dixie's mouth dropped open. "Is that who socked you? Lucas' brother? His dad?"

"His dad." Wayne could still hear the man's barrage of verbal assaults accusing the doctor of his son's death because he, the doctor, had not discouraged Lucas from going back to the "sissy ballet." Wayne wished he hadn't chosen to defend the discipline and strength required for dance. That's not what the family needed to hear, but he had to defend —what? The athletes, Lucas, or his sister?

"I deserved a swift punch in the face." Wayne hung his head. "Lucas nearly fainted in my office Saturday. I should've sent him down to ER right then and there instead of second guessing myself like an intern."

"That's heavy stuff, Dr. P." A tear trickled down Dixie's sallow cheek. "Lucas's death isn't your fault. No way."

"Look at me." Cassie bent over and grabbed his shoulders. "What would you tell me if I'd done the same thing?"

Wayne's stomach ached. Lucas's face flashed through his mind. That beautiful face. So young. Almost too pretty to belong to man. A life cut off way too soon. Wayne clenched his fists and let his gaze linger on Cassie's dark eyes. What *would* he tell her?

He took a deep breath and murmured, "I'd let you off the hook, of course. There's no way of knowing. Some people live with the disorder for years and some don't. I'd say, 'focus on your successes.'"

"There you go. Let yourself off your own hook." Cassie let go of his shoulders and dabbed her eyes with the back of her hand. "It never gets any easier, does it?"

"Yeah, what Cassie said." Dixie pulled her knees into her chest. "Don't blame yourself. I doubt Sigmund Freud could've turned on the lights for that knucklehead."

Cassie's laughter echoed through the room. "And the patient becomes the therapist."

The tension in Wayne's neck eased a bit. "Thank you for the reality check, Dr. Granger."

"I like the sound of that." Dixie lay back against the pillows. "When I get healthy, I think I'll go back to school and become a therapist to help fight Annie. Whatcha think about that, Dr. P?"

"If you're serious, I'll make sure you get a scholarship to the school of your choice and treat you to a steak dinner when you graduate summa cum laude."

"You're on. But for the time being, you should go home and apply a steak to that eye."

Chapter Twenty-Nine
Tony

Tony skimmed his index finger around the rim of his cup. "I don't know what changed, but Elise was different after I came back from Wichita."

He remembered the day he came home to Mom's house. There he could sort things out without a woman in his life to complicate things. As usual, it was all about timing. Hadn't finding his new girlfriend in bed with his roommate been bad enough? Here he had to come face to face with Elise. Pretty, petite Elise. Seventeen-year-old Elise—seven years his junior.

"Different? How?" asked Hank.

"Moodier. I guess it had a lot to do with her buddy Michael, who was killed in a car accident. It really messed with her head. But it was more than that. It's like she grew up. She wasn't a child anymore. After the way I treated her, I'm still surprised she took me back. And, to quote Rod Stewart, 'Mother what a lover, she wore me out.'"

"And they lived happily ever after."

That old ex-Marine knows how to deliver a sucker punch. I never was one to dwell on the past. "What's done is done" is my motto.

Tony glared at Hank, contemplating what to say next. "Right, Doc. That's why Elise is trying to starve herself to death, my son won't give me the time of day, and my daughter—I've no clue what's going on with

Gracie. One minute she's my kitten and the next she's throwing things because something don't fit right."

"Teenage girls are something of an enigma. Lennie put us through hell. There were times I didn't think we'd survive it. But we did."

"How?"

"Rode out the storm as best we could. As best any parent can. All the education in the psychology field doesn't amount to a hill of beans when it's your own kid." Hank took a framed picture of his daughter in a cap and gown from his desk. His ruddy cheeks glowed. "She'll soon be Leonora Rodgers, MD. Maintains a four-point-o in med school. I predict she's gonna be one sought-after pediatrician." He set down the photo. "But you're not here to listen to me regale you with my story. Let's get back to yours. You were telling me how you dropped out of Wichita State and moved back in with your mom. How did that work out?"

"It was pretty cramped. I ended up hanging out at my friend Denny's place more often than not. He was shacking up with his girlfriend and they had an extra bedroom."

"And she didn't mind?"

"Nah. Kate was pretty cool about it. Besides, she and Elise hit it off."

"Back up." Hank wrote on his clipboard. "Elise moved in with you?"

"Not exactly." Tony popped a stick of gum into his mouth. "Ya see, when we hitched back up, things got hot and heavy. Denny and Kate's pad was sort of a getaway place."

"You're lucky she didn't get pregnant."

"That's the funny thing. Her mom found out about us and sprang for birth control pills. Things were copacetic for a while until my crazy Jewish princess found Jesus."

"So, her newfound faith cramped your style. Is that it?"

Tony scowled. "Hey now, don't lay the blame on me."

Hank's pager buzzed. Looking at it, he said, "Time's up, Chief. I'm letting you off the hook for now." He offered his hand. "Friends?"

They clasped their hands. "Yeah," Tony muttered, an uneasiness rising inside. "Friends."

After their session, Tony stopped off at the corner bar for a beer.

He checked his watch. Twenty-two hundred hours already? Tomorrow he had to be at work by zero-seven hundred hours. Important meeting with the Master Chief. He gulped back his beer and left a payment on the table. A half hour later, without turning on the light or undressing, he fell into bed, his emotions waging war with his stomach.

His heart pounded. First Dr. Picard, then Hank. What had he done to push Elise into this insanity? *What if she dies like that dancer kid? I need her!*

He finally nodded off to one nightmare after another. Frankie cried out for him. Elise sank into the Mekong River, her eyes glazed over. His alarm blared at zero five thirty.

At zero six hundred hours, he rolled out of bed and dragged himself to the shower. Closing his eyes, he let the water wash over him a while longer before drying off and brushing his teeth.

After downing two cups of black coffee, he felt semi-human.

He buttoned his uniform shirt, checking out his reflection in the full-length mirror to make sure all creases were in the right places. Since his tour in the Gulf, he'd taken on the responsibility of doing his own laundry. Why expect Elise to do it when he had it down to a science? Besides, she'd said more than once that trying to get those creases right made her crazy.

He combed his hair and moustache. "A little gray in the temples, Chief. Distinguished." He grimaced, his head still pounding from lack of sleep. "Fifty in December. Old."

Pinning his gold wreath onto his pocket, he smiled at the newest star on his recruiting badge. It signified his being the top recruiter in the district. Tony took great pride in making those goals. "Not bad for trailer trash."

The sound of retching came from the bathroom. He hurried down the hall and knocked on the door. "You okay, Gracie?"

No answer.

He pounded.

"I'm fine. Go away!"

"You don't sound fine." He shimmied the knob. She'd locked the door. "Do I need to take you to the doctor?"

"NO!" The knob turned in his hand and the door opened. Gracie, her eyes red and puffy, greeted him with a coquettish pout. "I mean... breakfast didn't sit well, I guess."

He pushed her tousled hair from her face and held his palm against her forehead. "You don't feel warm. In fact, you're ice cold. I'm not so sure I shouldn't take you to the emergency room."

"I'm not sick."

"I ain't convinced." He peeked at his watch. He couldn't afford to miss his meeting. "Maybe you shouldn't go to swim practice. The flu's been making the rounds. Your mom's roommate—"

"Daa-aaad. Read my lips. I do *not* have the flu!" She slammed the door.

He went to the kitchen and poured a cup of coffee. Trembling, he eased himself into a kitchen chair. He set his cup on the table and dropped his head into his hands, choking back hot tears. Over the past couple of weeks, he'd learned more than he ever wanted to know. The signs were all there. His daughter's obsession with weight and food. Like mother, like daughter. Of course, Gracie didn't have the flu. He suspected her vomiting had nothing to do with how her breakfast sat either. What else could go wrong?

After Gracie left for school with her boyfriend, Tony called MEPs and told the XO he'd be running late. Tony dialed the hospital phone. Fuming, he checked his watch again. It took a good five more minutes to jump through their hoops to connect with the eating disorder unit. At last, a woman's voice answered, "Brookside EDU, Nurse Terry speaking. How may I help you?" She sounded way too cheerful. Probably that nutball who wore feathers in her hair.

"Get my damned wife on the phone."

"Chief Reeves?"

"Yeah."

She lowered her voice. "Hang on a moment. Elise is stepping off the scale."

"How much?"

"Privileged information, Chief. Here's your wife."

"Tony?" Elise's voice sounded strained. "Has something happened to Ben? Is Gracie okay?"

"I'm fine, thanks."

She paused. "Glad to hear it."

"Gracie's sick."

"Take her to the doctor."

"She's at practice."

"How could you let her go swimming if she's not well? Was she running a fever?"

"No. But after breakfast she puked her guts up." Anger and panic swelled in his chest. "I'm late for an important appointment. If this keeps up, I'm gonna lose my job. I don't know what to do, Elise. She needs her mother."

***

Elise hung up the phone. As she made her way to the dining room, Tony's tearful words repeated in her head, "She needs her mother. She needs her mother."

What else could go wrong? She took a seat between Felicia, the fashion model, and Irma.

A pall fell over the breakfast table after Cassie broke the news about Lucas to the patients. Felicia burst into tears. Irma's wrinkles deepened and her face paled to ashen gray.

An odd light flickered in Nyx's hazel eyes and she murmured, "Lucky guy. He escaped."

Elise's stomach threatened to empty itself of what little she'd managed to gag down. All she could think of was his mother, whom she had met briefly after his coining out. She would never forget the range of emotions playing at the woman's features when she embraced her son and ushered him out the door. What must she be going through now? Elise couldn't fathom it. What if it had been her Ben or Gracie?

Of course, the idea of Ben with an eating disorder was ludicrous. He'd never had to worry about weight. He ate whatever and whenever he wanted. But any number of things could rob a mother of her child. Accidents. Illness. The disturbing possibilities riddled Elise.

What about Gracie? She had been a chubby baby with a voracious appetite, nursing every two hours around the clock. Although the pudgy toddler slimmed down as she grew, Elise obsessed over Gracie's weight. She stocked the refrigerator with fresh fruits and veggies, avoiding the pitfall of rewarding her children with sweets. Had she put too much emphasis on diet and exercise?

The conversation with Tony came back to haunt her. Like Lucas, Gracie insisted nothing was wrong. Elise imagined her daughter following in Lucas's footsteps down the path of denial, waiting until she was old enough to escape her parents' care. Left to her own devices, Elise saw Gracie fixating on her swimming the way Lucas fixated on his dancing and Dixie fixated on her gymnastics. An image of Gracie emerging from the pool came to mind, her youthful plump cheeks replaced by hollows and her shapely legs reduced to twigs.

Without a single thought of its calorie count, Elise spooned soggy Cheerios into her mouth. Her tears splashed into the milk.

"Elise?" Cassie's voice startled her. "Are you okay?"

"No." She noticed Cassie's bloodshot eyes. "Neither are you. When you delivered Dixie's card, did you see Lucas?"

Cassie bowed her head and gave it a shake. "By the time I got to ER, he was gone. His poor, poor mama."

"Do you have children, Cassie?" asked Felicia, a faraway look in her eyes.

A proud smile graced Cassie's full lips. "Twin boys and a girl. One of my sons is a Marine and his brother is a college professor. Teaches history. And my daughter's in med school. She's not stopping at being a nurse, like her mama. She's going to be a doctor." Cassie's smile vanished. "No mother should outlive her child."

"I'm worried about my daughter, Cass." Elise shoved her bowl away. "I feel so helpless. I don't know what to do for her."

Cassie moved Elise's bowl back to her. "The best thing you can do for her is get yourself well."

Chapter Thirty

THE LOUNGE FILLED with present and former patients gathering for Wednesday night support group in the patient lounge. Elise compared the people, who ranged in age from middle school to retirement age. Tina-Louise had added some weight to her frame and would soon be leaving. Thirteen-year-old Yessenia, a wisp of a child who had been admitted that morning, huddled in an overstuffed chair, resting her chin on her drawn-up knees. Nyx hid behind her book. Irma sat in a straight-backed chair, grasping the seat with her bony fingers, her lined face sans expression.

Elise noticed Felicia, glass of *Ensure* in hand, was flipping through an issue of *American Baby.* At their last family group session, Felicia and her husband seemed more interested in each other than Saturday's speaker. Elise guessed the beautiful model had something on her mind other than high fashion.

At five minutes to seven, Gracie entered, giggling and chattering with Marissa.

Gracie didn't appear to be ill in any way. Her round cheeks bloomed, and her auburn curls cascaded over her shoulders. The picture of health. Nonetheless, Elise knew from talking to Tony not to be deceived by appearances. Gracie had a problem. The question looming in her mind was how long had it been going on?

Throwing her arms around Elise's neck, Gracie whispered, "You look awful, Momette."

"Love you too, kitten." Elise kissed her cheek. "Dad told me you spent this morning bowing to the porcelain god. How long before your teeth fall out?"

"That won't happen to me." Gracie stiffened. "At least I'm eating."

"Are you?" Glancing at Marissa, Elise asked, "Is your friend teaching you her tricks?"

With a frown, Gracie straightened and grasped Marissa's arm. The two girls found seats across the room, the farthest spot from Elise. Gracie whispered something in Marissa's ear. Marissa's eyes widened and she glared at Elise, mouthing "no" with her scarlet lips.

Why couldn't I just keep my big mouth shut? Elise bit back tears. *I always manage to say the wrong thing.*

Sharon, a tech on the unit, facilitator as well as a recovering bulimarexic, brought the meeting to order. "Hi, ladies. I'm happy to see Marissa, Bonnie, and Donna back for a visit. How's recovery going?"

Elise hadn't met the latter two. Bonnie, who sat to Sharon's right, looked to be in her forties with long salt and pepper hair. Tall and thin, she didn't appear to have recovered much. She flashed a stiff smile. "I'm doing—fine."

Sharon arched an eyebrow. "Yes. I can tell. Could you stick around after the meeting, Bonnie?"

Hanging her head, Bonnie murmured, "Okay."

Sharon patted Bonnie's shoulder. Then she shifted her attention to the plump lady on her left. "Donna? I haven't seen you in months. How's life treating you?"

In Elise's estimation, life was treating moonfaced Donna well.

Donna raked her fingers through her short brown hair. "Great! I'm on the dean's list at KU and I haven't tossed my cookies in nearly a year."

"Tossed her cookies?" Annie chortled. "Ha! I'll bet she eats more than her fair share of cookies every day."

Elise flinched. For the past few days, Annie had been mercifully silent. But then, who was this Beast with whom Elise wrestled? She chastised herself. How dare *she* judge someone by her own misguided imagery? Donna wasn't fat. A little on the *zoftig* side Elise's mother would say. *Nothing like Aunt Viv, may she rot in Hell.*

"Donna's about to earn her degree in veterinary medicine." Sharon explained. "We're so proud of her. Last year we weren't sure she'd live to see it."

Gracie cast a furtive glance at Elise then turned to Donna and asked, "How did you stop barfing, Donna?"

"It wasn't easy." Donna linked her fingers and rotated her thumbs. "But when I lost three teeth and started puking up blood…"

"She ruptured her esophagus," Sharon interjected. "Nearly died on the operating table."

The color drained from Gracie's face.

"It was my wakeup call, for sure." Donna smiled at Sharon. "I would never have made it through without the support I received from this lady and all the others here. I don't want to let y'all down."

"We're all glad you're okay now, Donna. Who wants to go next?" Sharon asked. "Marissa? How's life on the outside?"

"Terrific." Marissa's blonde curls bounced as she spoke. "We've had cheerleading workshops this week. Meredith and I've had some great twin time and I have a new best friend." She flashed a grin at Gracie.

"Awesome." Sharon swiveled her head to make eye contact with each person. "Just a reminder. What's said here, stays here."

"Like an AA meeting," said Felicia.

"Exactly," said Sharon, fixing her eyes on the chic young woman. "I don't believe we've met."

"I'm Felicia." Setting her magazine aside, she cocked her head to one side. "I'm a newbie here. As long as I've opened my big mouth, may I share?"

Sharon waved her hand. "The floor is yours, my dear."

"Thanks." Felicia took a deep breath and exhaled. "The truth is, my glamorous profession—I'm a model—required going to a few cocktail parties with the rich and infamous after fashion shows."

Sharon crossed her legs and leaned back in her chair, an expression of deep concern on her face. "I'm sure you experienced a lot of pressure to stay thin."

"Oh, don't you know it?" Felicia bit her lip and paused before continuing. "One ounce over the line and you're history. Dinner was a celery stick and dry popcorn. That's when Martini and Rossi became my best friends. Dulled my pain and filled my tummy. Until one day I woke up to boxed wine and orange juice for breakfast and couldn't remember the night before."

"Oh, how awful for you." Tina-Louise leaned forward, propping elbows on her thighs and her head on her hands. "What happened after that?"

Tapping her index finger against her lips, Sharon gave her head a slight shake.

"It's okay," Felicia took a sip of her *Ensure* and tilted her head toward Sharon. "I got nothing to hide. My agent found me an Alcoholics Anonymous group and I started doing the twelve steps. I'm clean and sober four years this summer. Now I'm tackling my food addiction. Gonna beat it, too."

"Thank you, Felicia." Sharon sat up straight. "I admire your courage."

Gracie raised her hand. "Which is harder? The booze or the food?"

"They're both ferocious tigers, aren't they?" Felicia's smile vanished. "It's like this: the alcoholic can lock up her tiger and throw away the key. The anorexic has to take her tiger for a walk three times a day."

Sharon wrote on the note pad on her lap. "May I quote you, Felicia?"

"Sure, it's not original. I know I'm taking a lot of time, but may I share my good news?"

"Of course."

"I have to get well because..." With a radiant smile, Felicia pressed her hand against her tummy. "I'm pregnant!"

"I knew it!" Elise clapped her hands. "I saw the way you and your husband were whispering and grinning Saturday."

"I wasn't quite sure about it then. The clinic called and confirmed it today. I guess our last fertility treatment took after all. I'm gonna call him tonight."

Irma's perpetual scowl deepened. "What's so wonderful about it? You clean their messes when they're babies, put up with them when they're ungrateful teenagers," she glared at Gracie and Marissa, "and when you're old, they banish you from their lives." Her voice cracked.

"Irma?" Sharon knelt in front of her. "What's the matter, sweetie?"

"Don't patronize me like I'm some doddering old biddy."

"Oh, this is about the new treatment facility, isn't it? Do you mind if I share with the group?"

Irma hung her head. "Go ahead, it's no big secret."

Sharon stood to address the rest of the group. "Irma's daughters have made arrangements to send her to a long-term care facility in California."

Nyx peered over the top of her book. "How soon are you leaving so we can plan a farewell party?"

Irma growled. "I hate parties."

"I meant for *after* you leave."

"I don't have to take this." Irma stood and headed toward the door.

Sharon followed her and took her hand. "Please Irma, we're nearly finished here."

Irma folded her arms across her chest, glowered at Nyx, and muttered, "Black-haired Goth witch."

Checking her watch, Sharon said, "We've covered a lot of territory tonight. I will be back next week. Thank you for a great meeting."

As the patients and visitors dispersed, Elise searched the room for her daughter. Gracie appeared to be having a meaningful conversation with Felicia. Marissa approached Elise with a folded piece of paper in her hand. Glancing over one shoulder and then the other, she handed it to Elise. "Please read this before jumping to conclusions about me and Gracie."

Later, back in her room, lonesome for Dixie, Elise unfolded the note. Marissa's penmanship left a lot to be desired. Elise did her best to decipher it.

Dear Mrs. Reeves,
Your daughter Gracie is cute and funny and is the best

swimmer on the girls' team. But like it or not, she's got an eating disorder like you. Only she binges and purges. I've tried to get her to stop but she only gets mad at me. I'm afraid if you die, she will too. Please let me be her friend. And please, get well before it's too late.

XOXOXO

Marissa Falcone

Trembling, Elise crumpled the note. Her pulse thudded against her temples. She couldn't deal with this now. If only Dixie was here to talk to.

Elise took her sketchbook and propped it on her knees. She drew her little self wearing a mime mask, smiling at her reflection. At her side her pixie friend, Hope, frowned.

"It's so easy to hide behind that smiling mask, isn't it?" Annie intoned. "No one wants to know you anyway. Tony certainly doesn't care." Annie screamed. "Look at the mess you've made, you fat cow! You can't even pretend to save your daughter. Your own baby girl"

Tightening her fist around her pencil, Elise pressed the point into the paper. It snapped before she could rake it across her drawing. Startled by her own outburst, she dropped the pencil on the bed and examined her artwork. No harm done. She would add color to the sketch.

She set aside the sketchbook. There was no point in trying to draw tonight. Taking the wadded note, she did her best to smooth the paper and read it again.

Chapter Thirty-One

THOSE DEEMED healthy enough were allowed to use the hospital's fitness facilities on Friday afternoons—under close supervision. Elise dipped her toes in the cool water, wishing she'd thought to have Tony bring her workout fins. Tucking her hair under her swim cap and securing her goggles, she prepared to make her EDU debut.

She knew it took thirty-six laps to make a mile in this twenty-five-yard pool. "Seventy-two lengths, here I go—cowabunga!" she uttered in a low voice to herself.

Taking her diving stance at the edge of the deep end, Elise flinched when Terry said, "Hold on there, sister." She folded her arms across her chest, wagging her head to emphasize her tone and making her butterfly earrings flutter on either side of her face. "No one's swimming a mile on my watch." She displayed her Mickey Mouse watch. "Twenty minutes for a *gentle* swim." She motioned her head toward her gangly assistant. "Behave yourself or Adonis will report to me. Now, I'm going to make sure Tina-Louise and Nyx aren't burning up the track." With that she turned and walked away.

Elise's heart thumped and she dove in at the deep end. Cold water swooshed around her. Dipping down, she planted her feet against the pool wall and launched herself forward. Alternating arms, she rotated her body from side to side and kicked. When she reached the shallow-end wall, she did a flip turn and propelled herself in the other direction. The water gurgled in her ears. She swam lap after lap, zooming from one end to the other and back again. She felt free. She felt weightless.

At the thought of weight, a sudden panic washed over her. Her suit seemed snug. She touched her stomach. It felt round and bloated.

"You're too fat to stuff into a swimsuit." Annie's laughter gurgled. *"Elise the sea cow."*

Images flashed through her mind in rapid-fire succession. Her mind tumbled back to the day Ben was born.

"It's a boy!" The tiny bundle all but disappeared in Tony's arms. "Hey, sailor boy. Let's call him Michael Benjamin after your friend who died in the car accident."

"No!"

The lifeguard blew his whistle.

Elise slowed to a breaststroke as her mind fast-forwarded a few years. Gracie was three, Ben was eight.

"Mommy," Gracie's chubby cheeks flushed scarlet. "Benny took my dolly and won't give it back."

"Gracie scribbled all over my homework."

"Did not."

"Did too. Little brat. I'm going to decapitate your stupid Barbie."

Tony unbuckled his belt. "Give your sister back her doll. Now!"

Whack!

"But Dad... My homework..."

"She don't know no better."

Ben's protests turned to painful cries as the belt smacked his bottom. "You never listen..."

"Stop that crying or I'll give you something to cry about!"

Holding her breath, Elise dove underwater to stop the awful waves of the past. Her lungs burned. Her heart pounded. Her safe place betrayed her.

The lap lines on the pool floor blurred and disappeared. The Kona Kai restaurant appeared. Her wedding night.

Elise gazed into Tony's gray eyes and then at the rings sparkling on her left hand. "We did it. We really did it."

He laid his hand on top of hers. "Elise, your dinner's getting cold and your husband's getting horny."

A combination of panic and dismay knotted in the pit of her stomach. She'd entered the cage willingly. Trapped. The final vestiges of childhood were behind her. A married woman at eighteen. She longed to drown in Daddy's arms.

Elise curled up on her side, careful not to disturb the IV needle in her arm, and stared out the window at the dark sky. Her head throbbed and her throat burned. The heart monitor next to her bed beeped. Slow and steady, between forty-five and fifty beats per minute. "One beat per day," a trainer at the Y had quipped a few years back.

Beside the bed, Tony took her hand and kissed it. His eyes, devoid of the anger she feared, brimmed. They glittered in the lamplight.

She almost preferred an angry tongue lashing to silent tears.

"I'm pretty sure it was a panic attack," Wayne told Tony. "But since she came close to drowning, I want to keep her under observation for the night. No one else is dying on my watch this week." The door shut behind him.

The aroma of Tony's Old Spice aftershave wafted over her. A soothing scent. Although his dark hair had grayed at the temples, his handsome face remained unlined. And those dimples. It was still the face she'd fallen in love with. Yet something had changed. A tangle of emotions made her heart ache.

"What kind of a crazy stunt was that, Elise? I'm surprised they even let someone in your condition in the pool. I suppose you wanted to show off your lap-swimming prowess. You need to stop and think for once."

"Please, don't lecture me."

His red-rimmed eyes blazed from his crimson face. "I ain't lecturing you. Someone has to be responsible. You need to stop this nonsense and think about how it's affecting everyone else for once."

There it was. His predictable reaction. The quintessential commanding officer with all the answers. She licked her parched lips, searching for the words to tell him how she felt. As usual, they eluded her. "You'd be better off without me."

With something between a growl and deep sigh, he sank into the chair beside the bed and rubbed his stubbled chin. He shut his eyes. "You're unbelievable, Elise. I just—"

Before he could say anything more, Dixie knocked on the open door. "Hey, Suzie-Q. I hope this isn't a bad time."

"Come on in." Tony stood, tucking his hat under his arm. "Everything's hunky dory.

A nurse's aide wheeled Dixie's chair into the room. "I'll be right outside the door, Ms. Granger. Let me know when you're done."

"Okay, honey bun." Dixie shifted her gaze from Tony to Elise. "Are you *sure* you're okay?"

"Yes—yes, I'm fine." Swallowing tears of shame, Elise raised the head of her bed, doing her best to sound cheerful. "Hey roomie. You look great."

While great might have been stretching the truth, Dixie did have a slight blush in her narrow cheeks Elise hadn't seen before.

Tony flashed his recruiter's smile at Dixie. "I'm speaking at a school rally tomorrow." He leaned over and brushed his lips over Elise's. "I'll leave you gals to it."

He pivoted on his heel and stalked out of the room.

"Hunky dory, eh?" Dixie peered over her shoulder at the doorway then turned back to

Elise. "What on earth happened, Elise?"

"I—I don't know exactly. I was swimming and it was wonderful, and the next minute, I woke up in the ER."

"Are you really okay or were you just saying what you thought Tony needed to hear?"

Feeling a little like a kid caught stealing cookies, Elise pulled the blanket around her neck. Tony's voice came from down the hall where he regaled the nurses with one of his many Navy stories.

Tilting her head toward the door, Dixie pursed her lips. "Trust me. I know his type. Always has to be in charge. Like my coach. Is there anything else you're not telling me? Does he beat you?"

"He's never laid a hand on me." Elise yawned. "Sorry. Meds are kicking in."

"Yeah, I get it." Dixie called out to the aide. "Home, James. I'll keep the light on for you, roomie."

"You're going back to EDU now?"

"Yeppers. I'm over the bug." Dixie grasped Elise's hand. "You and me, Suzie-Q. We're gonna show Annie who's boss."

Chapter Thirty-Two

A few patients from EDU and Psych filed out of the chapel. For some, it was a time to seek forgiveness or healing for their addictions. For the rest, it gave them a break from their units. This Sunday morning, Elise questioned her own motives.

She rose from her front-row pew and arched her stiff back. Before she could follow the others out, Chaplain Charlie approached her and offered his hand. His grasp was strong and warm.

"Good to see you here, Mrs. Reeves. I'm so glad you survived your ordeal."

"Yup, didn't drown—this time."

His ruddy cheeks reddened even more. Elise regretted her rapid retort. "I'm glad I survived, too."

Releasing her hand, he nodded. "I've kept you in my prayers."

"Thank you. It was scary. I really thought I'd swum my last lap —ever."

"I hope I didn't bore you too much this morning. I noticed you taking notes."

Hugging her sketch diary, Elise gave her head a slight shake. "Um. Not exactly. I was drawing."

"May I see?"

Elise's face warmed as she relinquished her open book. He pored over the page, a serious expression on his cherubic face. To her relief, he burst out into raucous laughter. "Is my nose really that big?"

"It's a caricature."

"A wonderful one at that." He ran his fingers through his auburn curls. "The burning bush could use a trim."

Taking the book back, she tore out the page and gave it to him. "You may have it, if you'd like."

"I shall cherish this. When you're famous I can say 'I knew her when.'" He winked. "I just won't say from 'where.'" He held the sketch at arm's length. "Did you sign it? Oh, there. I see you did. I'm going to frame this right away and put it on my office wall."

"I'm glad you like it. Not everyone has a sense of humor."

"When you look like me, humor is an essential virtue."

Elise turned to leave. "I guess I'd better get back upstairs before they come looking for me. We're coining out Tina-Louise this afternoon."

"Lovely child."

"She is."

"May she never return to this place. Let me accompany you. I need to administer the sacraments to Irma."

"Yes, she'll be waiting."

"Impatiently to be sure. A dear lady really. She doesn't want anyone to know." He gathered up his sacramental kit. "I hope she finds peace at the rehab center in California."

"She seems pretty happy with being miserable. At any rate, we're coining her out tomorrow."

He started toward the door. Then he stopped and walked to the back row of pews. He patted the seat. "Do you have a moment to chat?"

She checked the clock on the wall to see she had plenty of time. Sitting on the pew, she shrugged. "I guess so."

He sat beside her, leaving a modest space between them. "Your story intrigues me. How did a Jewish woman come to believe in Christ as her messiah, her savior?"

Elise's focus shifted from her sketchbook. She remembered the day as though it was yesterday. A tiny laugh escaped her lips. "Ha! It was my

Jesus freak friend Leslie who invited me to a prayer meeting. It was the last day of high school and I only went to get out of scrubbing the bathrooms." She smiled to herself and continued to explain. "In preparation for Mom's weekly sabbath mahjong service."

Chaplain Charlie's brow furrowed. "I guess I'm not as well versed in Jewish liturgy as I thought I was."

"Sorry, I was just being a smart aleck." Her cheeks warmed. "Mahjong is a Chinese game Jewish women play." Elise chuckled. "My mother played *religiously* every Tuesday and Saturday."

"Ah, I see."

"Anyway—the prayer meeting—everyone was so warm and happy. The pouring rain outside didn't bother those kids. They sang their Jesus songs and clapped their hands. I wanted what they had. They prayed with me. I challenged Jesus to show me He was real and somehow, at that moment, I knew."

Chaplain Charlie's smile put her at ease. "That's beautiful."

Elise wished she could experience the same happiness she'd known then. Life had stolen it from her. She felt old, older than she'd ever been. Older than she ever would be.

"Tony sure didn't think it was beautiful."

"So, he doesn't share your faith?"

"He does now—ever since he went down to the altar at a men's retreat when Ben was a baby."

"Wonderful."

"As I told you before, my parents thought I was *meshuggeneh*." She rotated her index finger beside her ear. "To tell the truth, Chaplain, I'm not so sure they were wrong."

The last well-wisher in the coining out ceremony for Irma, Elise let the bronze medallion rest on her palm and repeated the prayer by St. Francis of Assisi that she'd come to know by heart. She scanned the older woman's weathered face.

Is this me in twenty years—emaciated, lonely, and bitter?

Elise searched for something pithy to say, but words wouldn't come. The others had offered their best wishes, even Nyx choked out a "may the gods be kind to you."

"Enjoy California," Elise managed to croak. "Be happy."

"Nice work if you can get it." Irma reached over and snatched the coin from Elise. "You're still young, Elise. What I wouldn't give to be as talented and pretty as you." Leaning forward, she squeezed Elise's knee in her pincer-like grip. "*Illegitimi non carborundum.* Don't let the bastards get you down."

Chapter Thirty-Three

The chorus to "Manic Monday" played over and over in Elise's mind as she stepped onto the scale and turned her back to the beams. It was her third Monday on the unit and she still tried to decipher where the weights stopped. Her stomach growled in anticipation of breakfast. Damned appetite. She wished she had her aspirin to kill it.

Dixie ascended the scales after Elise. "Am I getting heavier? Can I ditch the wheelchair yet?"

"I'm not supposed to say." Terry wrote on Dixie's chart and nodded. "Keep up the good work and who knows?"

Elise tried to read Dixie's numbers, but Terry slid the weights to the ends of the beams. "Mrs. Reeves, you know better."

After their blood pressure and pulse rates had been recorded, Terry sent the patients to their rooms to change out of their breezy hospital gowns. Two new patients had been admitted over the weekend, a seventeen-year-old boy and a fifty-year-old woman. Thad and Helen.

Thad looked like the boy next door, towheaded and freckle-faced. His full cheeks didn't give away his secret, but the callouses on the back of his hand did. Elise's thoughts went to Gracie.

Despite her big-boned stature, Helen was decidedly underweight. Rouge didn't mask her cheek hollows. Her coifed black hair against her ivory complexion seemed unnatural. Heavy penciled brows gave her a fixed scowl. Perhaps Felicia could give her a few fashion tips.

Back in her room, Elise slipped into her blue jeans. "There does seem to be a wide age-span here, doesn't there?"

"Annie doesn't discriminate." Dixie fastened her bra. "I don't know why I bother."

"Maybe when you put on some more weight."

"Nah, I never had enough to fill an A-cup to begin with." Dixie donned a pair of black leggings. "I see you overthinking things every time you look at me, Suzie-Q. My recovery scares you. Wanna talk about it?"

Startled by Dixie's astute observation, Elise bit the inside of her cheek. "What makes you think it scares me? I think it's wonderful. I do. Really."

"Methinks the lady doth protest too much." Standing in front of the dresser mirror, Dixie slid her hand over the top of her head. "I hope my hair will grow back." She slipped on a sweatshirt. "It's intimidating to you Suzie-Q, isn't it?"

"No. I said—"

"Yeah, I heard what came out of your mouth." Fixing her gaze on Elise, Dixie refused to let up. "Why are you afraid of getting well?"

***

Dixie's words haunted Elise all through breakfast. *Why am I afraid of recovery? I'm afraid I'll get fat like evil Aunt Viv or Dad.* The scent of sausage tantalized her. Her stomach growled. She gulped her coffee to take the edge off her fickle appetite.

Yessenia, a raven-haired thirteen-year-old girl who had been admitted two weeks before, chugged back her *Ensure* and munched on a piece of bacon. Elise had heard through the nurse's grapevine that the girl had stopped eating after her best friend lost her life in a car crash. Her doctor had sent her to EDU before her depression and lack of appetite became something else.

Although her cheeks had already lost some of their hollows, Elise felt like there was more the girl wasn't saying. "Dr. Picard says if I keep getting better, I can go home next week."

Across from her, Helen picked the raisins out of her oatmeal. "God bless you, Yessenia. What do you want to be when you grow up?"

The girl pursed her lips and closed one eye. "A nurse, I think. Or a social worker. I want to help people."

"Then you better keep your scrawny little butt out of places like this," Dixie said, eyeing her. "Don't waste your precious life like me. Help yourself first."

"That's great advice," said Helen. "I wish someone had told me that when I was your age."

Dixie drenched her scrambled eggs with Tabasco and took a huge bite. "These are great. Nothing works up an appetite like starvation." She took a long swig of milk and dabbed her lips with her napkin. "Welcome to the nut hut, Helen. These are good people here at Brookside. Better than Menninger's. And I should know."

Helen's eyes sparkled. "Thank you. You're Dixie Granger, right?"

Yessenia's dark eyes widened. "You're… the famous gymnast!"

Dixie grinned. "You guys know me?"

"*Know* you?" Helen giggled. "I wanted to *be* you, but I was never any good at gymnastics. I still remember your Suzie-Q routine."

"Yeah, I fell off my balance beam to become a living, breathing skeleton. I'm getting better." Dixie turned to Yessenia. "Follow my lead to recovery, kiddo."

"Yes, ma'am. I will!" Yessenia moved her breakfast closer to Dixie. The two of them lowered their voices and continued to chat. No doubt Dixie was sharing her newfound wisdom with the girl. It made Elise smile inside to watch her friend blossom.

"I envy you, Dixie," Elise murmured to herself. "I don't know if I can do it."

"*'Cause you're a stupid slob,*" Annie intoned. "*No hope for you, you pathetic excuse for a woman. For a mother.*"

Elise turned her attention back to her untouched breakfast. She picked up a cold sausage link and nibbled at it while trying to come up with a topic for conversation to put Helen at ease. The weather was always safe. Or TV programs. Everyone had a favorite show, right?

Noting the ring on Helen's left hand, Elise asked, "Do you have any children?"

"One son." Helen popped a raisin into her mouth. "He lives with his father. The two of them deserve each other."

"Oh." Elise found herself at a loss for words. "Sorry."

"Don't be. My ex created our son in his own nasty image. I pity the woman who marries him." Helen gazed at her heart-shaped diamond. "My one-karat consolation prize. They left me four months ago." She shoved her cereal bowl away from her. "I haven't been able to eat much since. My sister had me admitted here. How about you? Children?"

Elise held up two fingers. "A son and a daughter."

"Go on! You don't look old enough."

"Ben's twenty-one and a senior at Harvard, majoring in journalism and psychology. Gracie's sixteen."

"A double major? That's impressive. What about your husband?"

"Navy recruiter." Elise drank her orange juice. "Works a lot."

"Lucky you. Exact opposite of my ex."

"Not sure which is worse. A lazy slug or a workaholic."

Helen arched one of her black-penciled brows. "I see. Nothing left when he comes home?"

"Bingo."

Chapter Thirty-Four
Wayne

DIXIE LAID one of her reed-thin legs across the other and leaned back in the wheelchair. Although her recent weight-gain thrilled Wayne, she needed to put on, at the very least, thirty pounds to be within normal range.

Mr. and Mrs. Granger, in Wayne's wingback chairs, flanked their daughter. Mrs. Granger brushed a stray wisp from Dixie's face. "You used to have such thick hair."

"Mr. and Mrs. Granger—"

"Please, call me Jim," said Dixie's father.

Mrs. Granger fixed her worried gaze on Dixie. "Has something happened? Oh my, have there been complications from the flu? She gave us quite a scare. I don't know what I'd do—"

"Ingrid, would you let the man talk?"

Turning her focus back to Wayne, she held Dixie's hand. "She's skin and bone. Forgive me. I'm so worried about my little girl, you understand. Of course you do. She was better after Menninger's, but it didn't last. She went downhill as soon as she came home. When we got your call last night asking us to come in this morning, I was afraid it was bad news."

Dixie rolled her eyes and wrenched her hand from her mother's grasp. "Mutti! Could you stop referring to me in the third person?"

"Mutti?" Wayne handed Dixie a can of *Ensure* and sat on his desk. "I thought I detected a slight accent. Are you from Germany, Mrs. Granger?"

"Austria. And you may call me Ingrid. My family fled the country right before the war."

"Mutti was a ballerina like your sister." Dixie opened the can and chugged it. "Mm. French Vanilla. It could use some whipped cream."

"My daughter has told me about your sister's battle with anorexia, Dr. Picard. Such a waste." Ingrid shifted her gaze to Elizabeth Picard's photo on the desk. "She was lovely. Excellent form. I'm sorry for your loss, Doctor. So, you can well understand my concern for our *schatzi*."

Jim leaned back in his chair and rested his right foot on his left knee. "I'm sure you didn't call us in to chitchat, Doc. Give us the bad news. What's up with Trouble here?"

Wayne frowned, but Dixie shook her head and grinned. "Daddy's always called me that."

"Ever since she used my jockstrap for a weapon."

Dixie pulled back the elastic on an imaginary slingshot and let it go. "Fa-wing! Not a dog or cat was safe."

Imagining little Dixie terrorizing neighborhood pets made Wayne chuckle as he picked up a folder. "I'm pleased to say I think your daughter has turned a corner. Her attitude has changed, and for the past two weeks, she's made some positive choices." He handed Jim a page. "Check out these weight charts."

Jim's eyes widened and he handed the sheet to Ingrid, who clapped her hand over her mouth. "Oh, *schatzi*, I—"

Holding his index finger to his lips, Wayne gave his head a slight shake. "I'd rather Trouble not know exact numbers for the time being. She's still fragile and has a long road ahead of her."

"Hello!" Dixie put her fists on her hips and scowled. "Still in the room. I might be scrawny, but I'm not invisible."

"That's for damn sure." Wayne took a book from his shelf and handed it to Dixie. "Here's some summer reading for you."

She thumbed through it and read the cover aloud, *"The Heart of Psychotherapy* by George Weinberg. Looks interesting."

"One of my favorites," said Wayne.

Dixie laughed. "So, you want me to do psychotherapy on myself?"

He smiled. "Consider me your personal library. When you finish that one, I'll lend you another. If you're serious about helping others, and I think you'll be excellent at it, I'd like to be one or your source references."

Ingrid dabbed her eyes. "Oh, *schatzi,* this is *wunderbar.* I'm so proud."

Jim handed the paper back to Wayne. "What school would you suggest, Doc?"

"There are a number of good ones. I went to KU myself. Close to home."

"Rock Chalk, Jayhawk! My alma mater, too."

Raising a flat hand, Wayne gazed into Dixie's sunken eyes. "Let's not get ahead of ourselves. You'll need to pace yourself. Same goes for you, Mutti and Dad. Encourage, but don't push too hard."

"Oh, yeah? You'll all be eating my dust." Despite her added weight, the chair still dwarfed the former gymnastics star. She squared her shoulders and set her jaw in a determined line. "Don't forget, Dr. P, you promised me a steak dinner when I graduate summa cum laude. You might as well make reservations at the Hereford House now."

Chapter Thirty-Five

Elise relished the morning downpour during art therapy. She found the sounds of thunder and rain comforting. Smushing sticky clay between her hands, she listened to her fellow patients' conversations. She enjoyed having her roommate beside her.

"I was never any good at this, so here goes nothing." Dixie slipped from her wheelchair to a seat at the table. She rolled a piece of clay in her hands. "Amazing what a difference the absence of one person makes."

"Yeah, it *is* refreshing." Nyx glanced up from her second dragon in the making. "Whatcha think of my sculpture?"

"It's really nice. He looks like he could start breathing fire any minute." Dixie chuckled. "I wonder if Irma misses you as much as you miss her."

Pam peered over Nyx's shoulder. "You really have a gift for this. Would you like me to get some iridescent paint for you?"

A rare smile parted Nyx's lips. "You'd do that?"

"Of course. Anything for a budding artist."

Nyx winnowed her fingers through her long black hair with its lengthening blonde roots. "I'm thinking of letting my hair go back to its natural color."

From across the table, Helen piped up. "Natural's a *grand* idea." She winked at Nyx. Putting down the lump of clay she had been struggling with, she reached up to her own hair. Elise's breath caught in her throat as she realized what was about to happen.

"This infernal thing itches like the dickens." Helen whipped off her wig, tossing it to the floor. A long gray braid cascaded to her waist. "I wore it for my ex. You think I should mail it to him?"

Elise couldn't remember a more pleasant day on the unit. As the class ended, she even found herself looking forward to lunch. The aromas emanating from the dining room enticed her and made her stomach growl.

Friendly chatter continued through lunch as they laughed about Helen's wig. Even Nyx joined in, claiming the hairpiece looked like a tarantula. Felicia erupted in a fit of giggles and promised to help Helen style her real hair.

After lunch, Elise entered Pam's office for her one-on-one. These twice-a-week sessions with the art therapist were easily Elise's favorites. Nowhere did she feel more validated and appreciated.

Sinking into one of the upholstered chairs, she handed Pam her notebook. Pam sat in the chair opposite and opened it. "I see you've been busy. Any illustrations to go with it?"

Elise revealed two new sketches she had in a separate folder. "Of course."

Settling back in her chair, Pam crossed her legs and read from Elise's notebook, "'It was then the little girl became aware that she was smiling and laughing a lot. She decided it was time to remove the mask. To her shock and dismay, it had become so much a part of her it would not come off. Elise tugged and pulled. Alas, it was no use. The mask seemed there to stay—forever!'" Pam glanced at the accompanying sketch. "Simply amazing, Elise."

"I can't claim originality." Elise drew up her legs and sat cross-legged. "My son took me to see Marcel Marceau at the Lyric a few years back. Even in his old age, he's astounding. Anyway, he did a pantomime where he'd found a smiling mask and put it on. Then he couldn't get it off. How he could hold a smile while every inch of his body reflected panic is beyond me."

"You've certainly captured those things in your sketch and your story. And I think you can claim originality in the way you're using it. Interesting that you refer to it as a false face." Pam turned the page. "May I?"

Elise nodded.

Pam read aloud. "'Oh no! What'll I do?' moaned the terrified child.

"'You look very happy,' offered the pixie in an attempt to comfort her friend.

"'I'm not happy. It's not me. No one will ever know how I really feel.'" Pam closed the notebook. Leaning forward, she locked her focus on Elise. "I must say, you've nailed yourself."

Winding a lock of hair around her index finger, Elise squirmed and shifted her gaze to the pictures on her lap. "I guess so."

"You do it well, you know—evasion is one of your 'gifts.'" Pam lifted another picture of the masked child from Elise's lap. She outlined the red mouth with her fingertip. "A smiling depressive. Always the clown, laughing on the outside, screaming for help on the inside."

Elise grinned in spite of herself. "Wayne says the same thing."

"What are you going to do about it?"

Despite Pam's challenge, Elise felt lighter on her way back to her room. However, the feeling didn't last long. Dixie met her with the news that Nyx, who had seemed uncharacteristically cheerful in the morning, had managed to swipe one of the sculpting tools from the art therapy classroom. Cassie found the girl on the bathroom floor right after lunch, blood pooling under her wrists.

Fortunately, Nyx hadn't cut deep enough for the wounds to be fatal. Nonetheless, she would be transferred to the psych ward, possibly to a different facility once doctors deemed her stable enough.

All regular activities for late afternoon had been cancelled. A debriefing session was planned for Nyx's stunned fellow patients to discuss their feelings after supper. Shocked by the news and given unprecedented free time, Elise went to the art room where airbrushing her latest illustration would offer a needed distraction.

The hallways were desolate. Only an occasional announcement over the loudspeaker broke through the silence. Even the nurses curtailed their normal prattle and gossip.

Hunching over her sketch, Elise turned on the airbrush. She switched it off when she heard Cassie talking in the next room. Elise strained her ears to hear what she said.

"I don't get it. I saw worse in Nam and never caved in like this. I should've seen the signs. That child made her decision this morning." Cassie paused. "I love you, too, Hank."

Elise felt a twinge of guilt for eavesdropping on the nurse's phone call. Hank? She seemed to be hearing that name a lot lately. She switched the airbrush back on and sprayed a thin stream of color for her picture's background.

The familiar and unmistakable scent of Cassie's perfume wafted over her. Switching off the airbrush, Elise turned to see the nurse, tears streaming down her bronze cheeks.

"Don't stop what you're doing." Sinking into a chair beside the table, Cassie asked, "Do you mind if I watch you, sugar?"

Without stopping to think about it, Elise said, "You couldn't have stopped her. Her mind was made up and, like it or not, you're not God."

Cassie dabbed her nose with a tissue. "You heard me on the phone?"

Heat rushing to her cheeks, Elise nodded.

Cassie shrugged. "My husband said the same thing."

Emptying the excess color from her airbrush into a paper cup, Elise inclined her head toward Cassie. "What's Hank like?"

"Let's see. I've told you my Hank's a Marine Corps Vet. What else can I tell you?" Cassie's expression reflected her devotion. "We met and married in Vietnam."

Elise found a chair and sat. "Go on."

"I'll never forget the look on his blue-eyed, blonde mother's face when he introduced us. Can you imagine?"

"Was she upset?"

"Her? Oh no." Cassie laughed. "Just surprised. When Martin Luther King Jr. led his protestors to Selma, Alabama in 1965, my blessed in-laws marched over the Edmund Pettus Bridge with them, waving an American flag and singing 'We Shall Overcome.'

"Honestly don't know what I would've done without Hank's folks when he returned from Nam without his legs. That was the hardest time. I already had twin baby boys to take care of. I wasn't ready for an invalid."

"That must've been terrible."

"Girlfriend, terrible doesn't begin to describe it."

"Does his mom stay with him while you're putting in long hours here?"

"Oh, my no!" Cassie's laughter filled the room. "Nothing holds my Gunny down. He went back to school on the GI Bill and got his degree. Became a licensed therapist. He's made it his personal mission to help his fellow veterans deal with their trauma. He facilitates meetings every Saturday morning at the VA Hospital."

Elise's heart skipped. Tony had mentioned the name Hank Rodgers more than once. It never occurred to her it was any kind of therapy session. Could this be the same Hank?

"Between eight-thirty and ten?"

"Why yes."

"Your last name is Chukwu, right, Cassie?"

"For professional purposes I use my maiden name." The nurse winked. "But at home, all the mail has Mr. and Mrs. Hank Rodgers on it, nice and proper."

Chapter Thirty-Six
Tony

T ONY PUMPED the stationary bike pedals. According to the display between the handlebars, he'd reached the three-mile mark. Two more to go. He leaned forward as the resistance increased.

Thinking back on his unusual session with his therapist, he shook his head. He had to hand it to Hank. The man had creative ways of going for the jugular. Not that Tony minded meeting at a Vietnamese restaurant for lunch. He enjoyed a good bowl of Pho and a spring roll every now and again. But, as always, Hank had an ulterior motive.

"Olfactory or smell is one of the most powerful memory triggers. What does it bring to your mind, Chief?"

Hank's plan had worked. Dropping a handful of basil leaves into his soup, Tony remembered exactly where he'd been the week after Frankie died. His CO sent him on shore leave in Saigon.

R and R had been the farthest thing from Tony's mind. All he could think of was that innocent kid. He had rambled the streets with no place in particular to go. He stopped at a little shop to buy some knickknacks for Mom and Jaimie.

Turning to leave he'd nearly fallen over a little girl, who grinned, revealing her missing front teeth. "Hello, Joe. I Kieu."

Tony pedaled faster, shutting his eyes. Images of the shanty town zipped through his mind. People living under cardboard and tin roofs. Ragged clothes hanging over lines strung from hovel to hovel. Food scents rose with the steam from cooking pots.

Leaning on a homemade crutch, Kieu had hopped to him on her one leg. Scars obscured half of her cherubic face. She tugged at Tony's pant leg. "Come with me, Joe. Má make you best pho in Saigon."

Kneeling to the girl's eye level, Tony pinched her unscarred cheek. "Hey sweetheart, I can't take food from you and your family."

"You no take." She grasped his hand. "You pay American dollar."

"Never could refuse a pretty girl." He followed her to where a woman bent over a huge cooking pot, stirring soup. She flashed a black-toothed grin under her conical hat. Aside from the lines around her weary eyes, she didn't look to be much older than her daughter. He took off his hat and bowed. "Good afternoon, Ma'am."

Kieu had rattled off a few sentences. Her mother bowed and dipped a hefty portion into a bowl. She placed it in his waiting hands and then held out hers, palms up. "Thank you, Joe."

Tony found a place to sit on the ground and dove into his savory meal. Kieu sat beside him, leaning her head on his arm. "You have good girl at home like me?"

"Nah. Not me. Maybe someday."

"You take me back to America with you? I be your good girl."

"What about your Má? She would miss you."

"Má have many children. Kieu always sick... cause much..." She paused and scratched her head, "... much bad-ship."

"Hardship?"

Kieu had nodded. "Má say no place for me. I am... bad luck. Má say I go to America because my father is G.I. She say American doctor fix me."

Tony raised his bowl to his mouth and swallowed what remained of his soup. Then he handed it back to Kieu and stood. "Tell her it was delicious."

"You come back tomorrow?" She struggled to stand. "You come back for Kieu?"

He had only taken a few steps down the road when he heard her cries. He turned to see an older boy grab the bowl and shove her to the ground. Tony didn't need an interpreter to understand the boy's words. Their intent came through loud and clear.

Every day, for the remainder of his leave, Tony had lunch with Kieu. He even toyed with the idea of adopting her, but he was just a kid himself and single. Not that it would have mattered. His last day in Saigon, Kieu's brother told him she had died in her sleep.

Tony shook his head, as if it would erase her. "Lying little bastard."

He checked the screen on the bike. One more mile to go. Concentrating on his workout, he watched people of all shapes and sizes run the track in the center of the building.

He and Elise had joined the fitness center not long after Gracie's first birthday. Elise had wanted to get back in shape and he had needed an outlet, having recently re-enlisted in the Navy. While he loved recruiting and the discipline of military life, the stress of meeting weekly quotas had taken its toll. He hadn't meant to take it out on Elise and the kids, but he couldn't seem to help it.

The fitness center became their Mecca. Elise loved the pool and the aerobics classes. They challenged each other with "super circuits", alternating between weight machines and running laps.

Elise had managed to drop the excess pounds she'd gained in pregnancy and then some. She had never been so slim. Her obsession with exercise hadn't concerned him. What could be healthier? She looked terrific. Nonetheless, he had had a niggling feeling something wasn't quite right where food was concerned. She had refused to eat meat, or anything fried. Healthy diet? Sometimes her "meal" would consist of a handful of M&Ms and a bowl of dry popcorn. She drank a pot of coffee a day by herself and, when she finished that, she'd fill up on Diet Coke.

Why didn't I do something back then? Maybe we wouldn't be in this mess.

What could he have done? He couldn't do anything when he was deployed to the Persian Gulf for two years. Things fell apart. Elise couldn't cut it alone.

Sweat dripped down his neck and back. He took a swig from his water bottle. *One more mile before I hit the weights.*

He shut his eyes and relished the burn. Frankie's face flashed before him, terror in his eyes as he gasped and disappeared beneath the murky Mekong water. Kieu hobbled through his mind. Her sweet lopsided smile—so innocent and trusting. Peddling faster, Tony gritted his teeth. *Forget about them, Tony. Stop dwelling on it. Get back to the here and now.*

"Tony! Tony, help me!"

"You take Kieu to America—land of free and brave?"

"Poppo? You okay?"

With a start, he snapped open his eyes to see Gracie standing in front of the bike. Dripping curls hung around her face and goggle imprints ringed her eyes. "Hey, kitten, good swim?"

"It was okay."

Beside her, Marissa raked her fingers through her wet hair. "Okay? Gracie's a dynamo in the water. I'm never racing her again."

Tony studied his daughter in her swimsuit, her colorful towel tied around her slender waist. Although not as well-endowed as her mother, her curvy figure had developed over the past year. "I can't believe you're growing up on me, Gracie."

She kissed his cheek. "I'll always be your kitten, Poppo."

"Touching. But I'm freezing." Marissa sputtered through blue lips. "Catch you in the locker room, Champ."

Following her with his eyes, Tony waited until he was sure the girl was out of earshot. He grasped Gracie's wrist. "I emptied the trash cans this morning."

Chapter Thirty-Seven
Gracie

GRACIE SLUNK DOWN in the wingback chair, shifting her gaze from Dr. Picard, to Mom, to Dad. Their collective glares bore through her. With a menacing scowl, Dad unveiled an empty Ipecac bottle.

Flushing with shame and wishing she had tossed that bottle somewhere else, she took a mental inventory of what she'd stuffed into her face for breakfast. Twinkies, two toaster waffles, a banana, three hard-boiled eggs, and a package of peanut butter crackers. She'd washed it down with Strawberry Quik in milk and an Ipecac chaser.

It only took twenty minutes for all of it to surge back up. She had gotten the idea for Ipecac from a book by a recovering bulimic. The woman's story, meant to be a testimony of her victory over her eating disorder, served as a dandy instruction manual.

Turning from Dad, Gracie looked to Mom, for what, she wasn't certain. "Momette?"

Instead of any kind of support, Mom cast her gaze downward, her shoulders slumped. "What do you want me to say, Gracie?"

"That you get it. That you understand me."

"I've never used Ipecac."

"Okay. What about all the pink Correctol pills? What's the diff?"

Mom covered her face with her hands. "I'm sorry, Gracie. I'm so sorry, I've failed you."

Dr. Picard caught Gracie in his soft blue gaze. "Has your mother failed you?"

"I love her," Gracie muttered.

"I should hope so, but that's not what I asked."

"Okay. Yes!" Gracie cast a sidelong glance at Mom. "She's always nag —*encouraged* me to eat healthy stuff and exercise."

"Nagged is the right word." Dad flung the empty bottle into the trash. "She drove the kid crazy about her body—from the time she was two. Toddlers are supposed to be chubby. What kind of mother makes a baby eat salad, for Pete's sake?"

Gracie wanted to scream, tell him to back off. Instead, she bit her lip and stared at the Ipecac bottle in the wastebasket.

"Is this the way you see it, too, Gracie?" asked Dr. Picard.

Memories flooded back to the night of Homecoming. By the time Mom had finished scrutinizing her figure flaws, Gracie had wanted to find a hole in the floor. Although Doug had assured her he liked her pink dress, she had felt it better suited to a ten-year-old's birthday party. Resentment had filled her when she saw another girl at the dance wearing the cute outfit with the bare midriff Mom wouldn't allow her to buy.

"Dad's not any better. If it was up to him, I'd never go anywhere."

Dad glared at her. Mom kept her hands over her face. Dr. Picard tossed Gracie a Tootsie Roll and smirked. "You're not going to puke it up, are you?" He folded his arms across his chest. "You heard Donna's story last week. Do you want to end up rupturing your esophagus, too? You might not be as lucky as she was. Do you have a death wish?"

Heat rose from Gracie's neck to her forehead. "Marissa asked me the same thing."

"Smart girl."

Gracie rolled the wrapped candy between her thumb and forefinger while searching for an answer. Did she want to die? No. The truth? "I don't want to get fat."

Dad jumped to his feet and brandished his index finger at Mom.

"See? That's what I mean! She gets her sick thinking from her mother. Look at my wife. Too skinny don't do nothing for a man. Now she's passing it along to my daughter."

Mom dropped her hands and narrowed her eyes in an expression of pure hatred. Gracie trembled, remembering all the times he had talked down to Mom or yelled at her as if she was a kid. Everything had to be his way, from TV shows to radio stations. Her chest hummed with so much rage she feared it would explode. Doubling her fists, Gracie rose and closed the distance between herself and Dad. "Shut up! Shut up, up, *up*! If you weren't such a friggin' control freak, none of this would've happened."

"I couldn't have said it any better, Sis-turd." Tall and lanky, her nemesis and sibling rival—her big brother Ben stepped into the room. He peered around the room through wire-rimmed glasses. "Sorry I'm late, Dr. Picard. I came as quickly as the law would allow."

Gracie's heart cratered to her stomach. Ben. Mom's favorite. He always took center stage.

Dad stepped toward Ben and extended his hand. "Glad you could make it home, son."

Ben accepted the handshake. "I'm here for Mom and Gracie."

Here for me? Ha! Mom, maybe, but not me.

Mom leaped from her chair and threw her arms around Ben's waist. "What are you doing here? What about school?"

"Finals are behind me. All As, exactly as you ordered, Chief."

Without cracking a smile, Dad nodded.

"Good God, Mom, you look awful." Ben swept her up in his arms. Setting her back in her chair, he turned to Gracie. "What've I missed?"

"Glad you could make it, Mr. Reeves." Dr. Picard offered his hand.

"Mr. Reeves? Nah. Call me Ben."

Dr. Picard pointed to an empty chair. "I'd say we have some work to do. Won't you have a seat, Ben?" Pushing a button on his phone, he spoke into the receiver. "Could you move my afternoon appointments back an hour?"

Dr. Picard eased back onto his desk and lifted his candy dish. "Tootsie Roll?"

Ben took two. "Thanks. Maybe you should give me the bowl. I haven't eaten since breakfast, and I'm famished."

Leaning back in his chair, Dr. Picard steepled his fingers. "Ben, what do you think is the problem here?"

With a wary glance at Dad, Ben sighed. "Dad's a drill sergeant. He barks orders and we're expected to comply. He's always talked to Mom like he talks to us. Like she's ten years old and doesn't have the sense to tie her own shoes."

"Do you think your dad loves your mom?" asked Dr. Picard.

"He says he does." Ben drummed his fingers on his knees. "Hard to tell sometimes. I mean, he's generous with gifts and flowers. I doubt he's ever missed an anniversary. A lot of guys could learn from my dad in that department. But it's like she's his property."

"Yeah." Relieved to be out of the spotlight, Gracie nodded. "He expects her to toe the line and if she messes up, he chews her out like she's a naughty kid."

Dr. Picard wrote something on his notepad and leveled a concerned gaze at Gracie. "We'll come back to Dad's control issues. For now, I'd like to keep the focus on you."

"Yeah, Gracie." Ben brushed back a lock of his dark, shoulder length hair. "What's this I hear about you ralphing up everything you eat?"

Chapter Thirty-Eight
Tony

No one served better Margaritas or burritos than Patrikio's Mexican Restaurant. Tony decided he needed both. Dunking a tortilla chip in chili con queso, he mulled over the afternoon session with Dr. Picard. What had begun as an intervention for his daughter seemed to have ended as an all-out offensive aimed at him.

He pondered the changes in the young man who sat across the table. He swore Ben had grown taller in four years. He had Elise's dark eyes and hair, which he wore pulled back in a ponytail. The shadow of a beard darkened his slender cheeks and chin. At the same time, Tony could see a lot of his younger brother Woody in Ben. Ben's laugh and lopsided smile were all Woody.

Tony's reason for putting in for the patrol boats in Vietnam, a virtual suicide mission, had been so his brother, who had joined the Air Force, wouldn't have to go. The cruel irony in all of that was Tony survived and a car accident in Germany had taken Woody.

Ben, who hadn't spoken more than a word or two since they left the hospital, sipped his Margarita, his midnight-eyes trained on Tony. "What now, Dad?"

"Whaddya mean, 'what now'?"

"Mom? Gracie?"

Gracie swirled her straw through her Coke and glared at Tony. "You're not gonna lock me away in the loony bin with Mom, are you? What about school? What about the swim team?"

"Dr. Picard seems to think the day program will work for you." Ben kissed the top of her head. "It's only for a little while. Do some calisthenics at home and you like to run. You can catch up in summer school. And if your coach really believes you're Olympic material, he'll welcome you back to the team. What's a month in the space-time continuum?"

Gracie groaned. "I'm going to flunk Algebra, I know it."

"Never fear, Big Brother the Math Nerd is here."

"But you're going back to school."

A slow smile spread his lips as he turned his focus on Tony. "I've earned all my credits." He dipped a chip in the cheese sauce and handed it to Gracie. "I'm finished with Harvard until commencement."

Tony's heart leaped. Maybe the military wasn't the answer for everyone. As much as he hated to admit it, his children were not meant to be extensions of himself or Elise.

"In case my opinion matters anymore," Tony raised his glass and grinned. "I agree with Ben. Proud of you, Son."

* * *

Tony drummed his fingers on the arms of his chair. He crossed and uncrossed his legs before bringing his right foot to rest on his left knee. Waiting for Hank, who had left word he would be delayed, Tony inspected the shadowbox on the wall. The oak-framed box displayed a tri-folded American flag, a photo of Hank in his dress uniform, and his medals.

"Sorry I'm late, Chief." Hank walked through the door carrying a folder. "Pretty impressive dust collectors, eh?"

Tony rose from his chair and saluted. "I'm gonna have to get used to seeing you on two legs. Like 'The Six-Million Dollar Man.'"

"The VA did a great job on these prosthetics." Hank sank down on the chair across from Tony. "Lee Majors wishes he was as good looking. You should've seen the look on my wife's face when I walked in the door last Friday night. First time we've danced in years." He set his notepad on his lap. "Let's talk about *your* family. You mentioned Elise's record. Elmwood Psychiatric Hospital three times, Hilliard General once, and now Brookside Memorial."

"She went into Elmwood twice while I was in the Persian Gulf. Seems she don't want to get well."

"Why do you think that is?"

Tony would never forget the way Elise had shut him out by not answering his letters or phone calls. Maybe she wanted him gone. One of her times at Elmwood fell on Labor Day weekend when he was home on leave. It seemed to him she had planned it that way, so she didn't have to spend any time with him.

"Don't look at me." Tony flinched. "It ain't my fault."

"Who said it was?"

"My kids. At the family meeting, they accused me of being a control freak—a 'drill sergeant', is what my son called me—especially when it comes to Elise."

"Do you think there's any truth to it? Do you order your wife around?"

"I don't order. I instruct."

Things were simpler in the Navy. Tony saw what needed to be done, gave instructions to his subordinates without explanation, and, bingo, mission accomplished. Why couldn't Elise understand this?

As if he could read Tony's mind, Hank asked, "Does she want to be, as you say—instructed?"

"I thought you were on my side." Grinding his teeth, Tony stood. "I don't hafta sit here and take this shit."

"No, I don't suppose you do." Hank stood. Leaning into Tony's face, he poked his chest. "But how long do your wife and kids have to pay for your trauma?"

Tony opened his mouth to protest but stopped himself. How many times had he scolded her in front of the kids? He remembered how he'd bawled her out for letting the dog on the couch or demanded dinner be ready at a certain time. Did Gracie and Ben have his number?

Hanging his head, Tony squeezed the arms of his chair. "I guess I got some work to do."

Chapter Thirty-Nine

Elise curled up in a chair in Wayne's office for her midweek session. Her thoughts went back to her conversation with Cassie in the art room. Then after that, the way the kids went after Tony in their family meeting. Even though he'd been somewhat defensive, something had changed.

Should she confront him about Hank, or should she wait until he told her?

Wayne must have noticed her distraction for he pulled out the big guns. Elise flinched when he said, "You've mentioned the effect your parents' deaths had on you more than once. Care to talk about it?" He held out his ubiquitous candy dish and raised an eyebrow.

Elise popped a Tootsie Roll into her mouth. She chewed the candy, savoring its sweetness. "Could you be more specific?"

"Tell me about the day your father passed."

"Right before he went to work, Tony yelled at me because 'your dog' pooped on the bedroom floor. I'll never forget it. My son said he didn't like the way Daddy talked to me."

"How did that make you feel?"

"Vindicated." She blinked back a tear. "Even a five-year-old could see it."

"I'm sure you resented Tony for that. Weren't you angry?"

"Furious."

She went on to explain how her dad would call every morning without fail since her mom had passed away three years earlier. That day Tony had lectured her before work. The kids were fighting. The house was a mess. Now the phone was ringing. Dad's call came later than usual.

"What's up, Dad?"

"I miss your mom."

"I miss her, too."

"How is Grandpa's sweetheart?"

"Spoiled rotten. In case you're curious, your grandson's doing well, too."

Dad favored girls over boys. He never hid his disappointment when Ben was born. After Gracie came along, poor Ben became an afterthought in his grandfather's eyes.

"Are you all right, Dad?"

"I'm rattling around this house alone. I'm dying. My son in Washington DC doesn't give me the time of day and now my daughter wants nothing to do with me. What could possibly be wrong?"

"Dad. We went to lunch yesterday."

"You didn't call this morning. You don't care."

"I had another phone call." Elise ground her teeth. "You know I love you."

"I'm tired. I'm going to take a nap. Will I see you later?"

There had been desperation in Dad's voice she hadn't heard before. "Look, Dad, I have some errands to run this afternoon. I'll try to swing by."

"Don't do me any favors." Click.

"Five hours later I found him dead on the couch."

After an uncomfortable pause, in a soft voice, Wayne said, "Finding your father's body must've been devastating."

Elise found the concern in Wayne's soft blue eyes unsettling. She cast her gaze to her hands in her lap. "I—I've had better days."

Wayne neither smiled nor shifted his scrutinizing focus on her. Taking a deep breath, she held it for a moment and exhaled a short puff at a time. "I believe God prepared me for that moment."

"How so?"

"After Mom died, Dad stopped living. He never took care of his diabetes—defied doctor's orders. Said food was his hobby, his profession, and his pleasure. No one was going to take that from him." She smiled and brushed a stray tear from her cheek. "He'd eat what he wanted and one day, one big burp and he'd die."

"That's not how it happened, is it?"

"Hardly. He became insulin dependent and developed congestive heart failure. Toward the end he hardly ate and fell asleep at the table. He wasted away to one hundred and eight pounds." Elise fingered her shirt hem, winding it around her index finger. "The doctor told me he would lie down to sleep one day and never wake up. About a week before he passed, I told a friend I knew I'd walk in one day and find him."

"And that's how, as you say, God prepared you?"

"Yes. Do you believe in God, Wayne?"

"My dad was a Lutheran pastor."

"You don't think I'm crazy then?"

"Depressed? Dysfunctional? Yes. Crazy? Not by a longshot, my dear. Keep going. What happened after you found your dad on the couch."

"Right. After he blasted me for being a terrible daughter. That really hurt. I was tempted not to stop on my way home, but I couldn't shake the eerie feeling that I needed to. I knew as soon as I walked through the door."

The details of the day came back to Elise with crystal clarity.

It didn't take a coroner to tell her dad had passed. She touched his chest. It felt like stone. Nonetheless, she called nine-one-one where an operator walked her through CPR. Knowing her father had been gone for a while, Elise merely pretended to follow instructions. What was the point? After a few moments, she told the operator he was unresponsive.

Tucking her feet underneath her, Elise sighed. "I called the Louis Funeral Home—where all Kansas City Jews go to be interred. The guy who answered sounded like he'd been drinking embalming fluid. He assured me they would send someone to pick up the body but they couldn't give me a time.

"About then, I think, Dad's next-door neighbor Marcia knocked on the door. She said she had a feeling something wasn't right. She offered to take Gracie as long as I needed her."

"I gather she was someone you trusted."

"Implicitly. Marcia and Ron moved in when I was fourteen. They had three little girls of their own."

Once Marcia left with Gracie, Elise went through the phone numbers in Mom's old rolodex. Of course, she called Eugene first.

"He's dead, isn't he?" Eugene said in a soft voice before Elise could tell him the news. "We'll be there in a couple of days so don't have the funeral right away."

"I take it he knew how gravely ill your father was," said Wayne.

"He'd come home a week before to introduce Dad and me to his new bride. We agreed that Dad had held on long enough to meet Arlene.

Next on the list was Aunt Viv who wailed so loudly, Elise had to hold the receiver at a distance. Elise imagined huge crocodile tears running down her full cheeks.

Raising an eyebrow, Wayne scratched his head with his pencil. "You doubted her grief?"

"Grief, my eye. The only person Aunt Viv cared about was Aunt Viv."

"Why'd you call her?"

"I don't know. Courtesy, I guess. She was still my mom's sister."

Wayne wrote on his notepad. "Something to discuss at our next session. So, you made all these calls and your dad's body is on the sofa the whole time."

"I did what I had to do. It wasn't like he was going to get up and walk away."

Finally, the attendants from the funeral home drove their hearse into the driveway around five. Tony followed. He took Elise in his arms. She clung to him allowing the tears she'd held at bay all afternoon to flow.

Wayne stood to indicate time was up. Elise stretched her arms over her head to ease the tension in her shoulders. "Was I wrong to leave the kids with Tony that evening and go straight to the fitness center?"

"Only you can answer that one."

Back in her room, Elise laid on the bed and relived the shock of that awful afternoon. The image of Dad reposed on the couch, mouth open, was indelibly etched in her memory.

He didn't budge when Gracie wriggled out of Elise's arms and toddled to him. She patted his shoulder, squealing "Pa Pa."

Numbed by the realization, Elise took some toys from the diaper bag to distract the baby. As if she understood, Gracie solemnly took her plastic cars and plunked down on the floor. Her soft auburn curls shone in the sunlight pouring through the window.

All these years later, the horror of the moment flooded Elise. She didn't recall ever crying after Dad died. Instead, she had lost herself in diet and exercise. She became the maven of calorie counting. How many in a cookie? She could even tell you the number of calories in a piece of chewing gum.

"You know the steps well," sang Annie.

Tears soaked Elise's pillow. "God in Heaven, please, help me stop dancing."

Chapter Forty

Since Felicia would be leaving after the Saturday family sessions, the staff agreed to have her coining out ceremony right after breakfast. Elise looked around the room. Their numbers had dwindled over the past week with Nyx's transfer to the psych ward and Yessenia's departure.

Elise had overheard Cassie and Terry discussing Yessenia's delusional mother who insisted that she'd never given her consent to Yessenia's "needless hospitalization." That the girl wasn't sick, and Mama needed the money for "other things." Both of the nurses feared sending her home after only one week. It could be a recipe for disaster.

Elise examined the coin in her hand. What words of wisdom did she have for Felicia when she couldn't even help herself? She settled against the sofa cushions.

Thad, who had eaten everything on his plate and then some, squirmed on his chair. It didn't take a clairvoyant to read his mind. He cast anxious glances at the door and raised his hand.

Cassie gave her head a shake. "No, Thad. You may not use the restroom."

"But I really have to go—honest."

Elise doubted his sincerity. She could tell Cassie did as well.

"If you have to go that badly," Cassie leveled her piercing gaze at him, "I'll take you."

He pursed his lips and settled back.

"Thanks for letting my husband sit in for my coining out, y'all." Felicia's cheeks glowed as she reached for her his hand. "I'm gonna miss all you guys. The past three weeks have gone by really quick."

Tall and lean, Felicia's husband had to have been one of the most handsome men Elise had ever seen. He was, beyond a doubt, the darkest man she had ever laid eyes on, with an almost blue-black tone to his flawless complexion. Maybe it was the artist in her that allowed her, or some might say, caused her, to notice the actual tinting. One thing everyone, regardless of artistic ability, could see was the adoration he held in his eyes for his wife. "I can't thank you all enough for what you've done for my wife."

"Don't underestimate your influence." Cassie squeezed his broad shoulder. "A good man is worth his weight in gold and Felicia's got herself a shining nugget."

They were the picture of the perfect couple, the kind one would expect to see on a magazine cover. Closing her fingers around the coin, Elise coaxed a smile. "Felicia, I'm so happy for you. You deserve a good life and a healthy baby."

Elise handed the coin to Helen whom she noticed had ditched the wig and gathered her long salt-and-pepper hair into a braided chignon at the base of her head. No longer penciled-in solid lines, her brows had a graceful curve to them.

Helen took the coin and studied it for a moment. "'The wisdom to know the difference.' That's a tough one sometimes. We can't control everything, can we? I have high hopes for you, Miss Felicia." She patted her hair. "When you open your own salon, I'll be your first customer." She passed the coin to Thad.

The boy held the coin and licked his lips.

"I... um... good luck on the outside." His cheeks turned crimson. "That's all."

"It's okay, Thaddeus. Not everybody's good with speeches." Dixie took the coin from him and flipped it in midair. When it landed on the back of her left hand, she clapped her right over it and flashed a sly grin at Felicia. "Heads or tails?"

Felicia widened her eyes and twisted her lips to one side. "No clue."

"Aw come on. Play along."

"Oh, all right. You won't give me a moment's peace until I do." Felicia rolled her eyes. "Heads."

Dixie lifted her hand. "Nope. Tails."

Elise shook her head at her roommate. "Enough with the games already."

Dixie's effervescent smile faded a bit. "Felicia, life is like the toss of the coin, or a box of chocolates, according to Forrest Gump. Just like you can't choose your baby's sex, you don't always know what you're gonna get.

"But you can choose whether or not to stay in recovery. That bun in your oven deserves a healthy mom." She handed Felicia a slip of paper with the coin. "This is my phone number. You call me when it's close to time. Suzie-Q and I are going to throw you the best baby shower ever, aren't we?"

"Absolutely!" Elise grinned at Felicia. "I'll even decorate the cake."

"Don't forget the punch with 7Up and sherbet." Felicia took the paper and the coin. "I'm holding you to it, my friends."

***

Later that night, Elise settled into bed. Lying back against her stacked pillows, she contemplated the week's events. So much had happened, including Irma's transfer, Nyx's attempted suicide and Felicia's coining out. "This place has a revolving door, doesn't it?

Without looking up from her book on clinical psychology, Dixie murmured. "There's a nifty revolving door downstairs in the lobby."

Elise rolled her eyes. "You know what I mean."

The turbulent meeting with Wayne came to the forefront of her mind. "I almost felt sorry for Tony."

"You talking about the family session you told me about?" Dixie glanced up at Elise. "It does sound like y'all kind of ganged up on him. But from what you've told me, he had it coming."

Elise analyzed her drawing. The child's smiling mime face with tears oozing from her eyes mirrored Elise's conflicting emotions. Coloring in the red lips, she twisted her own to one side. "I'm afraid she looks older than five. What do you think, Dix?" She turned the drawing so her roommate could see.

Marking her place in her book with her finger, Dixie pursed her lips. "Maybe. Say, closer to ten or eleven. But then it could be because of the mask."

"Okay." Elise set the red marker aside and held the sketch at arm's length. "Done for the night."

Dixie closed her book and laid it on the nightstand. Rolling over on her side, she tucked one arm under her head. "When are *you* going to shed the mask?"

Elise poked and pinched her own cheeks. "Mask? What mask? I don't got no stinking mask."

"Nice try, Suzie-Q. How'd that song go, 'No matter what you do, you'll never run away from you?' Isn't that what your sketches are about? Ripping off the mask? Yet you keep it firmly in place. Mark my words, as long as you keep it there, people, Tony in particular, are going to steamroll right over you."

"Hanging out your shingle already?"

"Ha! Face it, we're both getting our psych degree from the couch."

Elise reached across the aisle and grasped Dixie's hand. "You're an inspiration. I want to be you when I grow up."

"Start by standing up to that man of yours. I see the way he looks at you. He adores you. He just doesn't know how to show it. Work with him. You're a fighter, Suzie-Q. You're going to send Annie packing." Dixie turned out the light over her bed. She rolled onto her back and shut her eyes. "All this recovery's wearing me out."

Elise set her drawing pad aside and turned out her light. "Pleasant dreams."

She had almost drifted off when Dixie's voice cut through the silence. "Hey, Suzie-Q. Know why elementary art teachers use anorexics for models?"

"I'm going to regret this one, aren't I? Why?"

"Because kids can only draw stick figures."

Elise groaned. "Good night."

"Hey, Suzie-Q."

"What now?"

"Didja hear about the new anorexia café?"

"No."

"It's closed seven days a week."

"*Barrump bump.* Go to sleep, you nut."

"Elise, you're too thin."

"Look who's talking."

"I've gained."

"Hurray. You're still a stick."

"If I gain a few more pounds Dr. P's springing me from of the wheelchair. Go me!"

"Rah. Rah. Rah."

Dixie switched on her light. Elise blinked. Dixie sat up and raised her fist. "I hereby serve Ms. Annie Wrecks-Ya with her walking papers."

"Old news. You're repeating yourself."

"And I'll say it again and again until it penetrates the only fat part of your anatomy—your head. Don't you get it, Suzie-Q? Michael Gordon's still raping you from the grave. Repeat after me, 'I, Elise Reeves, do solemnly swear—'"

"I can't."

"If I can, you can."

Chapter Forty-One

Elise stirred peanut butter into her oatmeal and checked the clock on the wall. Half-past eight. Dixie was officially late. Where could she be? She had told Elise the night before she had a big surprise.

The morning group session would begin at nine-thirty. Gracie had been admitted to the day program. She would be arriving in a little over an hour.

Elise's stomach roiled. What a failure she'd been as a role model. She shoved her bowl away.

The door burst open. With Cassie at her side, Dixie walked into the dining room, arms extended over her head as if she'd completed a perfect ten floor routine. She flashed an exuberant smile. "Notice anything different?"

Thad winked at Elise. "New dress?"

"Change your hairstyle?" Helen buttered a slice of toast. "Very flattering."

"Yanno," Thad pushed a lock of hair off his forehead, "you're not much taller standing than you are sitting."

"Take a seat, Miss Thang." Cassie beamed. "We don't want you to overdo your first day out of the chair."

"Now that you mention it, I do feel like I just completed a strenuous workout on the uneven bars." Dixie sank down beside Elise. "What's shakin' bacon?"

Elise licked peanut butter from her spoon. "Getting there, roomie."

"That looks delish, Suzie-Q. I think I'll give your creation a shot. Garçon." Dixie snapped her fingers. "One bowl of oatmeal, extra thick, if you please."

Setting a steaming bowl in front of her, Cassie curtsied. "Your wish is my command."

Dixie plopped a dollop of peanut butter on top of her cereal. She stirred it and took a big bite. Her cheeks puffed as she chewed. "Shticks to da woof of my mowf." Once she'd swallowed, she chased it down with swig of milk. "Really good. Eat yours like a good girl, Suzie-Q, so you can grow up big and strong like me."

Elise took a small bite. It did taste good. She looked up at the wall clock again. Eight-thirty. Ben had promised to have Gracie at the hospital on time. Elise's heart thumped.

While she was overjoyed to have her son home, she couldn't shake the horrified expression on his face when he first saw her in Wayne's office. The tears in his eyes had made her heart ache. How could she do this to her children?

Dixie was right. Elise had a decision to make. She sipped her lukewarm coffee. The proverbial moment of truth had come. The clock seemed louder with each tick.

Elise broke out in a cold sweat. Sharing her innermost fears and feelings in front of strangers was one thing but opening up to her daughter was quite another.

Chapter Forty-Two
Gracie

GRACIE SQUIRMED in her chair beside her mother and surveyed the circle of patients in the room, noting a few new faces and the absence of others since her last meeting. The first group of the day was a get-acquainted session. Mom reached over and squeezed her hand. "It's going to be okay."

Shooting Mom a sideward scowl, Gracie jerked back her hand. "Like it's okay for you?"

Mom hung her head and folded her hands in her lap. Remorse surged through Gracie. *I shouldn't be so hard on her. She's doing the best she can, putting up with Dad and all. But...*

Nurse Terry took a bell from her hot pink lab coat pocket and jingled it. "Time for this meeting to come to order. Who wants to start?"

Silence answered her.

"I'm not shy. I will. This place sure does have a revolving door, doesn't it." Sitting cross-legged on her chair, Dixie winked at Elise and nodded at the new faces in the circle. "Welcome to Club Head, ladies. I'm Dixie and I'm an anorexic."

Straightening, Mom raised her hand. She flashed a smile at Gracie. "I'm Elise. I'm—I'm—I have an eating disorder."

"Hi, I'm Jeanie," said a chubby girl with short brown curls and a turned-up nose. "I'm fat and I don't belong here."

Gracie bit her tongue. *No argument there. What's she doing here, anyway?*

Terry shook her head, making her walnut shell earrings bob. "I'm certainly no Kate Moss either. Why don't you think you belong here?"

"Look at all y'all." Jeanie glanced at Dixie. "You're a box of toothpicks and I'm—"

"A Vienna sausage?" Gracie clapped her hand over her mouth. Her cheeks blazed. "I'm sorry, it popped out before I could stop it."

To Gracie's relief, Jeanie chuckled. "Yeah or a bratwurst."

"No one's here to judge you, Jeanie." Terry shifted her penetrating gaze from Gracie to the rest of the group. "Dr. Picard saw fit to admit you. Why do you think that is?"

"I make myself throw up." Jeanie looked down at her feet, clutching the seat of her chair, arms stiff at her sides. "I take whole boxes of laxatives and bottles of Ipecac. But they don't work for me. I'm still fat as Granny's hog."

"It's okay, Jeanie," said Gracie, hoping to cover for her mean crack with a joke. "Pobody's nerfect."

"Trust me, darlin'," Terry winked at Jeanie. "You're in the right place. Next. How about we hear from the rooster in this hen house?"

The boy rocked his chair on its back legs, then brought the front ones down hard. "Hi, I'm Thad. Me and you got something in common, Miss Jeanie. One of the guys on my basketball team showed me how puking kept him at the right weight. It worked for me..." his face contorted in anguish, "... until the night I passed out on the court—in the middle of a game. I've tried to stop throwing up—but—but..." Tears made rivulets through his freckles. "I need help."

"And that, my good man, is step one on the road to recovery." Terry nodded.

"Wow, you're really brave." Jeanie's eyes shone. "Thaddeus."

"You'll do fine here." Terry patted Jeanie's back and leveled her gaze at Gracie. "What about you, Ms. Reeves?"

Trembling, Gracie grasped Mom's hand. "Hi, I'm Gracie and I'm a bulimic."

Chapter Forty-Three

"THAT LOOKS JUST LIKE YOU, Elise. Is it supposed to?" Helen frowned at her own sketch of a vase of flowers. "I can't even draw a stick figure."

Elise put the finishing touches on the sketch she'd started Saturday night. "Kinda sorta. I'm a mime."

"She's smiling but those don't look like happy tears in her eyes. Why's the child wearing a mask?"

With a shrug, Elise grinned. "Dr. Picard says I hide my true feelings behind an invisible mask. Smiling on the outside. Crying on the inside."

Dixie's pointed question shuddered through Elise. *When do I shed my mask? How do I do that? Dear Lord, what will become of me if I do?*

Pam laid her hand on Helen's shoulder. "Nice start. Why flowers?"

"They make me happy." Helen filled in a rose outline with pink crayon. "And because I can actually make them look like flowers. I tried a dog but it looked more like a goose."

"Fair enough. Elise, this picture's coming along nicely. May I?" She lifted the drawing and peered at it over her glasses. "Of all the illustrations you've done so far, this one tells a story all by itself." She set it back down. "May I make a copy when it's finished?"

"Sure." Elise sketched the girl's hair. "I'd be honored."

"I'll need written permission of course." Pam looked back over one shoulder and then the other. "Where's your roommate? It's awfully quiet in here without her."

"She said she was really tired and had a splitting headache. Cassie gave her permission to miss. It's no wonder. She can't get her nose out of the last book Wayne loaned her. Read the night away. He's created a monster."

"True enough. She's going to be a terrific therapist. The ones who've been through the fire usually are." Pam glanced at Elise's sketch. "Maybe you should consider becoming an art therapist yourself."

"Not me. I never did well in school."

"You never know. That was a long time ago. You might surprise yourself."

Pam pivoted on her heel and made her way around the room. She stopped and bent over Gracie's shoulder. "Very nice. Like mother, like daughter."

After class, Gracie handed her sketch to Elise. "Will you give this to Dixie?"

Elise checked out Gracie's caricature of Dixie, pride welling up in her chest. She noted that Gracie had given the erstwhile gymnast a full head of hair. Dixie's exaggerated, yet unmistakable smile took up the lower part of her face. Gracie had positioned her upside down on a balance beam, her toes pointed toward heaven. Not only had Gracie captured Dixie's likeness, but the twinkle in her eyes as well. Elise couldn't wait for her roommate to see it.

"Why don't you give it to her over lunch, honey?"

"What if she gets mad at me?" Gracie's cheeks flushed. "Please, Momette."

"Dixie? Get mad over this?"

"I made her body a stick figure."

"*Hey, Suzie-Q. Know why elementary art teachers use anorexics for models? Because kids can only draw stick figures.*"

"I guarantee she'll love it."

"You sure?"

"Very sure."

"Pinkie swear?"

"Pinkie swear." Elise crooked her pinkie around Gracie's and pulled her into her arms, careful not to crumple the drawing. "I'm proud of you, Evelyn Grace. So very proud."

Pulling back, Gracie kissed Elise's nose. "See ya at lunch." She spun on her toes and ran after Jeanie and Thad. "Hey guys, wait up."

It never took Gracie long to make friends. She had a way with people that Elise envied. Apparently, she'd inherited that from Tony.

Elise opened the door to her room and tiptoed over the threshold in case Dixie was still sleeping. However, the bed had been made and Dixie was nowhere in sight. The sound of running water came from the bathroom.

"Hey, honey," Elise raised her voice to be heard over the shower, "I'm home. Wait 'til you see what *my* talented daughter did for you."

Dixie didn't answer.

Elise laid the sketch on the dresser. That was odd. Dixie always sang in the shower. Elise strained her ears to hear Dixie's off-key rendition of "Singing in the Rain."

Dixie called it Chinese water torture because it was like a steady drip in Elise's ears and there was nothing she could do to make it stop.

Maybe she forgot to turn off the water before she went to lunch. Elise's gaze fell to the clothes neatly laid out at the end of the bed. Dixie's flannel pajamas lay in a wadded heap beside them. A menacing wind shrilled through Elise. At the top of her voice, she yelled, "Dixie Dawn, if this is some kind of a joke, I'm not laughing. You hear?"

Running water replied.

Elise inched toward the bathroom. Her pulse thudded in her ears as she pushed open the door. Steam choked her. Water flooded the tile floor.

Dixie lay under the shower, face down. Curled up in a ball, she clutched her stomach. Had she overdosed? Slit her wrists? No, there were no traces of blood to indicate suicide. Heart pounding, Elise dropped to her knees and pushed Dixie over. Vomit covered the side of her face that had been against the floor. Hot water pelted Elise's back, soaking her clothes. She pressed her fingers against Dixie's neck, but couldn't tell if the throb came from her friend's carotid artery or her own fingertips.

Elise crawled from the shower. Somehow, she managed to stand and stagger to the hallway. The floor swayed beneath her. Someone screamed. "Help! Cassie! Terry!"

The intercom blared. "Code Blue to room 918!"

Room 918? That was her room. The room she shared with Dixie. This couldn't be happening. It had to be a bad dream.

The screaming continued. Her throat burned. Someone swept her up. She balled her fists and fought against them. A needle stung her backside.

Chapter Forty-Four
Tony

IN HIS SESSION earlier that day, Hank had handed Tony a leather-bound book with the Navy insignia on the cover. He went to explain it was a journal for Tony to write whatever he wanted. Events of the day. Poetry. Profanity. Whatever came to mind. Hank explained there was something about putting his feelings on paper that would keep Tony from bottling them up inside only to explode like a grenade later.

"No one else is gonna read it," said Hank. "Unless you give them permission."

Tony knew about journalling from having read Elise's writings. She was the poet, not him. He held his breath for a moment. What if someone should find his and read it like he had read hers—without permission?

He thumbed through the blank pages and thought back over the day. Perhaps that would be a good place to start. He wrote—"Dear Diary"—then tore out the page, crumpled it, and tossed it in the wastebasket next to his desk. Setting pen to paper, he started with the date.

> 25 March 1996 – Monday
> Since I'm on leave and Gracie and Elise are tied up with workshops, Ben and I went to see a movie and grab some lunch.

He called it male bonding. I think it's the first time we've done it since he was ten and that didn't go so good.

I let Ben choose the movie. Up Close and Personal with Robert Redford. It ain't often he wants to spend time with the old man.

After the movie, we went to TGI Fridays. I still can't get over my boy ordering a Glenlivet. It don't seem like he could be old enough. Guess he is.

I think that pretty server took a shine to him. I pointed out she had a nice butt. Ben said he didn't notice. I asked if he was gay or something. And he says what if I am?

Saved by the bell. Our plates came. He got a Reuben, and I got a burger. Like his mom he gave me a hard time about my ketchup.

After that he tells me he's got himself a job for the summer. Waiting tables at a dive in Westport. I started to say something about his Harvard degree and how I wish I had the opportunity he did. (I guess Elise is right. I do tend to lecture.)

Anyway, Ben assures me he's got some kind of job with a New York investment firm in Manhattan.

It was a good afternoon with my kid. I don't like to admit I cried at sad moments in the movie. But I did tear up some.

Tony shut the journal. "That's enough of that. Guess if anyone found it, they couldn't read it anyway. Elise says my handwriting sucks. She's right."

Setting the book aside, he opened a box of letters and photos he'd found tucked away in his dresser drawer. It had been years since he'd looked at them. He unfolded one of the letters and read:

October 3, 1968
    Dear Tony,

Sweetheart, I feel like a rat, since you're off in Vietnam. But I'm afraid you'll get killed and I won't have no one. I met this really nice guy named Ted. You'd really like him. We got married last night. I hope you understand.

All my love,

Caroline

"'You'd really like him.' Yeah right." He crumpled the paper in his fist. "Where's that bimbo get off calling me sweetheart?" He tossed the letter in the wastebasket by the couch. "Why the hell did I keep it?"

He riffled through the photos until he came to one of Frankie standing shirtless beside him in the jungle. "Not a hair on that kid's chest." He tucked the photo between the pages of his journal.

Shuffling through the pictures, he stopped occasionally to gaze at the guys he'd served with. One photo showed a tall, lanky guy mugging for the camera. "What ever happened to you, Winston? What a cut-up you were."

Tony set the snapshots aside and picked up another folded letter. This one was in his handwriting. Unfinished. As he unfolded it, a snapshot fell onto his lap.

"Huh," Tony said to himself. He had forgotten all about the photo he had taken of Kieu. She was leaning on her crutch, smiling that crooked smile. The scars on the one side of her face really caused her missing teeth to stand out more than he had remembered. "You'd be in your thirties by now." He kissed the photo. "Poor kid."

Propping the photo against the lamp on the end table next to his journal, he turned back to the letter.

3 February 1969

Dear Mom,

In answer to your question. I got your care package. Thanks for the fruit cocktail cake. It was pretty gooey from the heat. I shared it with the guys and they agreed it was great.

Hey, Mom. I got a huge favor to ask. It's about the little girl in the picture. I know you'd fall in love with her if you met her. Enclosed is an adoption form. As you can see life ain't been kind to her. It's tough for kids with G.I. daddies and local mommies.

The letter stopped there.

His mind traveled back to the day he went to ask Kieu's mother for permission to adopt her. It was a longshot, but he had to try.

The girl's mother met him with tears. She led him to Kieu's body. Fresh bruises covered her face and arms. No attempt had been made to camouflage the blood-soaked cot beneath her. The woman said something to her son. The adolescent, who didn't seem too concerned over his sister's death, shrugged.

"You little murderer!" Tony grasped the boy's shirt and shook him.

The boy kneed Tony's groin. "Go home, GI Joe. We don't want you here."

What could he do? He turned to Kieu's mother, who sank down beside her daughter and wailed. "Kieu! Kieu!"

So Kieu's mom did love her after all. Finding some comfort in that revelation, Tony wiped away his own tears. He knelt and fished a necklace from his pocket meant for the child. A golden heart. He placed it in the woman's hand. "You keep."

He set the letter back in the box.

Taking the journal from the end table, Tony opened it and took a pen from his breast pocket. He set point to page and wrote,

We came back home from Nam. But it didn't seem like home ~~no~~ anymore. Damn protestor spit on me. Called me a baby killer. Dumb shaggy sonofabitch. I socked him. Hope I broke his nose.

The telephone rang. Tony shut the journal and checked his watch. Twenty-two hundred hours. "It better not be Doug calling Gracie this late." Tony picked up the receiver wind in a stern voice almost yelled, "Hello."

"Chief Reeves," said a distressed sounding voice. "This is Dr. Picard..."

Chapter Forty-Five

"I screamed, didn't I?"

"And kicked." Cassie stroked Elise's hair. She spoke in a low soothing voice. "Mmhmm. Threw a tantrum like my Lennie when she was an itty-bitty squirt."

Rolling onto her back, Elise shivered and pulled the blanket around her neck. "I think I bit you. Are you okay?"

"I'm fine. You bit Terry."

"Oh, I—"

"No need to apologize. She understands. I'm so angry I'd like to throw a fit of my own."

Beside the bed, the heart monitor beeped. With a syringe, Cassie injected something into the IV tube.

"What's that?"

"Lorazepam. It'll help you relax." Cassie tossed the syringe in a sharps container. Then she popped the top on a can of *Ensure* and poured some into a glass. "Here's something to tide you over until supper."

"I'm not hungry."

"Would you prefer a feeding tube?"

"It's do or die, Suzie-Q. Which will it be?"

Elise stirred the chocolate drink with her finger and licked the tip. "May I have a straw?"

Cassie took one from the tray table and put it in the glass. "Now you're talking, sister." She raised the head of the bed. "Let's make you more comfortable."

Dr. Picard entered the room and approached the bed. He put his hand on Cassie's shoulder. "I'll take it from here, Nurse Chukwu. They need you on EDU."

"How are the Grangers?"

"As well as can be expected."

Cassie brushed a tear from her cheek. She patted Elise's hand. "Get as much of that down as you can." She turned and left the room, shutting the door behind her.

Elise gagged down a few sips of *Ensure.* The taste nauseated her. She set the glass on the nightstand. Laying on her back, she stared at the ceiling. Out of the corner of her eye she saw Wayne enter.

He eased into an empty chair beside the bed. "There was nothing anyone could've done. We'll know more after the autopsy, but my guess is Dixie expired at least an hour before you found her, Elise."

Rolling over onto her side, she stared out the window at the relentless sky. She could still feel the hot shower on her back and see Dixie's half-open, unfocused eyes. *Expired? Is that all he can say? How can he be so cold and unfeeling?*

Elise turned back and glared at him. "You make her sound like a carton of milk."

"All right then. Shuffled off her mortal coil. Better?"

"Poetic, Mr. Shakespeare." Elise smiled in spite of herself. "She'd like that."

Wayne's eyes were as red and swollen as Cassie's. His shoulders slumped and two days' growth stubbled his chin. He propped his elbow on the arm of his chair and dropped his head in his hand. His bald pate shone under the light over Elise's bed. She regretted lashing out at him.

Her mouth went dry in the awkward silence. "First Lucas. Now Dixie." She took a sip of her drink and forced herself to swallow. "How do you maintain your sanity, Wayne?"

He raised his head and reached for a tissue from the nightstand. "Who says I'm sane?"

A wave of exhaustion flooded Elise as the Lorazepam took effect. Putting her glass back on the stand, she fought to stay awake. "Why?"

"Why what?"

"Why do you do it? Why are you here with me right now? Why did Dixie have to die? Just—why?"

"As for why I do it… I made a promise." A tear slid down his cheek. "As for Dixie, well, there's only so much the human anatomy can endure, Elise."

Elise's eyes burned. "She *promised* me."

"And she meant every word." Pinching the bridge of his nose, he took a deep breath and let it out in heavy sigh. "She made promises her weary organs could no longer keep."

Chapter Forty-Six
Tony

TONY LEANED back in the chair beside Elise's bed and flipped through channels on the TV's remote. "Not a damn thing worth watching." He turned it off and set the control on the bedstand.

Folding his arms across his chest, he studied his slumbering wife. Curled up in a fetal position, she curved one rail-thin arm around her pillow, the one that "squished in all the right places".

She didn't look much older than Gracie. In her sleep, hugging her pillow like a doll, Elise seemed even younger. He reached over and pushed her dark locks off her face and rested his hand on her smooth cheek.

"Chief Reeves, do you consider your wife's eating disorder a life-threatening disease?"

Tony cringed now at the defensive words he had hurled at Dr. Picard in their first family session.

"Hey, Mr. Shrink. Don't try to pin her problems on me. She's the one hanging our dirty laundry out for the world to see. This is the thanks I get? I work hard to put food on the table. It ain't my fault she don't eat it. And now I gotta worry about the medical bills stacking up".

"Tony?" Elise opened her swollen eyes. She squeezed her pillow.

"What are you doing here? I thought you were heading for a school in Wichita."

"Master Chief Matthews is covering for me."

"Oh." She shut her eyes tight. A tear oozed from the corner of one. "It should've been me." Her lips trembled.

"Shh." He pressed his palm over her mouth and held there for a moment. "Listen to me, Elise. You need to get through this. The kids and I need you."

Her jaw clenched under his palm. She opened her eyes and glared at him. Prying off his hand, she turned her face toward the window. "You'd be better off without me."

A wave of nausea wafted over him. He couldn't imagine his life without her. His eyes burned with unshed tears. He wanted to take her in his arms and hold onto her forever. "Please, don't say that."

She turned back toward him and scowled. "Oh? What should I say?"

"You talk to Mom like you talk to us. You treat her like she's property."

Tony's heart thrashed against his ribs. Regret riddled him for the way he'd unwittingly treated her. "Elise. Honey. I'm the one who don't know what to say." He stood. "Come here."

"Is that an order, Chief?"

Careful of her IV, he enfolded her in his arms. Sitting back down on the chair, he gathered her onto his lap. "I don't want you to go the same way as Dixie. Why are you doing this to yourself?"

"I—I never meant to hurt you."

"Yes, you did. I have a confession. I read one of your journals. I know how much you hate me."

She stared at him, eyes wide. "And you don't want to divorce me?"

"Never. You're my world." He kissed her forehead. "I have another confession. I—I've been seeing a—shrink."

"Hank?"

"Yeah. Hank. How did you know?" His words tumbled over each. "That don't matter. Hank. He's quite a guy. A war hero. You'd like him. He's got me going to meetings at the VA on Saturday mornings—with other Nam vets with PTSD."

"Oh Tony!" A smile spread over her lips, and she wreathed her arms around his neck. "I wish you'd told me sooner. I would never judge you for getting help. I'm proud of you."

"Proud?" His pulse raced. "I was afraid you'd think I was a loser. I didn't know if I'd stick with it." He tightened his arms around her. "Help me help you, honey—" his tears spilled over. "—I don't know what to do any more."

"You're doing it. Hold me." She buried her face in his chest and snuggled against him. "Just *hold* me."

Chapter Forty-Seven
Gracie

"The Lord is my shepherd; I shall not want..."

Gracie clung to Ben's hand as the crowd at the funeral home gathered around the lavender casket and intoned the twenty-third Psalm in unison. She scanned the floral spray on the lid. White sweetheart roses and red carnations with a silver ribbon that read, "Beloved Daughter." Her heart fluttered when she noticed the framed caricature of Dixie among the flowers.

Ben squeezed her hand. "Nice work, baby sister."

"... His name's sake. Yea, though I walk through the valley of the shadow..."

Glancing at Mrs. Granger in the chair in front of the coffin, Gracie tried to swallow the lump in her throat. *Would mom cry like that if I died?* Peering over at her brother, she knew the answer.

Ben's narrow lips set in a taut line in his slender face. Afternoon sun glinted off his tinted eyeglasses. He looked so handsome in his dark gray suit, his glossy brown hair pulled back into a ponytail.

"... no evil for Thou art with me..."

Dr. Picard's red-rimmed gaze met hers. *Why is he crying? He's a shrink. It's just a job to him. Isn't it? I guess he's a human being, after all. Poor Dr. Picard.*

"... comfort me. Thou preparest a table before me..."

The scent of all the flowers overwhelmed Gracie. She stifled a sneeze with her tissue. Beside her, Cassie circled her arm around her shoulders.

Cassie's crying, too. I guess it's not just a job to her either. Oh, Lord, I don't want to die like Dixie. I'd rather people say all the nice things about me while I can still hear them.

"And I shall dwell in the house of the Lord forever. Amen." Chaplain Charlie bowed his head. "Let us pray. Dear Heavenly Father, we commit your lamb, Dixie Dawn Granger, into Your hands..."

It must be rough to be a chaplain. Poor guy's barely holding it together.

Gracie scanned the huge gathering. She recognized some of the girls who had come for the day sessions at Brookside. It seemed to her that all of Kansas City had come to give Dixie a sendoff—including a camera crew from Channel Five.

Closing his prayer book, the chaplain faced the group. "The Grangers hope you will join them for dinner at Mission Hills Country Club."

Gracie marveled at the elegant dining room, replete with crystal chandeliers. Buffet tables were piled with colorful salads, fresh fruit and all manner of bread and rolls. Steam rose from polished chafing dishes.

She dredged a piece of prime rib through horseradish sauce. *Wow, they must have mucho dinero.*

Sitting across the round table, Cassie buttered a roll. "I'm sorry your dad didn't come, Gracie."

"He didn't want to leave Mom today. Said his place is with her."

"Good for him." Dr. Rodgers nodded. "I'd say there's hope for the chief yet."

Ben took a sip of water, his eyes focused on the young woman beside him. "So, you're a physician, Miss Rodgers—sorry, Dr. Rodgers?"

Leonora flashed an even-toothed smile. "That's what my diploma says."

Gracie stifled a giggle. It didn't take a rocket scientist to see why her brother was taken with Cassie and Dr. Rodgers' daughter. Her huge gray-blue eyes, fringed with long lashes, complemented her tawny complexion. Like her mother she was slender and tall. Her tight black curls skimmed her shoulders.

She's a knockout. Go for it, big bro!

Leonora seemed to pick up on the same attraction Gracie had from Ben. She tilted her head toward the man beside her. "But even my diploma is half right. It's Dr. Washington."

"Call me Jason." His onyx eyes shone behind wire-rimmed glasses, his smooth skin was deep brown. "Happy to meet you, Ben. Sorry we couldn't meet under better circumstances."

Ben's smile vanished and his face colored as he extended his hand. "You're a lucky man, Doctor."

Poor Benny. I can hear his crest falling.

Floral-scented perfume wafted over Gracie as Mrs. Granger eased herself into the empty chair beside her. "May I join you, Miss Reeves?"

Startled by the sudden approach of the grieving mother, Gracie dropped her fork, splattering sauce on her new skirt. *Why does Dixie's mother want to sit by me?* "Oops, what a klutz."

"Nonsense." Although sunglasses obscured Mrs. Granger's eyes, her cheeks were pale and blotched. She lifted Gracie's fork and handed it to her. "Life's too short to—" She brought her handkerchief to her mouth. "There I go again." Lifting her sunglasses, she dabbed her eyes.

Cheeks flaming, Gracie fidgeted and shifted positions. *What do people say at a time like this? What should I say?* "I—I'm so sorry," she croaked in a hoarse whisper, "for your loss."

Mrs. Granger pulled Gracie to her bosom. Dropping her head on Gracie's shoulder, she held the girl in a crushing embrace. "Dear, dear girl."

Not sure of what else to do, Gracie circled her arms around the woman, breathing in her perfume.

Mom's image popped into her head. Although not as emaciated as Dixie, she was decidedly underweight. Last night Gracie had heard Dad crying, begging God not to take his bride. What if the next funeral was hers?

Unable to stem her own sudden tears, Gracie clung tight to Mrs. Granger. After a few moments, they both pulled back. Horrified at the splotch on the lady's fine suit jacket, Gracie tried to blot it with her napkin. "I got snot on you, Mrs. Granger."

"Ach, I'm sure I left some snot of my own on your little shoulder." With a slight smile, she shook her head and laid her sunglasses on the table. She cupped her hand around Gracie's chin. "*Schönes Mädchen...* such a pretty girl. Please, call me Aunt Ingrid. Jah?"

"Jah. I mean okay. Sure."

"*Sehr gut.*" Aunt Ingrid's inflamed gaze held Gracie captive. "Dixie spoke highly of you."

"Me?"

"You are a swimmer?"

Gracie squirmed. "Yeah."

"She worried for you. Like a gymnast, you wear a skimpy costume when you perform."

Dixie's gaunt image came to the forefront of Gracie's mind. How could anyone compare her to Dixie? Gracie braced herself for a lecture. But who had more of a right to deliver one than this heartbroken mother? Gracie cast her gaze downward to avoid Aunt Ingrid's red-rimmed eyes and murmured, "It's a swimsuit, not a costume."

"I don't see much difference."

Gracie reached into her purse and fingered the bottle of Ipecac she'd planned to use after lunch. One or two more times should do it to get down to her goal weight. Then she would stop. No harm. No foul.

Ingrid curved her slender hands around Gracie's forearms. "But you think you're too fat."

Aunt Ingrid's words hit like a sucker punch to the gut. Gracie hung her head. "Kind of."

"So, you stick your finger down your throat. How many times did my Dixie do that to herself? And when that didn't work, she took that horrible stuff. What you call it?"

Gracie's heart skipped. "Ipecac?"

"How many times have you used it?"

"Once."

Aunt Ingrid's hands tightened around Gracie's arms. "The truth."

"Three times—maybe four."

"Maybe? Look at me, Grace."

Gracie raised her head. Aunt Ingrid's eyes filled. "Have you ever heard of emetine cardiotoxicity?"

"No."

"Keep it up and you will. Rather, those who bury you will. It was on my daughter's autopsy report. Emetine is another name for Ipecac."

"But Dixie hadn't—"

"You're going to say she hasn't taken it for a long time since she was in hospital. How do we know? You anorexics, bulimics—however you call yourself—you're a sneaky bunch. You tell yourself, 'It won't happen to me. I'm young, I'm invincible.'" She lowered her voice and leaned into Gracie until their noses touched. "Stop it. Stop it now." She grasped the sides of Gracie's head. "Stop it while you still have thick red hair." She pressed her forehead against Gracie's. "Stop it while your cheeks bloom with health."

Chapter Forty-Eight

THE FRIDAY FOLLOWING the memorial service, Dixie's parents had come to speak to the group for a special evening meeting. Elise noted that most of the staff, including Wayne, were in attendance. Some faces she recognized from family meetings. Marissa and her parents, Felicia and her husband, and Thad and his dad were among them.

Beside her, Tony squeezed her hand. Without a word of complaint, he'd agreed to give up a Navy function. He claimed his presence here was much more important.

Leaning her head against his arm, Elise grasped a large manilla envelope that Mr. Granger had given to her before the meeting.

Tony pointed to it and whispered, "What's that?"

"Something from Dixie." Elise fingered the clasp. "Mr. Granger said they found this among Dixie's things the afternoon she died. It's addressed to me, so they didn't open it."

"Look at her message on the front." To her other side, Gracie pointed to the envelope. "Aren't you just dying to know what's in it? Open it, Momette."

"Later." Elise pressed her index finger against her lips. "Listen to the Grangers."

If the truth be told, Elise did want to rip into the envelope. What could Dixie have left her? Her last will and testament? Sage advice from her newfound knowledge of psychology? Elise didn't want anything. She longed only for her friend back at her side to navigate their way to health together.

Returning her attention to the Grangers, Elise admired their courage. Haggard and pale, Mrs. Granger stepped up to the podium. Mr. Granger joined her, his broad shoulders slumped.

"Thank you to Dr. Picard who asked us to come tonight and speak." She eyed the crowd. "Many of you are afflicted with this horrid disease known as an eating disorder. The rest of you struggle against it, as medical professionals or desperate family and friends."

Dixie had scrawled *To the amazingly talented Suzie-Q* in red marker across the front of the envelope. The words blurred. Elise sniffed.

Gracie nudged her. "Mom, are you okay?"

Wiping her eyes with the back of her hand, Elise nodded toward the front of the room. "Pay attention."

Mrs. Granger took a deep breath before continuing. "My daughter was a bright light snuffed out before her time." She paused. "Her performances wowed audiences all over the world. I was so proud of her. Too proud perhaps. You see, in my youth I was a dancer—a ballerina." She stopped to dab her eyes and nod at Dr. Picard. "My dreams of fame never materialized. According to the conservatory director in Vienna, I wasn't good enough."

Elise traced the letters on the envelope. She felt a bump under her fingertip. What could that be?

"Instead of ballet my schatzi fell in love with gymnastics." Mrs. Granger folded her hands on the podium. "Her coach told us she was Olympic gold material. So, we encouraged—no—*pushed* her. We hired tutors and made sure she never missed a practice. I lived vicariously through her. From the time she was six I monitored her every activity. I watched her diet. No sweets, no fried foods, and lots of salads.

"Once, I think when she was twelve, maybe thirteen, she snuck out of the house with a friend and went to Dairy Queen. When I found out, Gott forgive me, I paddled her and grounded her for a month."

"Can you forgive me, Gracie?" Elise hung her head.

Gracie leaned her head on her shoulder. "Don't worry, Momette, you've never been *that* bad." Then she pointed to the envelope. "Aren't you the least bit curious?"

"Gracie, please. You need to listen to the Grangers."

"I weighed her every morning." Mrs. Granger continued. "Never an ounce over one hundred pounds." She looked over at Cassie. "Forgive me for talking numbers." She glanced at Elise. "When her coach told her that her thighs were too heavy, she panicked." Mrs. Granger shifted her gaze to Gracie. "She hardly ate. And what little she did eat, she threw up. Well, you know the rest." Her voice quavered. "I beg you, parents, spouses, coaches, don't repeat my mistakes."

With that, Ingrid collapsed into her husband's arms. He swiveled his head to make eye contact with each person in the hushed audience. "I've nothing more."

Chapter Forty-Nine

After helping herself to a couple of Tootsie Rolls, Gracie sat and tucked her legs beneath her in one of Wayne's leather chairs. Noting the dark circles under her daughter's eyes, Elise refrained from questioning her about breakfast. Ingrid Granger's cautionary words still rang in her ears.

As if reading her mind, Gracie winked and raised her right hand. "I solemnly swear not to puke them up."

Wayne paced in front of his desk. Seemingly lost in thought, he folded his arms across his chest and tapped his lips with his thumb. He stopped and looked at the clock. "Is Ben going to be here this afternoon?"

Tony drummed his fingers on the arms of his chair. "He started a new job last night. He was out cold when I left for my meeting this morning."

"He dropped me off at the door and went to park the car." Gracie popped a piece of candy in her mouth. "The parking lot is really full this morning."

With a growing sense of hope, Elise smiled at Tony. "How did your meeting go this morning?"

Fingering the leather-bound book on his lap, his cheeks flushed. "Okay, I guess."

Sinking down on his desk, Wayne unwrapped a piece of candy. "Do you think the support group is helping?"

"Yeah. They're a great bunch." Tony grinned. "It's good to know I ain't the only guy on the planet who's been through the same hell."

"Atta boy, Chief! There's no shame in seeking help." Wayne shifted his red-eyed gaze from Tony to Elise. "We've all had a rough week. I had a long session with my own therapist yesterday."

A knock sounded on the door. It opened and Ben peeked around it. Elise noticed he hadn't shaved that morning. He looked exhausted. "Am I too late? I had trouble finding a parking space."

"You're right on time," said Wayne. "Come on in and pull up a chair. Let's get started. Gracie, how are you doing?"

"Mmf." She held up one finger while she finished her candy. "Ben took me out for breakfast while Daddy was at his VA meeting. I had two pancakes, scrambled eggs, and a couple of slices of bacon." She made an imaginary X across her chest. "Cross my heart. I kept it down."

Tony settled back in his chair. "You wouldn't lie to us, would you, kitten?"

Gracie pouted. "I crossed my heart, didn't I?"

Ben sank into a chair, pushing a lock of hair off his forehead. "I'll vouch for you, Sis."

Elise hunched over her pocket-size sketchbook and drew the flower vase beside Wayne, concentrating on minute details. The way the rose's petals fell, and the way fluorescent lights washed out the shadows. The conversation around her faded into background noise. "Elise!" Tony's voice jolted her. "You see what she does, Doc? It's like she's a million miles away."

"Yes. Your wife and I have discussed this tendency on numerous occasions. It's what we call the fight-or-flight response." Wayne's understanding gaze calmed Elise. "She detaches when she's uncomfortable. I'm willing to guess you've been doing this since you were a small child, Elise. Quite common for children. Her parents' fights terrified the little girl, so she crawled inside her head to escape."

"I don't get it." Tony shrugged. "We weren't fighting."

"Force of habit. In the worst cases, a victim might block out an entire childhood. When the flashbacks rage, which they often do at Elise's age, the inner child protects herself with self-destruction."

"What I don't understand is that I have vivid memories of my childhood." Elise drew up her legs and rested her chin on her knees. "How could I not remember the abuse?" She shuddered at impressions of Uncle Leo's groping hands.

"I agree with Elise." Tony frowned. "She's been through some pretty tough stuff to not remember."

"She's an artist." Wayne continued. "Her life is a pentimento."

"What the hell is a pentimento?"

Elise hugged her legs tightly to her chest. "A pentimento is a painting hidden under a painting. For whatever reason, say the artist wasn't happy with the first painting but doesn't want to waste the canvas, he paints over the first picture."

"Or because he has something to hide." Wayne raised an eyebrow. "Let me put this into perspective. When you were a young child, you went somewhere else when the abuse happened. In a sense, you painted over the ugly images. This became more difficult as you grew older, although you were still adept at revision."

Elise trembled. "That's what I did with Michael."

"Michael? Your buddy who got killed after the dance?" Tony frowned. "What about him?'

She glanced at Ben and Gracie who had stopped their antics and gave her their full attention. Debating whether to continue, she took a deep breath.

Ben stood and tugged Gracie's ponytail. "Hey Sis, let's you and I go for a walk and work off some of those pancakes. Would that be okay, Dr. Picard?"

Wayne nodded. "That's a splendid idea, if your folks agree."

Tony focused on Elise and waved to the kids. "Sure. Go ahead."

Once the door shut behind the kids, Elise returned Tony's gaze. "That's what I did. With Michael. I told myself it was my fault when..." her vision blurred "...he—he raped me."

Tony's face went from stony white to crimson. She dropped her head on her knees. "I'm sorry, Tony. Please, don't be angry with me."

A hush fell. Squinching her eyes shut, she waited for him to explode. Instead, his arms encircled her. She raised her head to see tears streaming down his face. He pulled her onto his lap. Laying her head on his chest, she wreathed her arms around his neck and breathed in the warm scents of Old Spice and soap. His heart thumped in her ears. A steady soothing beat.

After a few minutes, Tony said in a low voice, "If that little bastard hadn't already gone to his reward, I'd hunt him down and kill him myself. Listen to me, Elise, rape is *never* the victim's fault. Just ask Dr. Picard."

Wayne smiled and wrote something on his notepad. "I couldn't have said it any better, Chief."

Chapter Fifty

"THIS IS the day that the Lord hath made." Chaplain Charlie raised his hands. The backlit stained-glass panel behind him gave him a celestial appearance. "Let us rejoice and be glad in it. Does anyone have a good word of what He's done for you this week?"

Elise chewed her lower lip. Yesterday afternoon, as she had started to open Dixie's envelope, she'd received notice from the admittance department that her insurance had run out. The company refused to cover more than four weeks of treatment. She had dropped the envelope on the nightstand. This was week four.

She glared at the chaplain. *What He's done for me? Ha! I must be on his permanent ignore list.*

Beside her, open Bible on her lap, Helen flashed a radiant smile. "He's given me hope and strength to face life on my own."

A formidable man from the psych ward stood. His unkempt black hair framed a ruddy face with two days' worth of growth, which gave him the appearance of a bear. His voice boomed like a Pentecostal preacher. "God Almighty has delivered me from alcohol. Hallelujah! Been three days since I touched the stuff."

Clearing his throat, Chaplain Charlie's lips quivered. He motioned for the man to sit. "Thank you, Jason. Anyone else?"

A nurse accompanying a patient in a wheelchair yawned and shook her head. Her patient was a woman who appeared to be somewhere between eighty and a hundred. Although frail and ill, her gray eyes brimmed with life.

She patted Elise's hand. "I'm so thankful God gave me the strength to come to church this morning. It won't be long before I see my Jesus face to face."

"Thank you, Lorraine. Elise?" Chaplain Charlie shifted his gaze to her, compassion in his green eyes. "Do you have anything you want to share?"

"God's abandoned you." Annie's maniacal laughter echoed, "You're mine, Elise. I'll never let you go."

"No Suzie-Q. Don't listen to her. Stick with the program."

What program? The insurance company's cutting me off.

"Open my envelope."

"Nobody cares," Annie intoned. "Nobody."

"No, Chaplain," whispered Elise. "I've nothing to share."

After the service, Elise remained in her seat. With Dixie's absence, her room was the last place Elise wanted to go. All that remained of her friend was an envelope.

How unfair. Just when she was starting to see light at the end of the proverbial tunnel, the insurance company was going to block it. The idea of going home terrified her. It was too soon. She and Tony needed more time.

Chaplain Charlie took the chair beside her. "God cares about you, Elise. He loves you with all His heart."

"No, He doesn't." She wrung her hands. "He took Dixie. My insurance is running out."

"I have a gift for you." He held a book in his hands.

"For me. Why?" With her index finger she outlined the golden Hebrew letters which were embossed on the leather cover. "*Sefer HaB'ritot.* Book of the Covenants."

He flashed his endearing gap-toothed grin. "Indeed, it is. It's both Old and New Testament, in Hebrew and English. When I found it at a used book shop, I knew who was meant to have it." He placed it in her hands.

She opened the book to the eighth Psalm and mouthed the Hebrew words, wishing she was more proficient. *"Adonai adoneynu, mah adeer sheemkhah b'khol ha'aretz... Lord, our lord how mighty is your name over all the earth..."*

"Pretty book." Elise flipped through the pages. "Nice words. Wish I could believe them."

Chapter Fifty-One

ELISE FINISHED a snack-size bag of cheese popcorn. It tasted so good, she thought about asking for seconds. She laughed at *America's Funniest Home Videos*. However, without Dixie's silly comments, it wasn't the same. At nine, Bruno came in and turned off the television. "Time for bed, folks. Back at the daily grind tomorrow."

Back in her room, Elise undressed and stared at her reflection. She could almost hear Dixie tell her how skinny she was, even though she wouldn't believe it. Maybe someday she would.

Slipping on her nightgown, Elise blinked back tears. With a sidelong glance at the manila envelope on the nightstand, she pulled back the covers and slipped into bed. She reached over and stuffed the envelope into the drawer. Out of sight, out of mind.

She had almost drifted off when the door opened. "Knock, knock. May we come in?"

Elise turned to see Helen, suitcase in hand, beside Cassie in the doorway. "Do I have a choice?"

"Nope." Leading Helen to Dixie's bed, Cassie's expression reflected mixed emotions. "We're getting two new patients this week. Helen's your new roommate."

Helen set her suitcase on the bed and opened it. "I'm looking forward to getting to know you better, Elise. I've been kind of lonely since Felicia left."

Lying back against her pillows, Elise folded her arms behind her head. "Afraid you'll be alone again by the end of the week. My insurance won't pay for more treatment. And now that Gracie's coming for the day program..." A sob caught in her throat.

Cassie dropped open her mouth. "Say what? I was afraid of this. Child, you are in no way ready to go home. Surely Dr. Picard can make a case for you."

"He tried. Said he couldn't get to first base with them."

"I'm sorry, sugar." Cassie smoothed Elise's covers. "I'll bring you something to help you sleep. We'll talk some more in the morning."

Helen changed into her pajamas and crawled into bed. "I'm here for you, Elise." She turned off her lamp.

Cassie returned with a pill. Elise swallowed it. Then she curled up on her side and shut her eyes waiting for the med to send her to oblivion. Cassie turned off the light and left the room, shutting the door behind her.

A couple of hours later Elise lay on her back, staring into the darkness. Helen's rhythmic breathing with intermittent snores only added to her mind's restless wandering. Her tears dribbled into her ears.

Just when I make a little bit of progress, bam! The rug's yanked out from under me. Wham! Kicked to the curb like so much trash. If only Dixie—it's not fair. I'm six years older than she was. I'm the one who should've died. Oh God, I don't want to die.

Elise rolled over onto her side and opened the nightstand drawer, trying to keep it from squeaking. In the dark, she found the unopened envelope. Taking it out, she shut the drawer. As she did so, she knocked a half-full water glass to the floor. The envelope fell from her fingers.

Helen bolted upright and cried out. "Don't hit me!" She covered her head with her arms as if to ward off a blow.

Opening her eyes, she breathed a relieved sigh and pushed her hair out of her face. "What a dream." She turned to Elise. "Did I wake you?"

"More like the other way around." Elise switched on her light. She rolled out of bed and dropped to the floor to rescue Dixie's envelope from the puddle. "I woke you with my clumsiness. Thank goodness the glass didn't break."

"Can't you sleep, honey?" Helen swung her legs over the side of the bed. "You stay put. I'll go fetch a towel. I have to use the john anyway."

Elise dabbed the damp edges of the envelope with her nightgown hem. Helen returned with the promised towel and knelt to sop up the water. "I hope whatever's in that envelope wasn't ruined." Sitting back on her haunches, Helen patted Elise's arm.

"I only met her a month ago." Elise hugged the envelope. "Yet I feel like I've known her all my life."

"From watching the two of you, I suspect the feeling was mutual. What's in the envelope?"

"I don't know. It's from Dixie."

"Open it."

"I—can't."

"Aren't you the least bit curious?"

"I'm afraid."

"Of what?"

"I'm not sure."

"Oy vey, this position is death to my creaky old knees." Helen grasped the bed and eased herself up onto it. She patted the mattress. "Come sit. What've you got to lose?"

"Not my dignity, that's for sure." Clutching the envelope, Elise joined Helen. "I lost that the day I nosedived in the store and they brought me here."

"You'll have to tell me about that."

"I took a bunch of—"

"Later. Open that thing. I'm here for you if you need moral support."

Taking a deep breath, Elise held the envelope for a second and exhaled through her nose. She contemplated Dixie's swooping, slightly smudged writing. *To the amazingly talented Suzie-Q*. She turned the envelope over, pried up the edges of the clasp, and lifted the flap. "It's a photograph." She pulled it out. As she did so, a folded note on pink stationery and a ring dropped onto her lap.

Elise slid it onto her right ring finger. Perfect fit. The sapphire, surrounded by diamond chips, sparkled.

"Gorgeous!" Helen reached for her eyeglasses on the nightstand and leaned in for a closer look. "You should wear it in good health."

"You sound like my mom. Are you Jewish?"

"Italian. Roman Catholic. But I grew up in a predominately Jewish neighborhood in Brooklyn."

"That's where my Dad was from."

"Would ya quit stalling? Lemme see that picture. It's autographed."

Elise held it at arm's length. Dixie balanced on one leg. Her other leg, parallel to her upper body, was braced by Dixie's grasp around her ankle. Her toes pointing to the ceiling, she reached her free arm straight out in front. Despite the intense concentration evident on her face, her effervescent personality shone through.

Helen read the note on the photo aloud, "'Suzie-Q, you've been blessed with so many gifts and God has definitely chosen for you to live. You're so beautiful inside and out. Your friend always, Dixie Granger.' She spelled it d-e-f-i-n-a-t-e-l-y."

"She couldn't spell her way out of a paper bag. I teased her about it all the time. She'd laugh it off and say she'd pay me big bucks to edit her doctoral thesis." Elise unfolded the pink note. The cramped, almost unreadable handwriting lacked Dixie's usual dramatic flair.

Dear Elise,

I really thought I'd beaten the odds, but as you no by now, I didn't. The doctors at Menninger's warned me there mite come a time my body couldn't recover. ~~Too bad~~. I wish I'd listened. ~~Ironik,~~ Crazy isn't it? I finally decide I want to live. Don't laff at ~~my sepling~~ spelling. I'm so tired I cant think strait and I feel like I could thro up. Maybe a hot shower will ~~rejoovinate~~ wake me up. One last time, Suzie-Q. Please. Please, pull your head out

of your butt and get healthy before Its to late. Ware our birthstone and think of me.

All my luv, strenth and hope,
Your friend,
Dixie Dawn Granger

Chapter Fifty-Two
Tony

After switching off the TV, Tony set the remote aside. The kids had both gone to bed. Tony could hear Ben's snoring all the way down the hall. It was good to have his son home.

Tony took a swig of beer and opened his journal. Hank was right. Writing his thoughts did help. Good thing no one was correcting his chicken scratching or his grammar. He chuckled. "Gramatacide," is what Elise called it.

Thinking back to the session in Dr. Picard's office, Tony poised his pen over the blank page. Twenty-five years of marriage and Elise had never once mentioned that little creep had raped her. When he'd griped about it, Hank pointed out that Tony hadn't told Elise much about Frankie or Kieu. No argument there.

He wrote,

> *I guess leave the past in the past don't work so good. It's really coming back to bite us. If Michael Gordon was still alive, I'd put a bullet through his thick skull. He seemed like a good kid. Stupid me, I even suggested when we had Ben that we name him Michael Benjamin. No wonder Elise got so upset. I'd never of*

guessed it of Michael. Always polite—and Jewish. Don't forget Jewish. The kind of boy her mother wanted her to marry. Not a rough around the edges, piece of trailer park trash like me.

Now my baby girl's trying to be skinny like her mother. If that ain't bad enough, Elise is going to have to come home next week. Damned insurance company won't pay. If she dies, it'll be on their heads.

Tonight Ben called and asked if I could pick him up from work. He had to leave his Beetle in the shop.

Tony stopped and looked at his watch. Oh three hundred hours. More like this morning. He remembered the used Volkswagen he'd bought for Elise always had problems. She used to say the car was Hitler incarnate and knew there was a Jew at the wheel.

I got to Kelly's at 01:30 and had a cold one while I waited for his shift to end. It gave me a chance to watch Ben in action. Never would've figured him for a chick magnet, but they do like to flirt with him. One even slipped him her phone number on a napkin. I saw him toss it in the trash after she left.

Setting his pen down, Tony thought back on his conversation with Ben. He couldn't remember a time they had spoken so freely.

He picked up the pen and continued to write.

We just got home an hour ago. Some of the things Ben had to say hurt like a punch to the gut. But I did what Hank said. I kept my pie hole shut and listened.

"It's always about the money, Ben says. The hardship—on you. What about us? Mom's eating disorder might kill her. Gracie's headed down the same path. And all you can talk about

is your burden? Then he jumps out of the cab and slams the door.

"I felt like punching his lights out. Instead, I got out of the truck and ran after him. What else could I do? I sat on the stoop and cried like a baby and told him over and over how sorry I was.

"Then Ben sits next to me and he's crying, too. I hugged him and kissed him like I should have when he was a little boy. I tell him how much I love him.

"He hugs me back and lays a sloppy wet one on my cheek and says, I love you, too, Dad.

"Benjamin. Son of my right hand is what the Bible says it means. I ask myself how many years have I wasted? I'll admit, God in Heaven if you're reading this, I'm scared spitless. I'm more than scared. I'm terrified.

Chapter Fifty-Three

ELISE SET the envelope with Dixie's picture at the bottom of her suitcase. "I'll have to get a nice frame for it." With a sigh, she tossed a mesh bag of dirty clothes on top of it. "Looks like the first thing I'll have to do when I get home is laundry."

"I hate to see you go." Helen unfolded one of Elise's T-shirts and read the message printed on it. "'Escaped mom. Don't tell anyone you saw me.' I could've used this one when my spawn from hell was growing up."

"Tell me about it. Gracie was my tantrum thrower. Ben just gave me the silent treatment. What brought you here, Helen?"

"My sister, who came to help me tie up loose ends after my divorce. I went into a deep depression. Couldn't sleep, couldn't eat, and tried twice to overdose."

"I'm glad she brought you here."

"This place has been a godsend. But I feel guilty since I don't exactly have an eating disorder. But Dr. Picard thought I'd get the best care on this floor. He was right you know." Helen picked up Elise's sketchbook. "Don't forget this."

Taking it from her, Elise thumbed through the pages until she came to the last sketch she'd started for her story. It was a golden-haired angel with a rainbow circling her head. She held a bouquet of daffodils. "I guess I'll finish the pictures on my breaks at work since I'll have to return the airbrush. I could use an angel right now."

"Do you believe in angels, Elise?"

"Not anymore. Do you?"

"Yes, I do."

"How can you say that, after all you've been through?"

"I'm here, aren't I?"

Elise closed the sketchbook, set it on top of her clothes, and forced a smile. "I'll still be able to see Dr. Picard and Pam in their offices. The insurance will at least pay for a few more visits." She choked back a sob. "Poor Tony's so stressed over our finances. He's working so hard on his own recovery, I'm afraid this will cause a major setback for him."

Helen gathered her purse from the dresser. "You're worried about going back to him, aren't you? Seriously, I don't think you have anything to worry about. He's a good man who worships the ground you walk on." She fished out a pen and a small notepad and wrote on the top page. "I'll be going back to St. Louis with my sister when I'm released. But if you need me, don't hesitate to call—collect."

Terry peeked around the door. "Helen, you're late for art therapy."

Helen shrugged and winked at Elise. "At least part of the competition won't be there. But there's still your daughter, who makes me look just as bad." She embraced Elise and kissed her cheek. "Remember what I said, my friend."

As Helen left the room, Terry beckoned to Elise. "There's someone here to see you. They're waiting for you in Dr. Picard's office. He said to tell you it's urgent."

Tucking Helen's number in the pocket of her blue jeans, Elise walked down the hall toward Wayne's office, afraid of what the next bomb dropped on her would be. Had Gracie ruptured her esophagus? Maybe Ben crashed his crummy little Beetle. She dragged her feet as a thousand horrible scenarios raced through her head. The closed door loomed large before her. As she grasped the doorknob, light glinted off the sapphire ring.

"You got this, Suzie-Q."

"Dixie?" Elise swiveled her head to look over each shoulder. Save the nurses at their station, the hallway was empty. "Great. Now I'm hallucinating." She pulled open the door.

Wayne rose from behind his desk, arms open in welcome and a broad smile on his face. "Come in, Elise."

Tony greeted her before she could fully enter the room and engulfed her in his arms, pressing his lips against hers.

A familiar voice behind her said, "Gut morning, Elise."

She whipped around to see Ingrid Granger. Slipping Dixie's ring off her finger, she held it out. "If you're looking for this, Mrs. Granger, I didn't steal it. It was in the envelope your husband gave me."

"*Nein, nein.* Put it back on your finger where it belongs." Mrs. Granger pointed to the chair next to Tony. "Please, have a seat. And please, you call me Ingrid."

Sinking into the chair, Elise glanced at Wayne, who nodded his agreement. She pushed the ring back over her knuckle.

"Dixie—no—*I* want you to have the ring. It was her birthstone. She was born September fourth, 1959." Ingrid's eyes misted. "She would be thirty-seven this year."

Elise squeezed Tony's hand. "I'll be forty-three on the same day."

"You see? It's meant to be. I suppose I should cut to the chase, as Dixie would say, and tell you why I'm here. I've been told you are having financial difficulty. *Jah?*"

Tony's face flushed from the neck up. "Ain't there something in the books about patient confidentiality?" He turned to Elise; one eyebrow raised. "You been hanging out our dirty linens again?"

Wayne cleared his throat. "I'll take the blame for the violation. Please, Chief Reeves, hear Mrs. Granger's proposition. If you don't like what she has to say, then feel free to slug me. You won't be the first."

"I will require your consent, of course." Taking a folder from her bag, Ingrid fixed her eyes on Tony for a moment and then shifted her gaze to Elise. "Every time we spoke with Dixie over the past few weeks, all she could talk about was Elise this and Elise that. How beautiful. How talented. She told me she wanted to get well so she could help you get well, too. You gave her something to live for."

Elise's face blazed. "Me?"

"*You.* And she mentioned more than once how your insurance had failed you before and was likely to fail you again." Ingrid opened the folder and handed Tony a stack of forms from the admissions office. "All you both have to do is sign these forms authorizing Jim and me to assume financial responsibility for you and your daughter for as long as you require treatment in this facility."

Tony's eyes widened and filled with tears. They spilled over as he inspected the forms. His hand shook as he took a pen from his polo shirt pocket. "Are you—sure?"

"Surer than I've ever been of anything, Chief Reeves. Jim and I have more money than we know what to do with. What we don't have is our only child. Allow us to honor her memory." She raised her face toward the ceiling. "Nothing would make her happier."

Tony signed the forms and offered them to Elise. "What do you say, hon?"

Elise wiggled her hand, so the light made Dixie's ring sparkle. "I'd say I have an angel looking out for me."

Chapter Fifty-Four
Tony

TONY PEEKED over Ben's shoulder and breathed in the aroma from the clay pot on the stove. "I have to admit, it smells great. I can't tell what it's supposed to be or what it started out as though."

Ben stirred in chopped green onions to the pungent concoction. "Cá kho to."

"You do and you'll clean it up."

"I knew you were going to say that," Ben glowered at him for a moment, then turned back to his cooking, "and it's caramelized catfish."

"Am I that predictable?"

Gracie giggled as she set the table. "Yep, Poppo. You most definitely, most certainly, are. I've heard you say that a plethora of times."

"Listen to you." Tony tiptoed behind her and dug his fingers into her ribs. "Did my baby girl swallow a dictionary?"

Shrieking with laughter, she wrestled out of his grasp. "Help me, Benny!"

"Sorry sis, you're on your own. By the way, wasn't Mom supposed to be coming home today? Or did I hear it wrong?"

"No, you heard it right." Tony took a beer out of the refrigerator and popped the top. "Change of plans. I'll tell you over dinner."

"Does everything have to be a production with you, Dad?" Ben rolled his eyes and lifted a wooden spoon to his lips. "Mm. Almost done. As long as you're in the neighborhood, there's a plate of spring rolls in the fridge. Would you mind taking them out? There's also a plate of cilantro and bean sprouts for garnish."

"Yessir!" Tony saluted. His stomach growled. "I guess I'll give this fish stuff a try. Although I prefer my catfish rolled in cornmeal and fried."

Ben's grimace conveyed his disgust. "I don't know why I'm bothering."

Gracie wrinkled her nose and shuddered. "With great big globs of tartar sauce. Ugh."

"Mm-mm, good eats." Tony rubbed his stomach and tugged one of her russet curls. "Tell me, son. When did you become such a chef?"

Ben's cheeks colored. "I like to cook, that's all." He scowled at Tony.

"Don't go getting so defensive. I didn't mean nothing by it."

Taking a deep breath, Ben turned back to the stove. "If you must know, my girlfriend, well *ex*-girlfriend, taught me to make this dish. She's Vietnamese."

"No kidding? Bet she makes a mean pho."

"You're familiar with it?"

"First ate the real thing in the land of rice paddies and snipers." Kieu's scarred face and gap-toothed smile popped into Tony's head. "None better."

"Anh's grandmother in Ho Chi Minh City taught her how to cook." Ben's tense jaw relaxed. Putting the pot on a trivet in the middle of the table, he smiled "You haven't lived until you've tasted *her* pho."

"Come with me, Joe. Má make you best pho in Saigon."

Tony blinked.

This is no time for flashbacks.

He forced a smile. "If you say so, son."

Ben sat and motioned for Tony and Gracie to sit. "Dig in."

On impulse, Tony reached for his children's hands. "If you two don't mind, I'd like to say grace."

"That's my name, don't wear it out." Gracie snickered then bowed her head and squeezed Tony's hand. "Sorry."

Tony cleared his throat. "Lord, thank You for this food. Bless it to the nourishment of our bodies. And thank You for what You're doing for this family. In Jesus's name. Amen."

A pot boiled over on the stove. Ben jumped up and turned off the burner. "I forgot about the sticky rice."

Gracie spooned fish and sauce onto her plate. "Looks like it's going to be stucky-to-the-pan rice."

"Yuckety-yuck-yuck." Ben lifted the lid. "It's mostly okay. The pan's going to need a good soak." He scooped out three servings. "Dare I say, overnight?"

Tony rolled his chopsticks between his thumb and forefinger. "Will it offend you if I use a fork? Even over in Nam, I couldn't get the hang of these."

Taking his seat at the table, Ben twisted his lips to one side. "As long as you don't use ketchup."

In mock frustration, Tony snorted. "Well, if you're going to be that way." He dipped his spring roll in pepper sauce and bit into it. The commingled flavors of shrimp, cabbage, cilantro and rice melted on his tongue. "Not bad."

"Da-ad." Gracie made a face and dropped open her mouth. Rice and fish cascaded over her lips onto her plate. "Please! Don't talk with your mouth full."

Pursing his lips, Tony swallowed with an exaggerated gulp. "I ain't that bad, am I?"

Ben snagged a bit of fish with his chopsticks, eyes on his plate. "Um… yeah, Dad, you kind of are."

Defensive irritation threatened Tony's good mood. He mixed the rice with the caramelized fish. After being careful to chew and swallow with his mouth closed, he turned to Gracie. "How'd your mom do at lunch today?"

"Okay. They ordered in pizza for us and she managed to eat a whole piece." Gracie sipped her tea. "She seemed happier than I've seen in a while."

"You two have been grinning like a couple of Cheshire cats all evening." Ben wielded one of his chopsticks like a sword, poking Gracie in her side. "Will somebody please tell me what's going on?"

"What's going on is," Tony dunked another spring roll in pepper sauce, "your mom and sister have a benefactor."

"Dixie's parents are paying all of our hospital bills." Gracie clapped her hands. Then she pressed her finger against her lips. "But, you can't tell a soul. Aunt Ingrid wants it to be a secret."

"Miracle of miracles!" Ben raised his hands toward the ceiling. "But, if you ask me, the real miracle will be keeping Gabby Gracie's mouth shut."

Tony set the remote on the end table and looked at his watch. Twenty-three hundred hours. Almost midnight. The kids had long since gone to bed. After watching an old Chuck Norris movie, he turned off the television and opened his journal. He searched the coffee table for a pen and found one hidden under a stack of Gracie's sketches.

Picking up one of her drawings, he studied it. She had used colored markers to draw a graceful mermaid with a colorful tail. Her red hair floated around her. "Well, I'll be, she's almost as good as her mom."

He took the pen and turned back to the open journal on his lap. "Been a few days. What should I write?"

> 30 March 1996
> I can't believe I'm taking handouts. ~~Means I ain't~~ I feel like I ain't holding up my end of the deal. My God-fearing Gramma would say it's pride. Okay, I give up. Who am I to look a gift horse in the mouth? Thanks, God.
> It's been a good night with the kids. Gracie and Ben washed the dishes. We watched television.

Looking over what he'd written, Tony muttered, "This is like the papers we used write at the beginning of the school year, 'What I did on my summer vacation.' Good thing I ain't getting a grade for this." He started another paragraph.

My son's a great cook. We had a nice evening tonight, but I can tell he's still pissed at me. I reckon I don't blame him. I didn't mean to turn into my old man, but I guess I kinda did.

"All the Vietnamese food tonight sure did bring back memories. I wish I could of saved Kieu. When you come right down to it we didn't do nothing over there except kill a lotta people. We sure as hell didn't save the country from the Commies.

"I remember the night patrol when Steve Kowalski bought it. Figure the odds. Seems like every war movie I saw as a kid had a Kowalski. Steve was a big fella. Real gung-ho war hero type. The VC shot him so full of holes there wasn't much to put in a box and send home to his wife and kid. We—

The phone on the end table rang. Tony startled, sending a jagged line across the page. "Who the holy hell is calling at this hour." He yanked the phone from the charger. "Hello?"

"Is Benjamin Reeves there?"

"Young lady, do you realize what time it is?"

"Oh, I'm sorry. I forgot, it's only noon here."

"Noon? You wouldn't be calling from—?"

"It's okay, I'll call back later."

Tony looked up to see Ben hovering over him, ready to make a grab for the phone. Tony nodded. "He's right here, Miss."

Ben trembled as he held the phone to his ear. "Hello—Anh?" His smile lit up his face as he rubbed his eyes. "Slow down, I can't understand you.... Hey that's great. When?" He paced back and forth, his expressions reflecting his changing emotions. "Oh, sorry to hear that. When's the funeral?... He did? Seriously?... What about your mom?" He snatched the pen from Tony. "Flight number? What time should I pick you up?" With a sidelong glance, Ben lowered his voice. "I love you, too, and I trust you implicitly, *nguoi yeu.*" He kissed the phone and set it back in the charger. With a faraway smile, he sank down in the recliner across from the sofa.

Tony cleared his throat. "I thought she was your ex."

"Not anymore. She'll be here next Wednesday. Our relationship is back on."

"Why'd you break up in the first place?"

"Her grandma was dying of cancer and wanted to die in Vietnam. Anh's parents insisted she go with them. She wasn't sure for how long or if she'd be able to return or not. We had a huge fight the night before she left." Ben paused and combed his fingers through his hair. "They wanted to take her to a matchmaker so she could marry a nice Vietnamese guy."

"I take it Granny passed on and that changed things."

"When did you get to be so perceptive, Dad? I never thought Anh would stand up to her mother, but she did. Told her folks she's an American woman in love with an American man. I can't believe they not only relented but supported her decision."

Tony shut his journal and propped his feet up on the coffee table. "I guess I'd best get used to spring rolls and cá kho to."

"Wait 'til you taste her fried chicken with mashed potatoes and gravy."

Chapter Fifty-Five

A FEW DAYS had passed since Ingrid Granger's stunning proposition. She had asked permission to sit in on Elise's next session. Elise readily granted it. Ingrid's eyes glistened with tears as she held Elise in her penetrating gaze. "Promise me you'll work on your recovery."

Elise drew an invisible x on her chest. "Cross my heart."

Could she keep her promise? Her apprehension mounted. What was it they said in support group? "One day at a time." Sometimes "one minute at a time" and, in her case, "one bite at a time."

"You're going to get so fat; you'll look like Aunt Vivian." Annie sang, *"Big butt, big breasts, big cheeks, oh wo-on't that be loverly?"*

Elise twisted and untwisted the hem of her purple T-shirt. Wayne pointed to the white letters on it and read aloud, "'Denial, it's not a river in Egypt.' Cute. Where'd you find that? I need to order a few for some of my other patients."

"They had a gift shop at Elmwood Psychiatric where I spent my first three hospitalizations."

"Oh, my dear." Ingrid clucked her tongue. "Three times?" She sank into a chair. Elise sat beside her.

"Hopefully, this will be her last hospitalization." Wayne settled into the wingback chair opposite Elise, laying a folder in his lap. "You're one smart cookie, Elise. You're as witty and as gifted as anyone I've ever met. In fact, your sharp sense of humor might be what's kept you from jumping off a cliff."

"Not to mention, I'm terrified of heights."

"Touché." He glanced at the picture of his sister. "Yet, with all of your gifts and talents, you don't think you're worthy. You don't see yourself as anything special. Why?"

"Why indeed," tutted Ingrid.

Elise folded her hands, rotating her thumbs in a frantic choreography, unsure of how to answer them. Her artistic abilities had always been a part of her life and not necessarily a positive part. In elementary school, her classmates had called her a showoff. In high school, fellow students thought nothing of hitting her up to paint banners or draw cartoons for the school paper without offering friendship.

When she went to the Kansas City Art Institute, she didn't fit their mold. Her art was looked down upon as nothing more than "illustration."

Church friends were always asking her to work on decorations for social functions or pictures for the children's classes. No one offered any kind of remuneration. After all, it was easy for her. She should think of it as her ministry.

"Why don't you see yourself as anything special?" Wayne repeated.

Elise shrugged. "I don't know."

"Yes, I think you do. Without the insurance company breathing down our necks, we're going to work on your self-esteem issues." He checked his watch. "If I'm not mistaken, you have an art therapy session next."

Hugging her sketchbook, Elise stood. Ingrid rose from her chair and embraced her. "*Meine schöne tochter.* My beautiful daughter. I'm expecting a return on my investment. Make my Dixie proud. And tell Annie to shut her mouth."

Pam looked over Elise's picture of the angel. "This illustration is simply charming. I love the way you're integrating the different media between your pen and ink, colored pencils, and air brush. Have you written any more of the story to go with it?"

Elise opened her notebook and handed it to Pam, who put on her readers attached to a chain around her neck. "I already read this part. Ah, here's where I left off.

"'Elise felt lonely. Lonelier than she'd ever been. She and Hope the Pixie tried again to pull off the mask, but their effort was in vain.

"'Elise closed her eyes, tears oozing from them. She was a prisoner within herself.'

"Well put. This is sheer genius!"

"Genius?" Heat rose from Elise's neck to her forehead. "Maybe I am, after all."

"Don't go getting swellheaded on me." Pam peered over her glasses. "Where was I?—'Once more the daffodils sprayed magic dust into the air. Hope and Elise drank in the wonderful aroma from the bright yellow blossoms.

"'A soft, almost musical voice startled the child. "Don't be sad, Elise."

"'She opened her eyes and gaped at a golden-haired girl with eyes the color of a summer sky and dazzling silver wings. "I'm your guardian angel. My name is Cherish. Your Heavenly Father sees you're in trouble and sent me to help you."

"'Elise trembled. "Is He mad at me for taking something that doesn't belong to me? Will he yell at me?"

"'The angel laughed a laugh that tinkled like windchimes. "No, dear one. He loves you so much and only wants the best for you."

"'Elise's heart leaped for joy. "Can you take this mask off my face? It hurts."'

"That's it?" Pam pouted. "I want more. Get to work! You have to finish this draft before you're discharged." She shut the notebook, her gray eyes sparkling. "I'm so pleased *your* guardian angel bought you some extra time."

"You know about that?"

"The whole staff knows about the gift. Wayne won't divulge who's behind it, but we all have a pretty good idea." She returned Elise's notebook. "You're making progress. I expect a signed copy when it's published."

Chapter Fifty-Six

Supper weighed like a lump of iron on Elise's stomach. She made a mental list of all she'd eaten. Roast chicken breast, no skin. Baked potato with a dab of butter. Green beans. Salad with Italian dressing. Whole wheat dinner roll with butter—*that* was the deal breaker. Ronnie had insisted it was part of a "normal" meal. Despite her trepidation, the food had tasted good.

Curled up on the sofa beside Helen, Elise hugged her knees and tapped her feet against the cushions. How much exercise would it take to burn all those calories?

Helen reached over and pressed her palm against Elise's foot. "Stop it! You're giving me motion sickness."

Propping her elbow on the arm of the couch, Elise rested her chin on her hand and tucked her toes under the sofa cushions. The EDU lounge TV lit up with *Touched by an Angel*. At least it was a show she liked. The episode, "Portrait of Mrs. Campbell", resonated with Elise, particularly when Tess likened the characters to a pentimento.

On screen, Monica revealed her true identity to Mrs. Campbell. Elise mimicked her Irish accent when she said, "I'm an angel sent by Gawd…"

Helen poked Elise's thigh with her big toe. "Shh!"

Monica continued, "… fear has no place in your life."

"Are you listening, Suzie-Q?"

Cassie appeared in the doorway and motioned to Elise. "You have a visitor."

"On Sunday night?" Elise rose and tiptoed across the room, careful not to block anyone's view. "Visiting hours are over."

"I know," said Cassie. "But she insisted. Says she's family and it's urgent."

Elise followed Cassie to the visitor's lounge. Family? Mom and Dad were both deceased. Eugene and his wife Arlene lived in Virginia. If something had happened to him, Arlene would've called.

A far cry from the little nuisance she had been as a child, Elise's cousin had grown into a slender, attractive woman in her late thirties. Elegantly attired, Nancy looked up from a table in the corner. Her narrow cheeks flushed as she stood and embraced Elise. Nancy's heavy perfume threatened to suffocate Elise.

She stiffened. "Nancy. How'd you know I was here?"

"I called your house. Your daughter told me."

That's my Gabby Gracie. Be fair. Nancy's family. Why wouldn't she tell her?

"Of course. What's up?"

Nancy's face crumpled. "It's Daddy. He's here in ICU. His liver. Cirrhosis. His doctor gives him a few more hours, a day at the most."

Good. I hope the old guzzler's in excruciating pain.

Elise hoped her face didn't reflect her thoughts. "I'm so—sorry."

Nancy sank back down in her chair and reached for Elise's hand. "He's asking for you."

"Why?"

"You're his niece."

"So?"

"For Heaven's sake, Elise. Can't you let bygones be bygones?"

Bygones? He should rot in hell for what he did to me.

Studying her cousin's face, Elise noted her resemblance to Aunt Viv —the thinner version. She hadn't seen Nancy since Aunt Viv's funeral ten years ago. Her aunt's obesity had caught up with her. After having both legs amputated due to her diabetes, she had stroked out. Elise remembered feeling like a hypocrite attending the memorial. She hadn't spoken to the old battle-ax since her own mother's funeral five years before.

She would never forget Nancy's theatrics during Aunt Viv's service. Huge crocodile tears and loud sobs on her brother's shoulder. At the same time, Dan had sat motionless beside her in his dress Army uniform, his face a blank slate.

Elise searched for something to say. "Is Dan with Uncle Leo?"

Nancy pursed her lips. "You know he's stationed in Germany."

"How would I know? No one's communicated with me in ten years. Did you know Ben graduated from Harvard? With honors. Or that Gracie's an Olympic-class swimmer?"

"I should've known you'd get all defensive, 'Lise. You always were."

A knot formed in Elise's stomach. "Can't Dan get a hardship leave?"

"He refused to request one." Nancy dabbed her nose. "He told me I could use Dad for fertilizer because that's all he was ever good for."

Elise bit her lip.

I always loved Danny. Poetic justice. Couldn't happen to a nicer guy. At long last, Uncle Letch-O is getting his comeuppance.

"I'm not allowed to leave the unit." Elise looked over her shoulder at Cassie for confirmation. "Give your daddy my regards."

To her dismay, Cassie said, "We make exceptions for family emergencies whenever possible."

Uncle Leo's heart monitor beeped erratically, the display's graph showing deep valleys and sharp peaks. His blood pressure dipped from eighty over sixty to, at times, fifty over thirty. The hospital gown swallowed his once muscular shoulders.

Elise remembered him at Aunt Viv's funeral. Robust, with his ever-predatory grin, he had seemed less than grief-stricken. Even beside his departed wife's casket, he'd pinched Elise's behind as she went by. She would never forget the way he'd licked his lips and eyed her chest. "Bodacious as ever."

Back in the present, he opened his jaundiced eyes. "'Lise, my—girl-friend." He lifted a trembling hand. She linked her fingers behind her back. "I—understand. Won't—blame you—" he gasped, "—if you—hate me."

Nancy shoved Elise aside and bent over him. "Save your strength, Daddy."

He frowned. "So like your—mother. Get away—from—me, Viv. Elise…" He beckoned her. "You're—a good—girl. You always were—a good girl." He reached for her hand. "Please—forgive—"

Taking a step backward, Elise resisted the urge to slap a dying man.

His blood pressure dropped from fifty over thirty to thirty over twenty. His hand fell to his side. A straight line replaced the peaks and valleys on the monitor. Eyes rolling back, he arched his back and his breath whistled through his open mouth.

Elise shambled down the hallway toward her room beside Cassie, her thoughts like tattered paper on the wind.

Weak with exhaustion, Elise asked, "What time is it?"

Cassie checked her watch. "Five past eleven."

"Don't you mean twenty-three hundred hours?"

"Either way it's way past your bedtime." Cassie stopped at the nurse's station. "I'll be in in a few to check on you."

Elise pulled open the door, trying to be as quiet as possible. Helen sat up in bed, a book propped on her knees. "Are you okay?"

"I will be." Elise noted her nightgown laid out on the bed and the covers pulled back. "Thanks, Helen. You spoil me."

"Every gal needs spoiling once in a while. You look like you've been dragged through a knothole."

"Feel like it, too." Slipping off her clothes, Elise let them fall to the floor in a heap. She donned her gown and crawled into bed. Letting her head sink into her pillow, she yawned. "I'll brush my teeth in the morning."

Helen turned off the light over her bed. "Pleasant dreams, roomie."

Elise had almost drifted off when Cassie entered the room, medicine cup in one hand and flashlight in the other. "I almost forgot your evening meds."

"Stereotypical." Elise sat up. "Nurse wakes patient to give her a sleeping pill."

"Just doing my job, ma'am." Cassie's gaze lingered on Elise while she waited for her to swallow the pill. "Do you need me for anything else?"

Before Elise could reply, Cassie's pager went off. "I've gotta take this. I'll be right back." She hurried from the room.

Elise lay back, wide awake. Folding her arms behind her head, she stared at the ceiling. mulling over the events of the past four hours.

Where was the sense of victory? Nancy's melodramatic shrieks played over and over in Elise's mind.

Appearances had always been important to her cousin. Determined to be nothing like her mother, Nancy had forged a career as an actress. The irony of her starring in a couple of porno films didn't escape Elise. At any rate, Nancy married a successful stuntman and now enjoyed the affluence his alimony provided.

Helen's voice broke through Elise's musings. "I heard about your uncle. Want to talk about it?"

"Good news travels fast, doesn't it? There's nothing left to say except, ding-dong the wicked old letch is dead."

Chapter Fifty-Seven

"Wake-up, sleepyhead."

Elise rubbed the grit from her eyes and coaxed them open to see Helen clad in a hospital gown, with another gown in her hand. "You wouldn't want to miss vitals."

Pulling the covers over her head, Elise moaned. "Go ahead. I'll be along in a few."

"Suit yourself." Helen's fuzzy slippers made shuffling noises across the floor. "I put your gown on the dresser." The door shut.

Elise rolled onto her back. "Vitals shmitals. Blood pressure, ninety over sixty, temp, ninety-seven point three, weight, two hundred fifty. I'd better get up before the Gestapo swoops in."

She sat up and swung her legs over the side of the bed. Jagged light shimmered in her left eye, obscuring her vision. Heaving an angry sigh, she padded to the bathroom. "At least my migraines aren't as bad as some. As soon as the aura passes, I'll be hunky dory. Right? Of course, right. Always talk to yourself, Elise?"

Her stomach roiled. "Oooh no." Dropping to her knees beside the toilet, she threw up until she had nothing left but dry heaves. She laid her head on the cool porcelain and groaned.

"Elise?"

She opened her eyes to see Cassie kneeling beside her. Elise forced a smile. "Just a migraine. It'll pass."

"No 'just' about it. I get those, too. Nasty animals, aren't they?" Cassie pressed her cool palm against Elise's cheek. "No fever. But I don't think you're going to make it to breakfast this morning. Let's get you back to bed. Then I'll go get you some 7Up and saltines."

Shivering, Elise draped her arm around Cassie's shoulder. Cassie helped her to her feet. Elise's stomach growled. How could she be nauseated and hungry at the same time? "May I have some hot tea instead? And maybe a soft-boiled egg and dry toast—rye or whole wheat."

Cassie tucked the covers around Elise and laid a cool washcloth over her eyes. "Listen to you, girlfriend. Never thought I'd hear you ask for food."

"It's what my mom used to make for me when I was sick."

"I'll call Ronnie and see if she can't make that breakfast happen." Cassie clicked off the overhead light. "You don't need that. I'll see if I can't get the doctor on call to authorize some meds for that headache. You try to rest."

Pain shot through the right side of Elise's head. She shut her eyes against the welcome darkness and curled up on her side. "So much for not as bad as some."

The sound of Helen's slippers shuffled back into the room. The bathroom light clicked. Head pounding, Elise slipped the washcloth off her face and opened her eyes. She squinted.

"It's okay, Helen, you don't have to be quiet. I'm awake."

Helen pulled on a pair of stretch pants and then slipped a tunic over her head. Sitting on her bed, she brushed and braided her waist-length hair. The light from the bathroom formed a halo around her head. "Cassie told me. I understand. I used to get Allen-induced migraines on a regular basis. I'm no diagnostician, but I'm willing to bet yours is stress-related. Poor kid. You've been through hell and back lately."

"I'm glad Uncle Leo's dead." Elise put one arm behind her head and the other over her eyes to block out the light. "My cousin Nancy the drama queen. She never could see past her nose job. Even if I were free to go to the funeral, I wouldn't."

"Do you think maybe he did to her what he did to you?"

"I don't know, although it wouldn't surprise me. He didn't treat Nancy and Danny very well." Elise gulped back another wave of nausea. "He often told me—in front of her—he wished I was his little girl."

"Just what you wanted to hear, huh?"

"She put on quite a show last night. Threw herself across him and sobbed. It took two nurses to pry her off. I suppose it's her way of dealing with her own childhood abuse."

Elise could still smell Nancy's overstated perfume and the alcohol her breath mints couldn't camouflage. Her high-pitched accusations rang in Elise's ears. *He adored you and you turned your back on him—on Mom—on all of us. You'd better come to his funeral, or I'll never speak to you again.*

"Now there's a threat I can live with," Elise muttered to herself.

Cassie entered with a tray. "Helen, breakfast is waiting for you in the dining room."

"Good. I'm starved." Helen headed for the door. "I'll miss you today, roomie."

Shaking her head, Cassie's gaze followed her. "Hm-mm, she's ready to blow this pop stand any day now." Turning back to Elise, Cassie set the tray on the bed table. "As Madam ordered—hot tea, soft-boiled egg, and dry rye toast."

The hot liquid soothed Elise's raw throat. "Thank you."

Cassie eased into a chair beside the bed. "I caught the tail end of your conversation. You're probably right about your cousin. It doesn't sound like her childhood was a bed of roses, either."

Elise dunked a corner of her toast in the egg yolk and then took a bite. "Nope. She grew up in a snake pit. I don't know how Danny turned out so normal. Maybe the Army had something to do with it."

"Can you forgive him?"

"Who? Danny? Nothing to forgive."

"Your uncle. His final request was your forgiveness. You know it's not something you do for him, sugar. It's for yourself."

Elise eyeballed Cassie, poising her fork in midair. Could she forgive Uncle Leo for herself? She decided she wasn't ready to find out. Instead, she said, "This egg tastes so good."

Chapter Fifty-Eight
Tony

TONY THOUGHT back over his session with Hank that morning, glad he had requested leave from his recruiting duties. He wasn't sure he could do his job very well with everything going on inside his head. He opened his journal and read his latest entry. "This journaling thing is full of trap doors. I write one thing and more crap surfaces."

He turned to the next blank page and wrote:

> This morning I told Hank about Elise's uncle passing. Hank asked if Elise and me was going to the funeral. No I say, Elise and Gracie's got sessions at the hospital that are more important and Ben's working the late shift at Kelley's. Hell, why would I subject the kids to the old geezer's funeral anyway? He never had nothing to do with them. I only met him a few times at family gatherings. At our wedding he was three sheets to the wind, and I didn't like the way he looked at Elise. Ain't no way I'm going to waste my time paying respects to a man I ain't got no respect for.
>
> Then Hank changes the subject. Big jerk asks me about my stuff. Boy it's easier to talk about Elise's stuff. This talking

about my own ain't no picnic. Sunday night I had one helluva flashback. I haven't wrote about it yet so here goes nothing:

The boy. Binh. Friendly kid. Nine, maybe ten years old. Round face, like one a them cherubs in a painting. He followed us all over the place, asking all sorts of questions about the USA. We gave him candy and trinkets. He loved baseball cards and bubble gum. Said he wanted to play for the New York Yankees when he grew up. When Kowalski found out the kid was passing on info to the VC and told them our every move, he exploded.

Shuddering, Tony paused his writing. The page blurred. Wiping his eyes and taking a deep breath, he wrote:

I couldn't blame Kowalski. He always looked out for Frankie and Frankie bought it because of Binh.

"After we was ambushed, we went back to camp and got wasted. It wasn't enough for Kowalski. He went batshit crazy and swore he was going to wipe out 'every damn gook in the village.' We followed him. He aimed his M1911 and shot the kid between the eyes—and anyone else who got in his way. He had to be stopped. I emptied a ten-round clip—my God, the VC didn't kill him!

Tony scrawled the words, making deep grooves in the paper. He let the pen fall from his hand and mopped his eyes on his sleeve. "How the hell could I forget that?"

Ben paced back and forth in the crowded airport, stopping from time to time to look out the window and check his watch. "I hope everything's okay."

"Relax, Ben, her flight's a few minutes late." Tony closed his book. "Take a load off." He gestured to the chair beside him.

Wringing his hands, Ben sat. "Whatcha reading?"

"It's called *A Rumor of War* by a guy named Philip Caputo. This guy knows me."

"Must be tough."

"Tough don't begin to cover it."

Tony couldn't stop thinking about last night's flashback. For years he'd been able to block out the memory of Kowalski's rampage. Now he couldn't make it stop. He couldn't erase the images. Every time Tony closed his eyes, he saw the surprised look on Binh's face when Kowalski shot him. He was just a kid.

A sarcastic reply came to mind, pointing out shirkers like Ben had no clue. One look in Ben's serious brown eyes squelched his comment. Instead, he squeezed Ben's shoulder. "I'm glad you'll never know."

"Dad, I know you're disappointed I didn't go into the military."

"You're better off. Some guys ain't cut out for it. There was guys in my outfit who wasn't. They didn't make it out alive."

The speaker blared. "TWA flight eight-sixty-seven from Dulles arriving at gate eighty-five."

Ben leaped up. "That's us! I hope you like her."

"You go on. I need to use the head." Tony rose from his chair. "Besides, you two lovebirds don't need the old buzzard hovering right off the bat."

Tony headed toward the restroom. He stopped and watched people embrace their loved ones with cries of joy.

How different from his homecoming in 1969. Although Mom had hugged and kissed him with happy tears, more than one passerby had cursed him. One had called him a baby killer and spit on his uniform.

Tony shook his head as if he could shake the memories from his mind and watched Ben push his way through the crowd. A petite Asian woman ran to him crying, "Ben! Oh my Ben!"

Ben said something to her. With a squeal, she cried, "yes!" and threw her arms around his neck.

Tony didn't have to guess what his son had said. Loneliness surged through him like frigid winter winds. Forcing his wooden lips to smile, Tony walked toward the happy couple.

Ben towered over Anh, who couldn't have been much taller than five feet. Elise wouldn't have trouble looking her in the eye. Anh's sleek black hair under a Kansas City Royals ballcap went to her slender waist. Instead of the traditional Vietnamese dress Tony expected, she wore blue jeans, a hot-pink T-shirt, and green high-top sneakers.

"Dad, meet Anh Truong, my bride-to-be."

She flashed a small diamond on her left hand and extended her right. "Pleased to meet you, Chief Reeves. Ben's told me so much about you."

Tony took her hand. "I hope some of it was good."

Her speech bore traces of a Vietnamese accent, but reflected her East Coast upbringing more. "He told me you're a war hero."

"There weren't no heroes in that war, ma'am." Tony took her backpack. "Since my son's forgotten his manners, I'll carry this for you. Dinner's my treat. Hien Vuong?"

"No thanks." She wrinkled her nose. "I'm tired of Vietnamese food. I've been dying to try Kansas City barbecue."

Chapter Fifty-Nine

EVEN AFTER A MONTH of daily weigh-ins, Elise still tried to determine the numbers from the sound of sliding weights on the beam scale behind her. While the bagel with lox and cream cheese had been scrumptious at lunch yesterday, she figured it added ten pounds to each hip. Terry slid the beams back to starting position before Elise could sneak a peek.

"Give it up, Mrs. Reeves." Clucking her tongue, Terry wagged her head. Her copper disk earrings reflected the light. "Go get dressed. Breakfast's at eight."

Elise stepped off the scale. "Same old story, different day."

Back in her room, she slipped off the hospital gown. She put on her bra and noted she filled it out a bit more than a couple of weeks ago. "I'm getting fat."

"No, Momette." Gracie entered the room. "You're getting healthy."

Healthy. Why does that word scare you so much, Suzie-Q?

Elise pinched her Gracie's cheek. "Good morning, my little eavesdropper."

"That's what you get for talking to yourself out loud. How's your head? Feeling better?"

"Much better, thank you."

"I'm sorry about Uncle Leo—and kind of not. I don't remember much about him. I do remember he gave me the creeps."

"That's because he was a creep." Elise hugged her daughter. "Why so early?"

"Poppo has a breakfast date with Doc Rodgers. He was antsy to get there on time. Ben's still sleeping."

"Did he have to work last night?"

"Yeah. Anh made breakfast and brought me in. She said she had some early shopping to do. Going to make us a special feast tonight. Two days and she already knows her way around town. She's really smart."

Elise slipped on her sweatshirt. "Is she as beautiful as Ben says?"

"I'll say. Even without makeup she's a knockout. And she's a black belt in Taekwondo. She's going to help me earn mine."

Reaching behind her head, Elise French braided her hair. "I can't wait to meet her."

"She's dying to meet you, too." Gracie took Elise's hand. "I'll invite her to come with us tomorrow."

"Oh no. Not here. Not like this."

As they entered the dining room, an all-too-familiar face greeted her. Yessenia Chavez, who'd shown so much promise a couple of weeks ago, peered up at her from a wheelchair, even thinner than before. "*Buenos dias, Señora* Elise. Did you miss me?"

"Of course I did." Elise sank down beside her. "But I'd hoped one day we'd meet again under different circumstances." She reached out to touch the girl's leg.

Yessenia recoiled and glowered. "Like maybe one day we'll do lunch on your yacht."

"What yacht? I don't understand."

"Don't you?" The girl drew up her legs, her dark eyes flashed. She dropped her head on her knees. "Leave me alone."

"What happened, Yessenia? You were doing so well."

"I—don't know. I'm just not hungry."

"There's dedication. Where's your dedication, Elise?" whispered Annie. "Fat and lazy. Fat and lazy."

"Your healthy breakfast order, madam." Cassie set a plate of scrambled eggs and rye toast in front of her. "You go, girl."

"There's that word again. Healthy. What are you going to do with it, Suzie-Q?"

"Synonymous with fat!" screamed Annie.

"I'm going to enjoy this healthy breakfast. Every last bite." Elise dripped Tabasco sauce on her eggs and slathered butter on her toast.

"Don't put that in your mouth, Fatso. Too many calories. You're going to—"

Elise bit into her toast and savored the taste of rye and melted butter. "Yum."

Beside her, Yessenia whimpered. "I—I—can't do this. I wish Dixie was here."

"Do you want to die young like she did?"

"No."

"Dixie would want you to get well." Elise curved her arm around the girl's skeletal shoulders. "She would say 'don't let that bitch Annie win, my friend.'"

"Who's Annie?"

"Annie Wrecks Ya. Someone who wants only the worst for you. I'm going to tell you all about her."

"That's my Suzie-Q."

Chapter Sixty
Gracie

After breakfast, the group moved to the patient lounge, where Gracie sat in the so-called seat of honor. Cassie held up the traditional bronze coin and recited the serenity prayer. "Today we bid a fond farewell to Evelyn Grace Reeves."

"Sheesh, you make it sound like I'm dying or something." Gracie rolled her eyes. "I'll be back tomorrow for family day and Wednesday night for support group."

"Nonetheless, this is what we do for outgoing patients and that includes you. Gracie, you've done some good work over the past couple of weeks." Cassie placed the coin in Thad's hand. "You first, sir."

Closing his fingers around the coin, Thad twisted his lips to one side. "You know me and speeches. I'm just gonna say 'Good luck, Gracie.' Your turn, Jeanie."

Jeanie took the coin and turned to Gracie. "You're such a sweet thing. I wish y'all only the best."

Gracie couldn't keep her eyes off Jeanie and Thad. Had those two both lost weight? Whatever. They made a cute couple. What a crazy place to find love.

"Gracie, sweetheart, this is only a bump in the road." Helen took the coin, rolled it between her fingers. "You've got a lot going on, talent and personality to boot. Go for the gold, honey—be it as an Olympic swimmer or anything else your heart desires." She made a V with her index and middle fingers, pointing them first at her own eyes, and then at Gracie. "Like The Police sang, I'll be watching you." She passed the coin to Yessenia.

Yessenia peered at Gracie from under dark bangs that obscured her eyes. She hurled the coin to the floor. "I don't know why you were ever here in the first place. Like the tubby twins who don't belong here, either." She angled her head toward Thad and Jeanie. She leveled a hateful glare at Gracie. "Not everyone gets things handed to them on a silver platter."

The color drained from Mom's face. Clapping her hand over her mouth she jumped from her chair and headed for the door. Heart thumping against her ribs, Gracie grasped the sides of her chair. Cassie blocked Mom's path and whispered something in her ear. Mom nodded and went back to her seat.

"What's your mommy's problem, Gracie?" Yessenia snarled. "Truth hurt?"

"Yessenia, that's quite enough." Cassie crossed the room and took an empty chair beside the girl. Lowering her voice to a stage whisper, she narrowed her eyes. "Everyone belongs here, understand?"

"Yeah. I guess so. But Gracie's got it all."

Bile rising to her throat, Gracie stood, fists at her sides. "Why, you little brat."

Cassie placed her hand on Gracie's shoulder and pressured her to sit. "Yessenia, I repeat, everyone in this room has a reason for being here. We hope every patient is on the road to recovery. Now tell me why you think Gracie's had everything handed to her, as you say, on a silver platter?"

Yessenia glowered at Gracie. "Look at her. She's a pretty girl with nice clothes and parents who love her." Yessenia's lower lip trembled. Her eyes brimmed. "My mom deserted me."

Compassion overtaking contempt, Gracie softened her voice. "You didn't see my mom when she came here. She nearly died."

"Yeah? But she didn't, did she? My mom killed herself." Yessenia bared her gritted teeth. "Then Dixie died, too. I hate them both. I hate all of you."

"You know you don't mean that." Cassie reached for Yessenia's hand. "Why don't you tell the group about your family?"

"What family? You tell it if it will make you feel better. Could I go back to my room first?"

"Of course. Terry will stay with you." Cassie nodded. She handed Yessenia a can of *Ensure.* "One last chance, girlfriend. If you won't drink this, it's the feeding tube for you."

Head bowed, Yessenia curled up in the wheelchair as Terry wheeled her from the hushed circle. Cassie cleared her throat.

"Yessenia's mother was a cocaine addict. Yessenia's been living with a foster family. They've been concerned about her eating habits for a while. But when she heard about Dixie, she stopped eating altogether. I'm sorry she lashed out at you, Gracie. She has a long, hard road ahead of her."

Gracie ached for her. No matter how bad she had it, someone always had it worse.

"Now." Cassie picked up the coin and handed it to Mom. "We need to finish Gracie's sendoff before supper."

Mom scooted her chair next to Gracie's and whispered, "For a moment I thought she knew about you-know-who and you-know-what."

"It's a secret." Gracie flinched. "Surely, you didn't think I—?"

"The thought did cross my mind." Mom raised an eyebrow. "Give me your hand." Gracie held it out, palm up. Mom kissed it and laid the coin in it. "You and me, kid. We're going to get healthy together."

Chapter Sixty-One

Festive described Elise's mood this Saturday morning. Besides her own family coming to participate, she'd had a chance to meet Helen's older sister Sophia, who had arrived before any of the rest of the visitors.

"Helen's told me so much about you, Elise." Sophia pushed Elise's proffered hand aside and hugged her. "I feel like I already know you."

With her olive complexion and deep-brown eyes, Sophia bore a strong resemblance to her sister. She even shared the same resonant voice and big-boned stature. Elise liked her right away.

"I love sharing a room with Helen." With an exaggerated pout, Elise cast a sideways glance at her roommate. "I'm going to hate it when she moves to St. Louis."

Sophia heaved a melodramatic sigh and put her hands on her hips. "You haven't told her, have you? Helen-Tell-All, I'm surprised at you."

Elise mimicked Sophia's stance. "Tell me what?"

Helen's laughter echoed off the walls. "All right. It was going to be a surprise, but since my sister has the cat scratching to get out of the bag, I'll tell you now. My big, bad sister sold her place in St. Louis and already has a contract on a place in the area."

"Do you know anything about Mission Hills? Charming area."

Sophia opened a brochure to show Elise a picture of an older, two-story home that looked like something out of *Better Homes and Gardens*. "It's a few blocks east of the actual neighborhood and the perfect house for two spinster sisters."

"You two will get lost in it," Elise gasped. "It's only the wealthiest neighborhood in Kansas City."

"Let me have a closer look at that. Not sure I can live in such a shack." Helen took the brochure. "My brother-in-law, may he rest in peace...," Helen and Sophia crossed themselves in unison, "... had a few coins stashed away."

A crowd began to gather. A heavy-set woman with a blonde, 1960s-style pageboy sat beside Yessenia's wheelchair. Whatever she said obviously upset the girl. A man with bronze skin and black hair and mustache sat at Yessenia's other side. He adjusted the bag attached to Yessenia's feeding tube and kissed her cheek. Clearly, these people cared about her. The trick would be to teach the girl how to care about herself.

"What do you care, Elise? Admit it. You'd kill to be that skinny, wouldn't you?"

As if it were possible, Elise stepped backward in an attempt to escape Annie's mocking voice. In doing so, she bumped into the person behind her. "Sorry I'm such a klutz." She whipped around to meet the gaze of a pair of almond-shaped eyes.

"If only our creator had installed backup lights in his creations." The young woman smiled. "You wouldn't happen to be Elise Reeves?"

"Guilty as charged."

"So happy to meet you, Mrs. Ben's Mother." She threw her arms around Elise. "I'm Anh."

Wayne perched himself on his desk. Elise sat in one of the wingback chairs. Tony sat in the other one. Ben on a folding chair. Beside him, Anh leaned close enough to be on his lap, her hand in his, her diamond sparkling between his fingers.

Was this necessary? Although Elise was overjoyed to meet Ben's beloved, she hadn't wanted it to be here. She did her best to avoid eye contact with Anh.

After grabbing a handful of Tootsie Rolls, Gracie took the chair beside Tony. "Mind if I sit here, Poppo?"

Tony pinched her cheek. "Only if you're willing to share your candy."

The cuckoo clock chimed. "Let's get started." Wayne tucked his chin and caught Elise in his gaze. "As you know, your husband's been seeing a therapist. One I highly respect, I might add.

"A lot has happened these past few weeks. While you've made progress, Elise, I feel it's time for the two of you to open the lines of communication. Share what you're both learning. How do you feel about it?"

"Here?" Elise shifted her gaze from Wayne to Gracie, from Gracie to Ben and Anh. "In front of the kids?"

"Kids, too." Gracie peered at her around Tony. "We're all in this together."

"From the mouths of babes." Tony gave Elise's knee a gentle squeeze. "I'm game if you are."

Elise's heart fluttered. Dare she trust him with her innermost feelings? Would it backfire as it had in the past? She looked up to see tears brimming in his liquid gray eyes. The eyes that had captivated her all those years ago. Could the love that, somewhere between "I do" and diapers, had turned to loathing be rekindled?

She curved her hand around his. "I—guess so."

Wayne cast his gaze on Ben. "Could get ugly."

Ben snorted. "Uglier than it already has been? I'm in."

"Maybe I should wait outside," said Anh.

"Stay. You're part of this family now."

Tony raised an eyebrow. "Something I should know about?"

"We were waiting for a better time to tell you. But now's as good a time as any." Color rose from Ben's neck to the tips of his ears. "We went to the courthouse yesterday."

Instead of the tirade Elise expected from Tony, he laughed aloud.

"Well, if that don't beat all." He leaped out of the chair with his arms open.

Ben rose and the two men embraced.

Anh rose. "I know this is sudden, Elise, but—"

Elise stood and hugged her. "From now on the name is Mom."

"All righty then," Wayne rubbed his palms together. "We've quite a bit of ground to cover in the remaining time." He unwrapped a piece of candy. "Where should we begin?"

Gracie pointed to the candy dish. "Maybe we should start with your addiction to Tootsie Rolls, Dr. Picard."

Chapter Sixty-Two

A LETTER HAD ARRIVED right after breakfast for Elise, but she'd been too busy to stop and read it. She inspected the envelope with its German postmark. The name in the return address read, "Sgt. Major Daniel E. Rosen."

Waiting for the group to gather for the Monday afternoon session, she carefully opened the envelope. She unfolded the note to find a wallet-size photo. There sat her cousin in his dress greens. The same hazel eyes and blond hair she remembered. Beside him sat a pretty brunette with a tow-headed boy on her lap and a girl with golden curls beside her. They looked to be under five.

Elise put the photo back into the envelope, promising herself to buy a frame for it when she went home. She turned her attention back to the letter written in Danny's half-print, half-cursive style.

Dear Elise,

Greetings from Daniel, Klara, Keith and Evelina Rosen in Stuttgart.
Nancy told me about your situation. I hope you get well soon. You always were
my favorite cousin.
She's pretty pissed off I didn't make the effort to make it home for our sperm

donor's funeral. As far as I'm concerned, they could dump the old man in the garbage where he belongs and bury him in a landfill.

He deserves it for what he did to you.

I never told my sister or my mom what happened, but I'll never forget it. The old sot stopped drinking after Mom passed and he tried to make amends with me. After all those years of being his punching bag, I can't forgive him. When I left for the army, I socked him a few good ones and never looked back.

I love my wife and kids. I love my life.

Take care of yourself, cuz and write back when you can.

Love,

Your Lifer Cousin Dan

"That's my Danny." Elise made a mental note to write a nice, detailed letter when she had a chance.

She shut her eyes to stem stinging tears. Uncle Leo and Aunt Viv couldn't hurt her. No doubt they occupied a special place in Hell. She smiled at the image that popped into her mind.

"Now you're getting it, Suzie Q," whispered Dixie. "Let it go."

A few more patients trailed into the room. Elise folded Dan's letter and slid it back into the envelope. Helen eased into a chair beside her and pointed to it. "Good news, I hope?"

Cleansing tears slid down Elise's face. "Very good. The best."

"Everyone take a seat please." Terry sank down beside her. "This is not a spectator sport."

Elise raised her head to see the small group gathered around her. Helen curved her arm around Elise's waist. Elise shook her head and smiled. "No, no, I'm fine. Really."

With a skeptical glance at Elise, Terry addressed the group. "Before we start, let me set some ground rules for the sake of our newbies. We do not share numbers, for our worth isn't defined by our weight or how few calories we've consumed. Avoid comparisons. And it can't be stressed enough, what's said here, stays here. Any questions?"

Elise sat up and wiped her eyes on her sleeve. Three new patients had joined the circle, two teenage girls and one older woman. Jeanie and

Thad sat side by side, holding hands. Yessenia, in her wheelchair, folded her arms across her chest, lips pressed into a thin line.

Terry swiveled her head from side to side, her walnut shell earrings wagging to and fro. "Recovery takes determination. Some of you haven't made the decision, have you?" She locked eyes with Yessenia who lowered her gaze. "Who's brave enough to share first?"

"Those new girls sure are thin, aren't they Elise?" Annie crooned. *"If you recover, you'll balloon like your dad. Like Aunt Vivian. Fat—"*

Elise raised her hand. "I'll share."

Chapter Sixty-Three
Tony

"I HOPE we're almost there; this thing's breaking my back." Clutching one end of a hide-a-bed sofa, Tony followed Ben up a narrow flight of stairs. "Nice furniture for thrift store stuff."

"We don't need anything expensive," said Ben. "Five months and we'll be on our way to the Big Apple. The landlord said we can leave it all when we go. That way he can jack up the rent for a furnished apartment."

A lamp balanced on the cushions rolled off and thumped down the steps, landing at the bottom. "Dammit, son, I told you not to leave it there. Now it's broke."

"Sorry to disobey orders." Ben's face reddened and his nostrils flared. "Chief."

"I'm only trying to help."

"You mean it's 'brok-*en*.'" At the foot of the stairway, Gracie picked up the fallen lamp. "Cool your jets, Poppo. The only casualty was the bulb."

"Thank you for the English lesson, Teach." Sweat rolled between Tony's shoulder blades as they navigated the couch up the last few steps and through the doorway. "You're sounding more like your mother every day."

Gracie snickered. "Can I help it if your grammar sucks?"

"You leave my grammar out of it." Tony set the couch legs down and mopped his face with his forearm. "What's she ever done to you?"

Setting down his side of the sofa, Ben smirked. "That's like humor, only different."

Anh hunched over the sink, washing dishes. "I guess I don't get the joke."

"It's Dad's way of making a bad pun. Grammar. Grandma. Get it? A mini ha-ha."

"Have your fun." Tony eased down on the couch and surveyed his son's place. "Nice, but awfully small. Nothing like the dump your mom and I moved into when we was first married."

"'We was'? Is there an English translation for that, Dad?"

Anh finished setting dishes in the drainer and dried her hands. "Benjamin, why do you and Gracie gang up on your father so much?"

"It's fun. Like shooting fish in a barrel."

Tony massaged his aching neck with his fingers. "I'm used to it."

"Your father deserves respect." Taking a bottle from the refrigerator, Anh cast a sympathetic pout at Tony. "He's a war hero." She took a mug from the freezer and poured beer into it.

"I told you. I made it out alive. That don't make me no hero."

"You fought for freedom and democracy." Placing the frosted mug in Tony's hand, Anh sat beside him. "I'll bet you have many stories to tell."

"Dad's never told us any." Ben opened a beer for himself and sat on a stack of unopened boxes. "I, for one, would love to hear about it. Anh's parents have told me plenty."

Tony took a long swig of the cold brew. "I'm sure we left a bad taste in their mouths."

"*Cha* says there were good soldiers and bad soldiers. Like all people." Anh laid her hand on his. "My father's a wise man. He says we embraced the good when we became American citizens."

Gracie dumped a dustpan full of broken lightbulb shards into a trash bag. "Tell us your story, Poppo. Please."

A loud bang startled Tony. His heart pounded against his ribs and his glass fell from his grasp. Doubling over he covered his head. "Get down!"

In the ensuing hush, he opened his eyes to see Ben at his side. "It's okay, Dad. A car backfired, that's all."

Tony straightened. "Sorry... your floor..."

Anh knelt to mop up the beer. "No harm done."

"It's okay, Daddy." Gracie's eyes filled and she hugged him. "You don't have to tell us anything if you don't want to."

Images flashed through Tony's mind. Catching Anh in his gaze, he cleared his throat. "I met Kieu in Saigon..."

Chapter Sixty-Four

"This is my favorite so far." Pam held the picture at arm's length. "I love the way you've worked the daffodils into every scene. But this one. There's so much peace in it."

Elise pored over her latest illustration. In the upper right side, a pair of feet in red tennis shoes stood on the shore of a pond. Two faces smiled from the blue airbrushed water. Little Elise watched her reflection while the angel peeked over her shoulder.

"I find it interesting that we see only the child's feet and not the angel's." Pam laid the picture on the growing stack. "Was this on purpose, Elise?"

"I didn't really think about it."

"I'd say your subconscious did." Pam winked. "Have you written more story as well?"

Elise handed over her notebook.

"Oh goody," Pam clapped her hands like a child and then put on her readers. "Yes, I see where I left off. She'd just met the angel named Cherish." Pam read aloud. "'Cherish took the girl by the hand and led her to a nearby creek.

"'"If you wash your face in the water it will take the mask away." Elise obeyed. When the water stilled, the angel told her to look at her reflection. The child was happy to see her own face in the water with no trace of the horrible white mask.

""Elise, my special friend," said the angel. "You have a lovely face. Never hide it again. I hope you've learned that masks can be very tricky and will trap you unless you are very, very careful."' Profound state-ment." Taking off her glasses, Pam focused her eyes on Elise. "How does grownup Elise feel about that?"

Elise returned her gaze. "After being trapped behind her mask for so long, she's terrified."

"That's the first honest thing you've said to me since you've been here."

Chapter Sixty-Five
Wayne

PACING IN FRONT of his desk, Wayne analyzed the petite woman curled up like a puppy in the chair. Her slight gain over the past week encouraged him. He wouldn't mention it to her, of course. Experience had taught him one ill-spoken word could highjack a recovery. Elizabeth smiled at him from her photo.

Such a puzzling disorder. While skewed body image fueled it, the reasons were as individual as the sufferers themselves. Why is it some can be helped while others lose the battle? Do Dixie and Lucas' deaths make me a failure as a psychiatrist? I know better. I can't force them to decide to live. I've seen dozens walk out of here and go on to lead healthy, productive lives.

"Yoo-hoo, Wayne?" Elise waved at him. "Are you in there?"

"I'm a little preoccupied this morning." He sat in the chair opposite hers. "Do you remember the joke I told you early on in your stay?"

"Which one? You've cracked a few." She twirled a loose curl around her finger and shut one eye, twisting her lips to one side. "Hm. Could you be referring to 'How many therapists does it take to change a lightbulb?'"

"You must be psychic. And the punchline?"

"One. But only if the lightbulb is willing to change."

"And?"

She stretched her arms over her head. "I'm going to buy a set of these chairs for my birthday. They're so comfortable." Shifting her position, she trained her chocolate-brown eyes on him. "You want to know if I'm willing to change—to recover—to face my demons and move on. Am I getting warm?"

"You're red hot, my dear."

Linking her fingers behind her head, she turned her face toward the ceiling. "I'm afraid if I put the weight back on, I'll get top-heavy again."

"If your breasts are truly an issue, plastic surgery might be an option."

"Ha. Tony would never go along with that."

"Have you ever asked him?"

She lowered her head and shook it. "I just—"

"You just assume." He made a note in her file. "We'll come back to this, if the need arises. I will continue to see you after your discharge if you want."

"Of course. Thank you."

"We'll cross that bridge when we come to it. Back to the matters at hand. Talk to me about your uncle. You told me when we spoke last, he begged your forgiveness on his deathbed. How do you feel about that?"

Her face flushed. "Don't you dare tell me forgiveness is a choice and not a feeling. I can't."

"I understand. If someone did to my daughter what your uncle did to you, I'd rip off his balls and make him eat them." He waited a few moments before continuing. "You have every right to bear a grudge. But you can't let the weight of it sap your will to live." He tossed a Tootsie Roll into her lap. "Here's food for thought. I once heard a holocaust survivor say that living a good and productive life was her best revenge."

Chapter Sixty-Six

ONCE A WEEK, the unit treated the EDU patients to a carryout lunch from a local restaurant. Today, it would come from a nearby delicatessen. Cassie and Ronnie entered the room with grease-stained sacks containing each patient's order. Dividing the bags between the two of them, they passed them around the table.

Yessenia, whose feeding tube had been removed the day before, took out her sandwich and made a face. "It's so big."

"One bite at a time, sugar," said Cassie. "Eat what you can."

"Better than nasal fuel." Helen tore into her sack. "Ham on sourdough with American cheese and mayo. What's yours, Elise?"

"American isn't even real cheese. Swiss on mine." Elise held her open sack to her nose and breathed in the aroma of corned beef on fresh rye bread. Her stomach growled. "I hope they remembered the horseradish."

One of the recent arrivals scowled at Elise and Helen. "Isn't it enough we have to eat this crud? Must you all discuss it, too?"

Remorse flooded Elise, dulling her appetite. There were few things she hated more than her meal being a topic of conversation. "I'm sorry, Janet. I wasn't thinking."

"We all have different likes and dislikes, don't we?" Ronnie sat at one end of the table and lifted her own sandwich to her lips. "Mm. Tuna salad with tomato slices. I know it's hard to accept, Janet. People discuss food on their own plates and the plates of others. Normal human behavior."

Janet pecked at her sandwich and glared at the dietitian. "So, what you're saying is, it's normal behavior to be rude and nosy."

Tears ran down Yessenia's face. She tore off a tiny chunk of her cheese sandwich and put it into her mouth. Elise didn't realize she'd been staring until the girl glowered at her and snarled. "Mind your own business."

"You going to eat your pickle, Elise?" Helen reached over to make a grab for it.

Thankful for the diversion, Elise slapped Helen's wrist. "Hands off my pickle. I'm saving it for last."

Out of the corner of her eye, Elise caught Cassie grinning at her. Elise returned her smile as she bit into her sandwich. Fear mingled with pleasure—the same way the pungent horseradish stung her tongue while the corned beef made her taste buds sing for joy. Cassie winked and gave her a thumbs up.

"Good afternoon, ladies and gentleman." Cassie gathered the group in a circle for the afternoon session. "For Janet, Miriam, and Patricia, our new kids on the block, role play might be something new."

"Is this like an April fool's joke?" Janet folded her arms and slunk down in her chair, stretching her spindly legs in front of her.

"So thin. So beautifully thin," intoned Annie.

Elise refused to compare herself to the flat-chested, ultra-slim seventeen-year-old. For the first time since Twiggy entered the fashion scene, Elise didn't see that level of skinny as attractive. In fact, with her straight, center-parted black hair, pointed chin, and sallow cheeks, Janet resembled the Wicked Witch of the West.

"You want to be that thin, Elise," Annie whispered. "You know you do."

No... No. I don't know how I ever saw that as pretty.

"You're going to get—"

Shut up, Annie!

"Atta girl, Suzie-Q."

The light glinted off Dixie's sapphire ring.

"Elise," Cassie's voice rousted her from her epiphany. "You've been here over a month. I'd say it's high time for you to take your turn."

Elise shrank back against her chair. "I played Irma's little sister. What about Jeanie and Thad? They haven't taken a turn yet."

"Excellent suggestion." Cassie gestured for the young man to come to the middle of the circle and sit in one of two chairs. "Thad, you're going to be Elise's Uncle Leo."

Beside him, Jeanie giggled. "Go, Uncle Thad."

As Thad sat in one of the chairs, Elise's heart cratered to the pit of her stomach. Had Cassie lost her mind? "No. Please. I—"

Patting the seat of the vacant chair, Cassie's intense glare left no room for argument. "Come on, sweet pea, we don't have all day."

Elise squared her shoulders and made her way to the menacing chairs. She sat opposite sweet-faced Thad. How could he portray her vicious uncle? No trace of evil in this boy. She gasped. Although devoid of malice, Thad's eyes matched Uncle Leo's to a T—amber with flecks of crimson and a charcoal border around the iris.

"A couple of weeks ago, Elise's uncle passed away right here in Brookside Memorial. Elise was with him in ICU," Cassie told the group. She turned to Elise. "I thought there might be something more you wanted to say to him."

Elise returned her piercing gaze. "You know very well what I want to say to that monster."

Thad scooted an empty chair next to his own and butted the seats together. Then he laid across them, straddling his long legs on either side with his feet flat on the floor.

"Elise—my dear niece." He wheezed and coughed. "It won't be long." He reached for her.

She recoiled and linked her hands behind her back. "Don't touch me, don't you ever touch me again."

"Please...," he sputtered and drew an exaggerated breath. "Why do you—hate me?"

"Why shouldn't I hate you?" Elise choked on bile. "You're an animal." She trembled. "You put your awful hands in places no child should be touched." She raised her voice. "You're despicable."

"Elise?" Thad acted as if he were ready to take his final breath. "Can —you—find it in your heart—to forgive me?"

Thad disappeared and Uncle Leo took his place. Elise's chest burned and her face blazed. Cassie and Wayne's words about forgiveness flooded her. She shook her head and lowered her voice to a raspy whisper. "I'm glad you're dead. Forgive you? Are you kidding me? Forgive you for making my childhood a living hell? I'll dance on your grave before I'll forgive you!"

In a torrent of unstoppable emotion and sobs, her words tumbled over each other. "I forgive my parents for never knowing who you were and allowing you near me. I even forgive Nancy for being your daughter. Most of all, I forgive *myself* for letting you affect me."

"Cry all the tears you need to, sugar." Cassie gathered Elise into her arms then turned to the stunned boy. "Thaddeus, for a man who's no good at speeches, you sure can act."

Chapter Sixty-Seven

"I'M NOT sure I'm ready for this." Elise squeezed Cassie's hand. She set her pillow on the chair. "I don't need this as much as I did when I came in."

Cassie's smile shone. "You've worked hard for this day, sugar plum. You're as ready as you're ever gonna be." She took the medallion from her scrubs pocket and handed it to Chaplain Charlie. "Father, will you bless this and start the ceremony?"

"Nothing would please me more." His round cheeks glowed and his eyes sparkled. He raised the coin toward the ceiling and bowed his head. "God, grant Elise the serenity to accept the things she cannot change, courage to change the things she can, and wisdom to know the difference. Amen." Opening his eyes, he flashed a warm grin. "Elise, you're an inspiration to me. Never lose your faith."

"Thank you for helping me find it again," whispered Elise.

One by one, her fellow patients took the coin and offered her their best wishes. Elise relished every one of them. Although she hadn't really developed relationships with the three latest arrivals, she felt an affinity for each of them. She silently prayed for their victories over the beast.

"We're in this together, Suzie-Q."

When the coin came to Helen, she bit the corner of her lip, her dark eyes glittering with unshed tears. "I'm going to miss you, my diminutive roomie. I know you're going to succeed. I see art fairs and awards in your future."

"Stop it." Elise sniffed. "You can't get rid of me that easily. We'll keep in touch. I promise."

Next Thad took the coin. "My little niece." He winked. "I'm still no good at speeches, but I wish you the best."

"You'd better brush up on that skill." Elise returned his wink. "You'll need it someday when you accept your Oscar."

He snorted and passed the medallion to Yessenia. She flipped it in the air and caught it on the back of her hand, clapping her other hand over it. "Call it, Suzie-Q. Heads or tails."

Elise's heart fluttered. "Heads."

Yessenia lifted her hand and shook her head. "Tails. You're gonna win anyway. One of these days I'll walk out of this place. What say I call you and we'll do lunch?"

"I don't have a yacht."

The girl's thin cheeks flushed. "How about Red Lobster?"

"It's a date."

Yessenia rose from her wheelchair. "The next time you see me, these wheels will be history."

"I'm holding you to that." Elise stood and pulled her into an embrace. Skimming her fingers over the girl's back she felt every bone. "Red Lobster's one of my favorite places."

Why did Tony insist on House of Hunan for Elise's first meal on the town? Trembling, she reached for a pair of tongs. The aromas of forbidden foods caressed her nostrils. She took in the myriad colors and contemplated her choices.

"Too many calories," whispered Annie.

"Rice noodles, my favorite." Elise laid a small pile of them on her plate. Next, she added a few stir-fried green beans.

Tony waved his hand over the buffet, furrowing his brow. "What?

No meat?"

"Don't worry." Elise's stomach rumbled. "I'm trying to decide between beef with bok choy and chicken with pea pods."

"Why not have both, Momette?" Gracie spooned a dab of each medley on Elise's plate. "We're celebrating."

Elise's hands shook. "I don't want to overdo my first night out."

"One day at a time. One minute at a time. One bite at a time," Wayne had reiterated when he signed her discharge papers that morning. *"The feelings might never completely go away, Elise."*

"The alcoholic can lock up her tiger and throw away the key. The anorexic has to take her tiger for a walk three times a day."

"I hope you don't mind if we join you, Chief," said a man's voice. She turned to see a tall, heavyset man with a bushy white beard and moustache. He grinned. "We happened to be in the neighborhood."

"Checking up on me, Hank?" Tony led the way to a large, round table, set down his tray, and embraced him. "There's always room for you, buddy." He turned to Elise. "This is my shrink, Dr. Henry Wadsworth Longfellow Rodgers."

Cassie looped her arm through Hank's. "My Gunny."

"I'm sure we can rustle up a couple more chairs." Tony held a chair for Cassie. "I'm delighted you came."

Elise sat between Cassie and Tony as everyone around the table joined hands and bowed their heads. Without being asked, Hank led the prayer with, "Rub-a-dub-dub, thanks for the grub. Yay, God!"

Cassie shook her head. "You see what I have to put up with?"

Tony raised his water goblet. "A toast to the Reeves family, to the newlyweds Ben and his lovely Anh, and to Gracie, who has achieved the rank of red belt."

"Thanks to my new sister." Gracie grinned at Anh.

"And last, but always first in my book, my beautiful wife, Elise." Tony kissed her ear. "L'chaim!"

Elise's chopsticks quivered in her hand as she poised them over her plate, feeling the vigilant stares of everyone at the table. She picked up a piece of chicken and popped it into her mouth. Savoring the blend of pungent seasonings and meat, she swallowed. "Perfect."

Acknowledgments

It takes a village to write a novel. My village includes the following people who have supported me along the way.

First a special shout out to Lia Wu, owner of Ozark Hollow Press who was willing, even excited to share Elise's story. Thank you, Lia, Hallah Butcher, and Tricia Wu for your patience in editing.

To therapist, Audrey Rice, wherever you may be. You were the one who helped this scarecrow find her brain. I hope you'll see this book and smile.

How fortunate I am to have a doctor like Constance Irick. Through the past thirty years, you've been so much more than my concerned and often flustered MD. You're not only my cheerleader, but also my friend.

To my nine pairs of eyes: Dale Rogerson, Jean "Taffy" Hays, Diane Yates, Linda Kreger, Na'ama Yehuda, Lonnie Whitaker, Kimberly Pennell, Sarah Potter, and Lori Wilson who graciously read, found typos, and made some great suggestions.

A special thank you to author and friend Kathleen Rodgers for your encouragement and understanding of my journey.

I end my acknowledgments with the most important one to Avinu Sh'ba'shamayin, Our Father in Heaven, Who saw fit to let me live to tell the story.

מודה אני לפניך מלך חי וקים

שהחזרת בי נשמתי בחמלה

רבה אמונתך

I thank you, Living and Eternal King

For restoring my soul to me in love
Great is Your faithfulness.

About the Author

Rochelle Wisoff-Fields is an award-winning artist and author with numerous published short stories and several books to her name.

Her own struggles with, and ultimate victory over, clinical depression and anorexia nervosa as an adult inspired her to write *Last Dance with Annie.* By telling a fictionalized story of a middle-aged woman's battle, she hopes to bring her struggles and those of others to light.

Rochelle's books include her historical trilogy, *Please Say Kaddish for Me, From Silt and Ashes,* and *As One Must, One Can.* Her short stories have been published in several anthologies. More of her illustrations are included in her own short story anthology *This, That and Sometimes the Other.*

She studied painting and lithography at the Kansas City Art Institute. Her preferred media are pencil, pen and ink, and watercolor. She has painted most of her book covers and created illustrations for *A Stone for the Journey,* the coffee table companion volume to her historical trilogy.

Rochelle and her husband Jan Fields, a retired Navy Chief, live in Belton, Missouri. They raised three sons. Rochelle enjoys painting, sketching, and swimming. Her weekly blog challenge "Friday Fictioneers" has a worldwide following.